The Night of the Rambler

BY Montague Kobbé

Published by Akashic Books
©2013 Montague Kobbé

ISBN-13: 978-1-61775-181-3
Library of Congress Control Number: 2013907455

Lesser Antilles map courtesy of the Perry-Castañeda Library Map Collection, Universtiy of Texas Libraries

Akashic Books
PO Box 1456
New York, NY 10009
info@akashicbooks.com
www.akashicbooks.com

to Peter Holleran

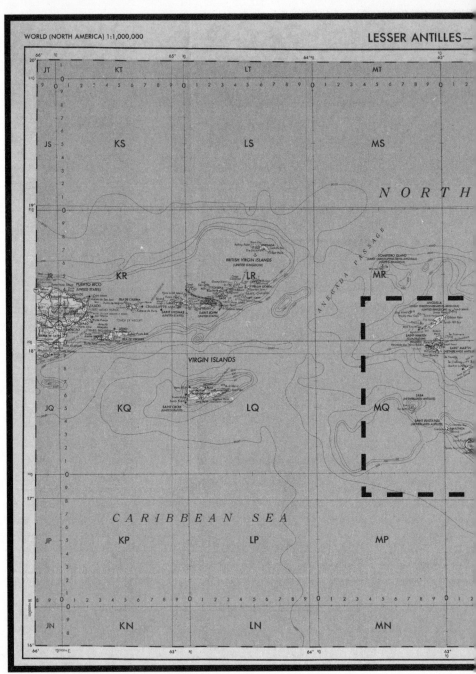

United States Army Topographic Command Map of the Lesser Antilles, North (1971)

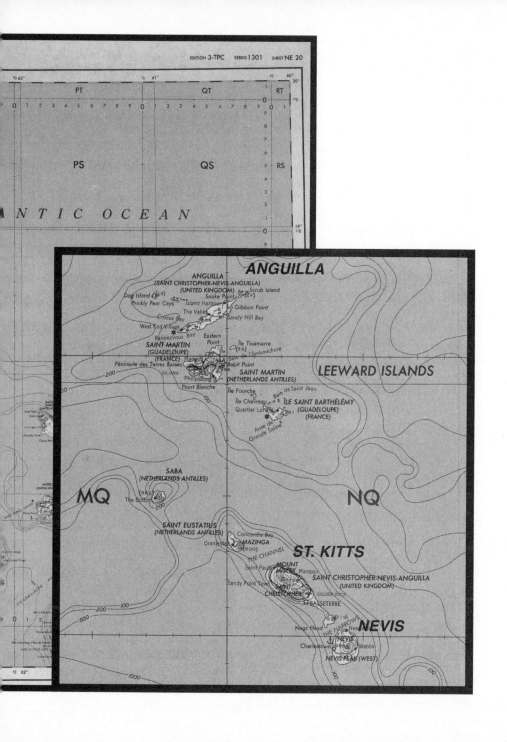

Student today don't mean na', but in a Latin America whipped into a frenzy by the Fall of Arbenz, by the Stoning of Nixon, by the Guerrillas of the Sierra Madre, by the endless cynical maneuverings of the Yankee Pig Dogs–in a Latin America already a year and a half into the Decade of the Guerrilla–a student was something else altogether, an agent for change, a vibrating quantum string in the staid Newtonian universe.

—Junot Díaz, *The Brief Wondrous Life of Oscar Wao*

PREFACE

THE BURNING QUESTION

AND THEN THE UNTHINKABLE HAPPENED: on May 29, 1967, a crowd of Anguillians gathered to protest, not unlike they had done in January of the same year, upon the arrival of the British local government expert who was forced to depart the island before delivering his message—whatever that might have been. They gathered and expressed their discontent at the notion of shared sovereignty within the tripartite state of St. Kitts-Nevis-Anguilla, much like they had done during the Statehood Queen Show of February 1967. It was precisely on that occasion when the image of Alwyn Cooke, hanging precariously from the edge of his truck, holding a wild ball of fire in his right hand, provided the people of the island with the first symbol of a revolution that had not yet started. They gathered to listen to their leaders' appeals, alternatives, solutions, ideas. They gathered at Burrowes Park, at the heart of The Valley, the "capital," and then they took matters into their own hands. On May 29, 1967, the people of Anguilla flocked to the streets, en masse in the park, marched toward the police station, and, spontaneously but vehemently, demanded the thirteen-man police task force leave the island, never to come back. Less than twenty-four hours later the last few policemen were boarding the freighter that would take them on their sixty-five-mile journey back to St. Kitts. Just like that, an insignificant speck of coral on the northeastern corner of the Caribbean had revolted.

At that point the situation was critical: hardly anybody was aware of the existence, let alone the whereabouts, of Anguilla; a fifteen-man peacekeeping committee acting as provisional government fruitlessly sought protection from Great Britain, from Canada, from the USA; the state of affairs on the island was precarious, and an invasion from St. Kitts seemed imminent. Intrepidly, Anguillians took the initiative, devised a shambolic attack on St. Kitts, and on the morning of June 10, 1967 embarked upon what must stand out among the most naive failures in the history of military enterprises.

When the men within St. Kitts's Defence Force camp heard the distant drumming of the shots fired outside, they didn't have the slightest clue of what was happening. Despite the fact that hundreds of Kittitians had been informed of the insurgency in an effort to foster local support for it, not one member of St. Kitts's police and security forces had been privy to this particular piece of information. Not long afterward, though, once they heard the loud roar of the dynamite setting the world alight, they knew that someone had opened wide the gates of hell. Nobody cared to ask who. The pertinent question at that time was whether to run for their lives or to put in place a plan to stifle the momentum of the rebels.

As it turned out, hell was not all that adept in running loose. By the time the faux coup had crashed against the walls of its own incompetence, looking for the people responsible for this minor embarrassment was no longer relevant. Instead, the local government jumped at the opportunity to declare a state of emergency, immediately implemented measures to tighten its (already watertight) grip on the country's structure of power, and wasted one month persecuting its political enemies.

The question as to who had let hell loose in the early hours of the morning of June 10, 1967 went down in history begging.

And yet, fortuitously, the mission achieved its goals. Faced with the threat of an armed uprising—faced, really, with the unthinkable— Premier Bradshaw focused on settling the score at home first, spent the following month turning St. Kitts into a 100 percent safe, absolutely invasion-resistant bunker. Now, in the 350 years of colonial history of Anguilla, its inhabitants have not exactly built a strong reputation for the pace and efficiency of their work. Or, to put it more obliquely, if Costa Rica is the Switzerland of the Americas, Anguilla is unequivocally *not* the Germany of the Caribbean. However, whether it was due to the urgency of the matter, or to the whimsical turnings of Providence, the peacekeeping committee acted in all haste, with uncharacteristic foresight and prudence, to build the institutional edifice required to rule a country. By July 11, 1967, one month and one day after the attempted attack on St. Kitts, Anguilla already had a small "army" of fifty servicemen, an anthem, a constitution, a revolutionary leader, a patriarch, and a foreign advisor.

The provisional government had also organized an internal referendum to decide upon the question of secession from the state of St. Kitts-Nevis-Anguilla. The overwhelming result of 1,813 votes in favor to five against, out of 2,554 registered voters, forever changed the course of Anguilla's destiny. Most importantly, though, Anguilla caught the eye of the world while Bradshaw's attention had drifted toward internal affairs. By the time St. Kitts looked back in the direction of Anguilla it was too late to use force—and diplomacy was not going to lead anywhere favorable. This was the extraordinary legacy of one of the most ridiculous episodes anyone will ever find in the annals of revolutions. This was the beginning of the first success of a country whose history, up to that point, had been little more than a catalog of hardship and failure.

The following is a fictionalized and utterly false account of the events that most definitely did not happen on June 9–10, 1967. And yet, while all characters in this story are little green men and women running around inside my head, the events that served as inspiration, the historical *facts*, as it were, must be considered no less than a sibling of the tale contained in these pages: the story I didn't write, but could have written—the book this could have been, but isn't.

PART I

CHAPTER I

MAY DE LORD BE WIT' US

WHEN A NEW POCKET OF LIGHTS FLARED farther to the east through the deep blackness of the night, Sol Campbell finally vented the rage that had been eating up his insides, and with an intimidating *Yo Rude!* issued the prelude to his duel. He seemed to stand on higher ground as his voice rose above the rest to ask, *Wha' dem lights over dere be? Tell me, nuh—wha' dat light yonder be, if it ain' St. Kitts?* Instantly, the roar of the engine receded and the surge behind the boat caught up with its hull, softly thrusting the sixteen passengers forward. Awash at sea, *The Rambler* drifted helplessly in no particular direction. The calm Caribbean waters rocked the boat melodiously, intensely, in the middle of the night, as its 115-horsepower diesel engine gargled on idle. Every now and then a wayward wave or ripple crashed against the underside of the hull, letting out an empty thump that reverberated inside the men aboard. There was no moon. The night, dark and clear all at once, was made thicker by a sinister haze which veiled the stars and the lights in the distance. Behind the wheel, on the bridge of the thirty-five-foot boat, a bitter argument ensued.

Rude Thompson, captain for a day, had been entrusted to take *The Rambler* to the northwestern shores of St. Kitts in order to meet local members of the insurrection at the stroke of midnight. But that very stroke had gone at least half an hour earlier, as they'd seemingly found themselves off the coast of, not St. Kitts, but the neighboring St. Eustatius.

The men had gathered at Island Harbour, on the northeastern end of Anguilla, that very day to pack the boat with guns, ammo, and a few provisions for the journey. The mission had been kept secret and the men involved had camped near the training site at Junks Hole Beach for the past three days, away from their families for added security. *The Rambler* was loaded for the sixty-five-mile journey southward on Friday, June 9, shortly after lunch. Alwyn Cooke, the mastermind behind the plan, showed up uncharacteristically late. He wore his usual gray pressed trousers and white cotton shirt buttoned up to the top. Yet there was something ragged about his looks—something that went beyond the three-day beard and the sunken rings around his eyes. He brought with him the dark green canvas bag in which, ten days earlier, the police task force had intended to take their guns, before they were expelled from the island.

At that time, Inspector Edmonton, head of the police task force, had carried the bag to the Piper Aztec that was supposed to take him and the remaining four members of the force back to St. Kitts. On his way from the small wooden building that was Wallblake Airport to the equally small propeller aircraft sitting on the dust strip, he was met by Rude Thompson, Gaynor Henderson, and the collective indignation against the man whose ill judgment had led to widespread violence months before, during the Statehood Queen Show. Rude's first request for Inspector Edmonton to *drop de bag an' go on* was more of an order. The inspector's reluctance to obey gave Gaynor the opportunity he craved to restore the pride that had been taken from him three months earlier, on the evening when he was thrown in the dungeon. So, emboldened by the circumstances, Gaynor took a .32 pistol from behind his back and shoved it right inside Inspector Edmonton's mouth, until it polished his uvula. *You ever taste de taste of lead in you mout'?* Inspector Edmonton had no chance to reply. *You better drop de bag unless dis is de last t'ing you ever wan' taste.*

Alwyn Cooke had thought the gesture excessively violent, but ten days had shaken Anguilla's world, and he presently approached with the same bag, except that it now looked heavier, bulkier. *Come to de back of de truck. Is t'ree more of dem back dere.* His shrill voice cut through the air and opened up the silence. By three in the afternoon, *The Rambler* was loaded with most of the equipment the police force had left behind: six Lee-Enfield Mk III* .303 rifles, such as the ones used during World War I; five Winchester Model 54 .30-06 rifles, the predecessor to the famous Model 70, launched in 1936; four M1 Garand .30-06 semiauto-matic rifles; four M1 .30 semiautomatic carbines; eight hundred rounds of ammunition; two boxes of dynamite; four detonators; and four cans of tear gas. In addition to the material confiscated from the task force was a supply of more modern equipment from the USA, including five automatic .25 handguns, three .32-caliber pistols, and, crucially, two M16 automatic rifles and two Browning M1919 .30-caliber machine guns, both of which were popular at the time with the American army, particularly in Vietnam.

However antiquated, *The Rambler* was equipped with an arsenal big enough to arm a small militia. Which is precisely what Alwyn Cooke, Rude Thompson, and the rest of the organizers of the operation expected to find in St. Kitts that night awaiting their aid. They would be in for a surprise—but not yet. Right now, burdened with the weight of sixteen passengers plus five hundred pounds of guns and ammo, the main con-cern was how much the boat could carry without sinking. Therefore, provisions for a trip that was to last at least nine hours were kept to a bare minimum: a demijohn of water, some dry crisps, and homemade johnnycakes—a local delicacy made of cornmeal and traditionally baked by women for their men to eat on the journey (later transfigured into *johnny*)—freshly prepared by some of the more diligent wives.

The *Rambler* was loaded and ready to go by about three in the afternoon, but the sun wouldn't set until some four hours later. The island, in complete control of the rebel government for the previous ten days, had been inaccessible to foreign traffic for forty-eight hours. Oil drums were carried in pickup trucks and lined up on the dirt strip of the airport to prevent any aircraft from landing, and all beaching points (there were no ports in Anguilla) had been guarded and officially closed to the outside world in an effort to keep any news of a plan which was largely unknown to the population in the first place from leaking to the enemy.

Consequently, at three in the afternoon of Friday, June 9, 1967, The *Rambler* became the first boat to leave Anguilla's territorial waters in two days. It sailed eastward from Island Harbour, and faced the tough Atlantic tides off the northeastern part of the island, before making the choppy journey past the cliffs of Harbour Ridge. Then it reached the treacherous seas off Captain's Bay, only to drift into the narrow passage between Windward Point, the easternmost part of the island, and Scrub Island, a midsized cay to the east that still housed a dirt strip built as part of that obscure episode of World War II—the Destroyers-for-Bases Agreement.

By four in the afternoon, The *Rambler* was cutting across the strait between Anguilla and Scrub, steering away from the waves that rolled in all the way from Africa, and heading in the general direction of St. Kitts and the rest of the Caribbean atoll. The first three miles of the passage were expected to be among the roughest of the day, but the sun still burned ferociously in the sky and the men aboard *The Rambler* still itched with desire to reach St. Kitts and get to the task at hand as the boat left Scrub Island behind on its port side and stopped challenging the high crests of the vigorous sea in order to roll with them toward Tintamarre, a.k.a. Flat Island, about ten nautical miles away.

Like Scrub, Tintamarre is a midsized cay just off the (northwestern) coast of its bigger sister island, St. Martin, which had little of interest for honest citizens outside one or two unspoiled beaches of white sand and turquoise water. Like Scrub, the island is flat enough to home a dirt strip, but with facilities in Dutch Sint Maarten to the south, Scrub Island to the east, and Dog Island to the north, the American army felt adequately prepared to monitor the traffic and disrupt the passage of German U-boats through the Anguilla channel. Perhaps understandably, their plans did not foresee the apparition of Jan van Hoeppel, a mercenary adventurer—half Quixote, half Saint Exupéry—who, in collaboration with the Vichy government across the French Caribbean, would foil the American initiative and develop a sophisticated replenishing station in Tintamarre for the Nazi navy to enjoy fresh fruit and water from Martinique, from Guadeloupe, from Dominica, while their submarines were refueled and replenished.

Alas, German interest in the Caribbean was short-lived, so when the traffic diminished and, indeed, the bad guys were defeated, van Hoeppel turned to aviation for inspiration: he already owned a four-seat, high-wing, single-engine Stinson Reliant, which he dubbed *La Cucaracha*, so he flattened the ground in Tintamarre, invested the money he had made collaborating with the Vichy in two ten-seat Stinson Model A trimotors and a six-seat Stinson Detroiter, and, just like that, established the first operational airline in the northeastern Caribbean: Air Atlantique.

Van Hoeppel had long shifted his focus from airplanes to real estate, and the role he plays in this tale hangs in the balance of untyped
words, but as sixteen restless men approached the western shores of
Tintamarre on the first stage in their voyage, the remnants of a fleet
that had been reduced by frequent accidents and decimated by a severe
hurricane more than fifteen years back glowed with a rare air of gran-
deur, of relevance, as if, somehow, one impossible dream could be mirrored in another. Then Alwyn Cooke intervened. *Cut de engine*. Rude
Thompson looked at his comrade with a trace of disbelief, but did not
venture as far as to question the order. A few seconds elapsed before
Wha' we do now?—a voice so anonymous echoed that it seemed to each
of the passengers in the boat as if they had all asked the question at
the same time. *We wait for night to fall*, and the ensuing silence filled
the air separating the flat soil of Tintamarre to the starboard and the
angled hills of St. Barths in the distance, shadowed in the center by a
thick pocket of rain that poured down somewhere at sea, between *The
Rambler* and the island.

It had just gone five when the diesel engine of *The Rambler* fell
silent. The first ten miles of the journey had taken a good two hours,
but the sun still hung high in the sky, far above the horizon line. Alwyn
Cooke intended to minimize the chances of being caught crossing the
St. Barths channel by lingering near Tintamarre until night had fallen.
On Friday, June 9, 1967, the sun set at 6:46 p.m. The tropical crepuscule, short-lived and dramatic, shed daylight for another half hour.
Hence, *The Rambler* and its crew had to sit tight and wait out at sea,
off the eastern end of Tintamarre, for two full hours. Of which, the first
thirty, forty minutes were spent in utter silence, as if Alwyn Cooke's
instruction had dropped a tacit curfew on words.

But it had not been Alwyn Cooke, nor anyone else, who had imposed the silence. Instead, it was the simultaneous reaction of sixteen men, all far too absorbed in their own worries to notice the world outside. To the three American mercenaries aboard *The Rambler*, all scarred from their exploits in Vietnam, this might have seemed like a natural reaction. However, to the average West Indian, a group of sixteen men sitting in silence for this long in a small boat was an aberration. A talkative people steeped in a long tradition of humor and faith, West Indians are not prone to fall silent—to let pass an opportunity to lambaste one another with a copious dose of pique—on any occasion. But this was more than just an adventure, and more was at stake than any of them would have cared to admit: here were joined at once interests that were national and personal, common and individual; here was invested much hope, much time, and much money—money to pay for guns, money to pay for experienced men of war, money that in Anguilla in 1967 simply did not exist. Many of these thoughts never even crossed the minds of any of the sixteen men aboard *The Rambler*. Nevertheless, the tension, the fear, the uncertainty that reigned was adequately represented in this drawn-out silence that lasted from the moment Alwyn Cooke uttered his order to wait for night, until sometime after six, when the red sun approaching the horizon inexplicably triggered in the young Walter Stewart a need to hum the melody of "The Lord Is My Shepherd."

Walter Stewart sat at the back of *The Rambler*, where the fumes of the diesel engine had sent him on a dizzying slumber from the start. But the boat had been drifting for a good hour, and, if anything, the pervading smell was of sweat and salt, of men at sea, and Walter had often gone out fishing with his grandfather, Connor, the head of the Stewart family from Island Harbour, and sometimes they had traveled as far north as Sombrero Island, forty miles away from Anguilla and right in the middle of the Anegada Passage, so Walter knew for a fact that what he was feeling was not seasickness, and yet he could not help the vacuum in his stomach, and the spinning inside his head, and the dryness in his mouth, the taste of bitter fullness in his larynx.

Although Walter was merely a kid—barely fifteen years old—he had been part of the revolution from the start. He had been there, getting his placard smashed on his head, in January 1967, when Rude Thompson and Alwyn Cooke recruited people to follow Chief Minister Bradshaw during his official visit to the island; he had proved one of the most vociferous hecklers at the speeches the statesman from St. Kitts had tried to deliver in Anguilla to "discuss" the concept of statehood; and he had been there again, watching from a safe distance, as the very same policemen who had so magnanimously shared their tear gas with the crowd left the island in an equally gallant gesture, on the morning of May 30.

Ten days later, the commitment and loyalty of Walter Stewart toward the revolutionary cause was neither challenged nor questioned. What was being put to the test, however, was his stomach—until the sun, hanging low over the horizon, reddened by a thickening mist, put a hymn he loathed in his mind. Then, slowly, he let out a wail, which turned itself into a quiet hum, which led to a whisper. By the time he started whistling the tune, Mario Gómez, one of the American mercenaries onboard, had had enough. *What the hell are you singing that for, boy? The only lord who can help you now is this:* and he held the long, angular shell of a .30-caliber missile upright in his left hand, between his index finger and thumb. His pale young face squirmed in a failed attempt to look tough. *Who the hell would put all that junk in a deserted rock, anyway?* asked Gómez, referring to the carcasses of whatever remained of the fleet of Air Atlantique. Corporal Gómez did not think Walter Stewart would be headstrong enough to go on with his gospel, but he did not want to risk it either, nor did he feel in the frame of mind to allow the protracted silence to continue. Meanwhile, Glenallen Rawlingson, a quiet, determined young man with bulging eyes, inward-folded lips, and an anthropoid gait, was also happy to break the silence. He was tall and thin, and darker than the average Anguillian. Unlike most of the men in the expedition, he did not stem from the eastern end of the island, but from the more central South Hill. In a spontaneous burst of energy, he explained, maybe to Corporal Gómez, maybe to everyone else, how once, not too long ago, Flat Island had been an important source of income to Anguillians. *My uncle did till de soil of dat land, when it belong to Mr. D.C.* Glenallen spoke the truth, but for those who did not know the story it was hard to imagine, adrift, awaiting the end of the day, that anything at all might have ever taken place on that godforsaken rock. Yet Glenallen's voice was less abrasive than the silence it replaced, so Corporal Gómez and the rest of the crew allowed him to continue his tale about an eccentric Dutch heir who had come to this far corner of the earth to dissociate himself from the civilized world and who had decided to set up his kingdom in Tintamarre, where he built a luxurious palace and raised cattle and grew cotton and, implausibly, became a major purchaser of Anguilla's one and only export: labor. Alas, there was to be no happy ending to the fairy tale. D.C.'s death was mysterious, sad, and, as all death must be, lonely, but also categorical, because he failed to plant in Tintamarre or in the womb of his beloved Elaine Nisbet, or anywhere else for that matter, the seed of his spring and consequently brought with the end of his life the end, too, of his lineage and of a Caribbean extravaganza like no other. But this episode is too important to be dispatched as an aside. So let's press the pause button and allow D.C. van Ruijtenbeek to linger in space for the time being, while we call upon the voice of the great Héctor Lavoe to put an end to

Glenallen Rawlingson's anecdote with the unmistakable melody of *Todo tiene su final / nada dura para siempre* . . .

Back in *The Rambler*, where it's unlikely that anyone had ever heard of Héctor Lavoe, except perhaps for Corporal Gómez, who had Borinquen running through his veins, the atmosphere on the boat loosened somewhat, awarding an air of normality to a situation that was anything but normal. When the sunset arrived it caught most of the men off guard. The tide had taken *The Rambler* slightly to the north of Tintamarre and the sun could be seen sinking in full behind the mass of water separating Anguilla from St. Martin. There was no afterglow. There was, however, a significant glow emanating from the fully restored and expanded electricity lines in St. Martin, which, since the devastating passage of Hurricane Donna in 1960, had been carefully developed on both sides of the island. Anguillians living on the southern shores were confronted with this sharp reality daily, but the men aboard *The Rambler* were mostly from the north and the east. Ahead of them the calm sea, tainted yellow, orange, pink, served as background to the silhouette of St. Martin towering above the pitch-black outline of flat little Anguilla, where not only had the government deemed it economically unviable to supply electricity to the six thousand islanders, but even the archaic telephone system which had been in place prior to Hurricane Donna remained, seven years later, derelict and unrepaired.

Invigorated by the beauty, by the powerful symbolism of the scene, Alwyn Cooke entrusted the mission to the heavens with a *May de Lord be wit' us* and gave the order to *Le's go*. The intrepid bunch was on its way again to meet its unlikely destiny.

The night had settled, there was no moon, and *The Rambler*, slow and overloaded, rocked between the dim lights of St. Barths, barely visible behind a curtain of mist to the east and the small pocket of life by

St. Martin's Orient Bay to the west. It was not until two hours after they had departed Tintamarre that the first major crossroads of the night was reached. The lights of Gustavia, the main settlement in St. Barths, had been left behind a good half hour earlier, and Pointe Blanche in St. Martin could barely be seen in the distance behind the boat. *The Rambler* had been cruising smoothly at the desired speed, just over ten knots an hour. Rude Thompson knew that all he had to do was point the ship due south and in less than three hours they would see the lights of St. Eustatius, at which point he would steer gently to the west, just a few degrees, not more, to take the sloop through the channel between St. Eustatius and St. Kitts and come straight into Sandy Hill Point. Here a friendly motorboat was supposed to be awaiting their arrival to escort them to the final meeting point at Half Way Tree.

All this sounded plain and simple, and it would have been so, had *The Rambler* been equipped with the most rudimentary of navigational tools, such as a compass. But *The Rambler* was a boat used exclusively to bridge the seven-mile channel between Anguilla and St. Martin, which never required anything more than mediocre eyesight, and it had never been intended as anything other than a means of transportation for leisure purposes or a smuggling run, which in Anguilla at the time was as much a national pastime as a way of earning a living. And Rude Thompson, captain for a day, had never stepped aboard *The Rambler* before the afternoon of Friday, June 9, 1967, when the boat had been floated at Island Harbour and loaded with a small arsenal of old guns.

Everybody had been too busy then, minding their own business, to realize the instrumental void on the bridge of the thirty-five-foot boat, and Rude Thompson had not thought of it until he found himself at the helm of a drifting vessel off the coast of Tintamarre. Before the fall of the night, and with Anguilla to the north as his point of reference,

Rude picked up an old piece of orange chalk and marked the cardinal points on the wheel of the boat. So once he heard Alwyn's coarse *Le's go*, he fired the engine and pointed *The Rambler* in the direction that his makeshift compass told him was south, using as frame of reference the lights along the eastern coast of St. Martin and those on the western side of St. Barths to make the appropriate corrections.

But Rude Thompson had not considered the effect of the tide, rolling at full strength from east to west once *The Rambler* hit the waters south of St. Barths. Or, if he did, he underestimated the force of the sea, such that, despite holding the helm steady within the lines that marked his south, *The Rambler* drifted somewhat—just marginally, not even a few degrees—to the west. The consequences of this minor inaccuracy would prove to be calamitous when, two hours later, as *The Rambler* soared through the northern Caribbean, the first tenuous lights flickered in the distance, dead ahead. *Da' oughtta be Statia right dere*, announced Rude Thompson, oblivious to the fact that at the speed they had traveled and with a mist that grew thicker as the night grew colder, they could not yet be within eyeshot of St. Eustatius.

It did not even occur to Rude Thompson that this could be so, because in Rude Thompson's mind all he required to confirm that, indeed, it was "Statia" right ahead of them, was for the lights of St. Kitts to loom in the horizon, marginally to the west of the lights which could already be seen. Never doubting he was right, Rude steered *The Rambler* to the east of the electric lights, roughly where he expected St. Kitts to appear. Less than half an hour after that, what he thought was St. Kitts emerged from the dark, farther still to the east than he had expected. It was not yet ten p.m., and at this rate Rude predicted they would reach the lights in an hour's time at the most, putting them just about an hour ahead of schedule.

The announcement was greeted with excitement by the younger ones among the militants, but Solomon Carter had long shed the candid ingenuity that so often accompanies youth, and he had never been known for his optimism in the first place, and he had lived long enough to be aware that when life deals you a hand with a surprise card in it, seldom does it turn out to be a pleasant one. But Solomon was no alarmist—nor was he a fool: often the man behind the scenes, he allowed the attention of the people of Anguilla to focus on the more charismatic figures of Alwyn Cooke and Rude Thompson, while he was allowed to exert his influence on them behind closed doors. Solomon Carter had been the first man to whom Alwyn Cooke had revealed his plans to invade the island of St. Kitts, before, even, Rude Thompson, precisely for the sober attitude and levelheadedness that took an apprehensive—nervous, really—Sol Carter right up to the corner where Alwyn Cooke stood. *Wha's our speed, Al?* Alwyn Cooke had not seen Solomon Carter approach in the darkness of *The Rambler*, and was startled by the question. He thought of scolding Solomon as he hesitated to give his answer. Then he thought better. *Ten and a half knots.* Solomon Carter knew they had kept a steady pace throughout the night—he had listened out for the engines—but he knew he still had to ask: *We slow down?* Before he saw Alwyn Cooke shake his head he'd already let out a long sucking noise, as he kissed his teeth in disgust. *In dis sea an' dis speed, how come we be ahead of schedule?* Alwyn gave no thought to Solomon's question, immediately passed it on to Rude Thompson.

Now, Solomon Carter was no expert in matters of seafaring, but it took more an elementary course in geography than a lifetime out at sea to understand that the latest set of lights populating the horizon could not be St. Kitts. When he explained to Rude Thompson that he thought the lights ahead of them came from Statia, and those to the west from

Saba, he was greeted with a patronizing chuckle and an impatient *Sol, when you last notice S'Martin behind?* The dim lights at the southern end of St. Martin had disappeared an hour or so after *The Rambler* had sailed past Pointe Blanche. *Wit' dis mist you havin' tonight you kyan't see all da way to Saba out west. Dem lights west Statia, an' dem in front St. Kitts.*

Solomon Carter was not convinced by Rude Thompson's explanation, and he made him aware of his concern, but before bothering to give the question further thought Rude found the need to emphasize his authority and discourage any further questioning by rhetorically asking, *Who de captain, Sol? You or me?* Solomon let out a fiery stare that ripped open the dark canvas of the night as he looked straight into Rude Thompson's eyes before turning away from him and heading back to the aft of *The Rambler*. There, he waited patiently for the next set of lights to appear on the horizon line.

But Sol's wait was cut short a few minutes later, when the lights ahead, brighter, larger by the minute, added to the numbing growl of the diesel engine, the violent rocking of the boat, and the dark flatness of the night chipped away at Gaynor Henderson's spirit and broke his will. From the bottom of his burdened, frightened chest, *Boy, too many people goin' dead* could be heard. The unexpected lament put an end to every idle conversation, to every useless motion meant to make the wait for the arrival in St. Kitts less tedious. For a moment, even the 115hp diesel engine went mute and toiled in silence. Until Harry González, the man sitting to the right of Gaynor Henderson, let out an exasperated *What the fuck?*

Too many people goin' dead wit' dis crazy plan, man, revealed a terrified Gaynor Henderson, who was, quite literally, scared shitless.

(The Plan)

T OO MANY PEOPLE GOIN' DEAD WIT' DIS CRAZY PLAN, MAN, cried
  Gaynor Henderson; and the whining tone in his voice put tears
in his words which did not yet run down his cheeks; and it traveled
through the thick air in the middle of the night, making its way past
Corporal Gómez's anger to wake Glenallen Rawlingson from his slumber; and it crossed the brain of each of the men aboard *The Rambler*
as it entered their system through one ear, only to depart it almost immediately out the opposite one; and it spread not so much outrage or
surprise but, rather, fear.

Fear for themselves, fear for the other, fear of God, and fear of death
took hold and spread among each of the members of a crew of amateurs
who had been so absorbed in the adventure of toppling a government
that they had not yet realized it was highly unlikely they would all be
taking part in the journey home the following day, even if their ploy
was successful. *I ain' go blow up no fuel depot: too many people goin' dead!*
Gaynor, of course, was referring to the tally of *other* people who would
die, more concerned about his record in the eyes of the ever merci-
ful God Almighty than about his most immediate future. However, his
spontaneous deliverance struck a note far more selfish, more individual, in his fellow Anguillians, all suddenly seriously threatened by the
arrival of death.

Meanwhile, the next repetition of his too-many-people-goin'-dead

nonsense was one too many for Harry González, who took his automatic .32 out of its holster, loaded it, cocked its hammer, got on his feet,
and with a *You fucking moron* lifted Gaynor by the collar of his T-shirt
with his left hand as he aligned the barrel of his gun with the large,
hyperventilating nostrils of the Anguillian. But by this time the whining tone of Gaynor's first wail had already found its way to the bridge of
The Rambler, where it tolled the alarm bells inside the head of Alwyn
Cooke, who, despite the darkness, could see very well what was going
on as he approached Harry González and ordered him, unequivocally,
to *Put da' away an' save your aggression for de Bradshers.*

Harry González was the leader of the three American mercenaries aboard *The Rambler*. He too had been to Vietnam but, unlike Mario Gómez, the war had not so much diminished his human sensibility
as emphasized the perversion of his already-cruel disposition. He had
come across Alwyn Cooke by mere coincidence one day on St. Thomas
in the US Virgin Islands, when he overheard the man explaining to an
official of the US Postal Service the serious impasse at which Anguilla
found itself after it had expelled the full extent of the police task force
from the island and, along with them, any semblance of allegiance, or
even suzerainty, toward St. Kitts. The central government in Baseterre
had subsequently frozen all Anguillian bank accounts and suspended
the postal service between the islands, effectively isolating Anguilla.
Therefore, the breakaway country had set up official PO boxes in both
French and Dutch St. Martin, which remained the only means to communicate and send funds to the island.

After a long conversation that was more monologue than negotiation, all that Alwyn Cooke achieved was an *I'm sorry, Mr. Cooke—I'm
afraid there's nothing I could do for you and your government, other than
to suggest to all customers wishing to mail something to Anguilla to do so*

to either of your addresses in St. Martin. That, along with a promise that a large, clear notice would be hung in all post offices in the Virgin Islands, advising customers of the situation in Anguilla, an assurance— *Believe me, Mr. Cooke, when I tell you that we understand the importance of your struggle and we wish you all the success*—and, on his way out of the post office, a chance meeting with Harry González, who had overheard the word *Anguilla* and had been intrigued enough to linger nearby and eavesdrop.

Harry González was a small man with a strong, square body and an eminently forgettable face. His hair was short, his hands tough as a fisherman's, and his clothes untidy. But there was something about his voice, deep and meaningful, or perhaps just evil, which demanded attention when he spoke. As Alwyn Cooke gathered himself and got ready to depart the post office, Harry González set off at full speed in a roundabout way that took him to the same exit that Alwyn was approaching, but from the opposite direction. The coming together that Harry González intended to make seem inevitable was, in fact, rather clumsy, and Alwyn Cooke, not the strongest-framed man by any stretch of the imagination, almost stumbled to the ground. Harry González's apology as he helped Alwyn back to his feet was almost sincere. *Mr. Cooke, isn't it?* and he looked wilily to one side, then the other. *From the rebel island, the new Cuba in the Caribbean, right?* Alwyn Cooke was perplexed, both by the blow that had nearly decked him and by the sudden notoriety he seemed to have gained since the expulsion of the police task force from Anguilla, just three days before. *I've been following the case closely,* Harry González whispered, in response to the shade of surprise which he saw cloud the eyes of Alwyn Cooke. *Follow me—don't be afraid, I'm a friend of your cause, and I think I can offer you something that will be of help.*

Harry González was making it up as he went along. He knew little about "the cause" and was not at all certain about how much he could help, but he sensed the opportunity to make a buck, and as he escorted Alwyn Cooke down to the harbor and back behind the docks, all he could think of was the prospect of a newfound benefactor. *Hey, mister— da' far enough, nuh.* Alwyn Cooke, not quite versed in the art of revolution and liberation, suspended his judgment momentarily and allowed a perfect stranger to lead him to the darker part of town in the hope that he would find a clue, a tip, a helping hand. But enough was enough already, and had Alwyn Cooke not known that he carried just about nothing worth taking from him, and had he not been quite sure that the Lord was there with him to protect him and guide him onto the path of righteousness and deliverance, had Alwyn Cooke not been dead certain about the fact that God was on his side, he might have feared for his safety, because, despite the fact that it was the middle of the day in early June, the hill to one side of the harbor and the tall warehouses before the two men cut large, sharp shadows that fed an air of lowlife into the atmosphere. On the other hand, Alwyn Cooke thought this might be precisely the kind of setting, of environment, as it were, where Providence would have him find the help Anguilla needed right now.

Just as Alwyn Cooke finally came to understand what Rude Thompson had been trying to explain all along, what he, Rude, had been trying to put to practice since the antics surrounding the failed Statehood Queen Show in February that same year—that, at least for the time being, Anguilla found itself on the side of the crooks, the hoodlums, the gangsters, and, indeed, the rebels—as Alwyn Cooke finally saw sense in Rude's words, Harry González turned on his heels and burned right through Alwyn's ingenuity with his fierce eyes. *Okay, okay—you're right. This will do right here just fine.*

At this point Alwyn Cooke half expected to see the knife or dagger that would turn this stranger into a Caribbean Mack, but the intentions of Harry González were far more mercantile than he thought, and as the man began his spiel, Alwyn became more comfortable with his skin, blood flowing back to his cheeks, the light brown returning to his complexion. *You have a family?* It was the third time Harry González asked Alwyn, but he was too immersed in his own thoughts to follow the conversation. Finally, Alwyn nodded gently and Harry González, *Right. You love your family, right? You would do anything for your family, right? To protect your family, right? C'mon, man—talk to me, man. Stop being so paranoid.* Alwyn Cooke nodded again, this time more vehemently. *You own a gun? You need a gun to protect your family, right? You own a gun?*

Harry González gave Alwyn Cooke no chance to explain that things didn't quite work that way in Anguilla, that violent crime was close to nonexistent, and that if anyone did anything to his family or to anybody else, everyone in the community would know who had done it, and where to find him.

Yes or no, man—do you own a gun? Yes! There you go, man. This is no different than having a gun to protect your family. You need guns to protect your island.

That's where Alwyn Cooke's recollection of the meeting blurred into a blank. That's where the penny actually fell, where Alwyn Cooke became convinced that *In trut', no soul ain' go hear not'in' we says, only if we go make one big mess dem go hear us.* That's when he realized that the efforts by the fifteen-member peacekeeping committee governing the island since May 30, 1967 to attain international recognition—indeed, to attain a minimum level of respectability—had to be accompanied by a parallel statement that would firmly entrench the rebel nation within the quarters of the rogues for it to be considered seriously.

Don't you for a minute think they won't attack you. They will attack, and if they know you're unprepared they'll attack even sooner. Think of Bay of Pigs—you think they won't do something similar to you? So your island's smaller than Cuba: don't worry, they'll just call it Bay of Piglets, or something, but be sure they'll find a way.

Harry González didn't very well know who he meant by "they," nor who Alwyn Cooke would associate with it, but it didn't matter anymore, because Alwyn was already absent and incapable of answering anything Harry said.

You need guns, you need a plan. You love your people, like you love your family—but can you protect them? I'm your man. I can get you guns, I can show you how to use them. Just call this number when you're ready and ask for Harry, or just come around here when you're next in town. Everyone knows who I am.

Alwyn didn't care to explain that he could not call, because there were no working telephone lines on the island. He just took the piece of paper Harry gave him, shoved it inside the right pocket of his pressed gray trousers, and turned back, without uttering a word, burdened by an urgency he had not felt before. Alwyn flagged the first cab he could find—*Take me to de airport.* He did not listen to the driver's chitchat, nor did he answer any of his trivial questions. Once at the Harry S. Truman Airport, he tracked down Diomede Alderton, the pilot of the Piper Aztec that had flown him into St. Thomas earlier that day, and gave him unequivocal instructions: *We mus' get back to Anguilla tonight.* Which meant before nightfall. And so, with the last light of the crepuscule, the same Piper Aztec that previously had ridded the island of its police task force landed on the dirt strip at Wallblake Airport, where the "ground crew" had recognized *The Pipe*, Diomede's plane, named after his copious smoking habit, and had cleared the runway of the cars and oil drums that obstructed it for protection.

As soon as Alwyn Cooke stepped off the plane he sent out a few boys to call the fourteen other members of the peacekeeping committee to attend an extraordinary session that night at his home in Island Harbour. By call, he meant, quite literally, *Run to dey house an' shout dey name till dey hear you.* Less than two hours later, fourteen curious, confused, and even angry men assembled at Alwyn Cooke's residence, where the rumbling of the generator indicated to them that he meant business. He had been sent to St. Thomas to put forward Anguilla's position to the regional government, and to persuade the US Postal Service to provide Anguilla with a means of communication with the outside world other than through the antagonistic St. Kitts. Whatever the outcome of his mission, it was hard to fathom why he found it necessary to discuss it in the middle of the night. Then came Alwyn with his report, which did not mention the regional government of St. Thomas, or the US Postal Service. Instead, he went on and on about the threat of invasion, the need to obtain more and more modern weapons, and the even more urgent need to deploy a contingency plan, in case foreign forces (read, Kittitian) were to approach the island.

Now, Alwyn Cooke could not have been aware of the news that had arrived from St. Kitts earlier that day, together with the four-man delegation which had been sent there one day after the expulsion of the police task force, because Alwyn Cooke had been between flights when the men in question returned from their frustrating journey not so much empty-handed as openly challenged. On May 31, 1967, a four-man delegation headed by Aaron Lowell, the representative of Anguilla in the parliament of St. Kitts-Nevis-Anguilla, took a concise and categorical proposal to Premier Bradshaw in St. Kitts, to allow the secession of Anguilla from the tri-island state, and to encourage the rebel island's return to direct British administration. The official government response delivered the following day not only ignored most of the proposal's content, it also called for the end of violence in Anguilla and a return to the constitutional order of the nation. Disappointed, the delegation headed back to Anguilla on June 2, 1967 to report their failure to affect any kind of reaction from Bradshaw, together with their fear that, while the premier dismissed them politically, he would simultaneously seek assistance from other Caribbean countries to invade the island and take it back by force. The fact that Alwyn Cooke echoed the same fears on the very same day without any firsthand information of the events deeply impressed the rest of the peacekeeping committee, which unanimously and immediately reached an obvious conclusion and declared him the minister of defence of the island of Anguilla.

Despite the fact that there was no newspaper, no telephone, no local radio station, news traveled fast around the island by word of mouth. It took less than eight hours for the leader of the opposition of St. Kitts-Nevis-Anguilla, who happened to be in Anguilla at the time of the revolution and who had been unable to leave the island since, to find out that his good friend Alwyn Cooke had become the island's minister of defence. So, the very first visit Alwyn Cooke received in his new capacity on the morning of June 3, 1967, just barely after the crow of the first rooster had made its way past yards and fences and had been echoed in the throat of every competing rooster up the hill to the east, en route to Harbour Ridge, and in the opposite direction, along the shoreline toward Welches Hill, was that of Dr. Crispin Reynolds, leader of the opposition and editor of the *Speaker* newspaper, the only outlet where Anguillian issues had been discussed over the past four months or so.

Indeed, that was precisely how long Dr. Reynolds had been acquainted with Alwyn Cooke, going back to the day when he, Alwyn, had approached the politician at his place in South Hill with a request to feature a regular column in the *Speaker* involving matters related to Anguilla. Hence, ever since the official birth of the "Letter from Anguilla" section in the newspaper, a visit from one to the other was not to be considered out of the ordinary. However, the time of day invested the occasion with a sense of importance that was mirrored in Dr. Reynolds's somber, almost lugubrious tone of voice. The meeting was brief and, seemingly, inconsequential. It served only as a means to test the waters of the disposition of each toward the other. It had started with a statement of solidarity by Dr. Reynolds—whose party held the sole seat allocated to the island in the parliament of St. Kitts-Nevis-Anguilla— with the Anguillian people, and had ended with an assurance that if the rebel government were to back Dr. Reynolds's political initiative against Premier Bradshaw, he, in turn, would do everything in his power to grant the people of Anguilla their wishes, whatever those might be. Most importantly, however, Dr. Reynolds departed Island Harbour with the impression that his party and the rebels were on the same side, and that they could count on each other in the future. *We mus' meet again, Mr. Cooke. Dere are some important matters we mus' discuss.*

Alwyn Cooke did not have to wait long for that next meeting to take place: later that evening Crispin Reynolds knocked again on his door, this time with a folder full of important matters they needed to consider. Alwyn Cooke did not expect any visitors at home that evening, and he had not slept a full night since the revolution of May 30, four days earlier, so the generator was silent and he was more than ready to crash when he heard the knock on his front door. He slipped back into his pressed gray trousers and his clean white shirt while his wife, Ylaria, attended to the call.

Ylaria was more than ten years younger than Alwyn, but at twenty-eight no one in Anguilla would have said she was young. She had beautiful round features sharpened by the darkness of her skin, her eyes, her hair, gently coiffed into long plaits. Despite the beauty of her face, Ylaria's temper had awarded her something of a reputation among locals. To go with her fiery personality, she had a full, plump body, which inspired intermittently extreme doses of lust and fear. Dr. Reynolds had not expected to find the corpulent presence of Ylaria Cooke on the doorstep of her and her husband's home. Startled, he did what no one should ever do before a woman of her temperament: he hesitated. *Wha' kinda time dis is to come knock on a man's door?* Dr. Reynolds's quick presence of mind provided him with the perfect riposte to get out of trouble, *Di kind fo' serious business*, and before he could send Ylaria to go fetch her husband, Alwyn Cooke emerged from the shadows and asked his wife to start the generator.

Neither man felt an apology was necessary. *Jus' come dis way, doctor*, and business began in earnest. *Wha' I come to show yer, Mr. Cooke, is for yer eyes an' yer eyes only*. Alwyn Cooke was a man of his word, a man whose integrity had never yet been questioned, a man so proper very few people indeed had ever heard him utter an indecent syllable. Dr. Reynolds knew that if he was not stopped then and there it was because Alwyn, intrigued about what he had to say, would trade the information he came to offer for secrecy. So Crispin Reynolds took a short pause, gave Alwyn a chance to get out of the meeting, and, when he didn't, continued his speech, explaining how Robert Bradshaw was a resourceful man, how *He finally get to power, now he develop a likin' for it*, how people in St. Kitts were still too ingenuous to live up to the responsibility of democracy, how Robert Bradshaw was a loquacious speaker and an experienced politician who had manipulated the sentiments of voters in St. Kitts in order to favor himself and his cronies, *Like dat good-for-not'in' Paul Sout'well,* the country's deputy premier. *Ain' no one in St. Kitts go get rid of Robert Bradshaw by peaceful means.* Alwyn Cooke listened quietly, hardly blinking, awaiting the moment when something in Dr. Reynolds's speech would point in the direction of Anguilla. *Maybe yer t'ink this ain' got not'in' to do wit' yer an' yer republic, Mr. Cooke, but yer republic is only four days ol', an' I coin't see it reach di age of ten days ol', unless yer do somet'in' to stop Bradshaw an' his men from comin' over.*

Alwyn Cooke was far less experienced than Crispin Reynolds in political affairs, but he knew enough to understand that nobody would come knocking on his door late at night only to warn him—threaten him, almost—about the dangers that lay ahead on the road toward freedom, unless there was a benefit to be derived from it. So Alwyn Cooke waited a little longer, played his role expertly, and allowed Dr. Reynolds to unfold the plans contained within his folder.

Le' me show yer some numbers, Mr. Cooke. Dr. Reynolds produced a series of charts mapping the division within the electorate of St. Kitts, which made his party look a lot stronger than was evidenced in the elections of 1966, where despite earning the only seat awarded to the island of Anguilla, and the two seats appointed to the island of Nevis, the party had lost all the seats disputed in the seven constituencies of the island of St. Kitts. *I ain' questionin' Bradshaw's popularity wit' di cane-cutters out in di fields.* Yet Crispin Reynolds was more than keen to demonstrate how in the more urban areas of the country—hardly anything, not even Basseterre could merit the name *city*—Robert Bradshaw's victory had been marginal, if at all legitimate.

The hour was late, and Alwyn Cooke had had enough of listening to the political problems of an island with which he wanted his people to have no links whatsoever, but before he could ask what all of this had to do with him or Anguilla, Dr. Reynolds explained: *I guess wha' I tryin' to say is if I organize a rally in St. Kitts, yer could count on one to two t'ousand people showin' up, an' if I demand more drastic measures, at least some hundred of my supporters would take part.*

Throughout the year of 1967 the antagonism toward St. Kitts had escalated on the island of Anguilla, reaching the point where political intervention and pure lobbying had been sidestepped in favor of crowd mobilization and active protesting. Alwyn Cooke had been instrumental not only in the planning but also in the practical execution of a number of these protests. However, the goal behind the uncharacteristic activism that had dominated the lives of all Anguillians in the past five months had been to voice the dissatisfaction of the people, and to demonstrate to Britain, to the central government in St. Kitts, to anyone who cared to listen, really, that effective—peaceful—administration would be impossible in Anguilla so long as the island's artificial association with St. Kitts remained in place. The ultimate consequence of this process, and indeed its greatest success—i.e., the expulsion of the police task force from the island on May 30, 1967—had been nothing more than the spontaneous resolution of an incensed mob, empowered by its size, encouraged by association, who had marched to the police station the day before, demanding the unthinkable. Escalation had reached its peak, and Anguilla found itself, very much by accident, "independent."

Even so, what Dr. Reynolds had come to suggest was an altogether different kind of activism to that in which Anguillians had been involved through the auspice of their leaders. Dr. Reynolds had come to propose a joint operation by Anguillian and Kittitian forces in an effort to abduct Premier Bradshaw and Deputy Premier Southwell, to neutralize the military forces of the island, to seize the media, and to install a new government, spearheaded by the leader of the opposition party, Dr. Reynolds himself. In short, Crispin Reynolds had come knocking on Alwyn Cooke's door late at night to ask for his help in a sinister plan to carry out a coup d'état. Now, Alwyn Cooke was a man of principles, and in any other set of circumstances he would have shown his indignation in a forceful, brusque manner, before throwing his visitor headfirst out of his house. But Alwyn Cooke presently found himself in an unusual position, where he had to think about the good of his country, not only the categorical nature of his principles; and he was still concerned about the need to be recognized at an international level; and the threat of invasion from St. Kitts seemed evident to him, and had been confirmed by the rest of the members of the peacekeeping committee the night before. So Alwyn Cooke convinced himself by the minute of the need to make a definitive statement, to make one big mess, that would firmly entrench his rebel nation within the quarters of the rogues and be considered seriously.

Crispin Reynolds finally produced the small red folder he had kept inside the larger folder all this time, and spread out the blueprints of a yet-uncommitted crime. A group of fifteen to twenty Anguillians would be in charge of jump-starting the operation with their arrival, late one night, into a safe port where they would be able to distribute guns and ammunition among a large crowd of Kittitians. From that point forward, the idea was to split the rebels into three separate groups, which would all arrive in the capital, Baseterre, simultaneously. At this stage the groups would take different paths, one positioning itself by the main police station, another covering the grounds of the Defence Force (the name chosen by the government for its makeshift army), and a third heading toward the town's main fuel depot. The coordinated attack would begin at the Defence Force camp, where dynamite sticks would blow a hole into the building, allowing access to the rebels. As soon as the blast was heard, the group deployed by the police station would lay siege on it, using to its advantage the chaos produced by the explosion of the fuel depot, which would also be set alight as soon as the Defence Force camp was taken. The combination of speed with the element of surprise would allow the rebels to take control of the military forces on the island with minimal resistance. Subsequently, the group in charge of blowing up the fuel depot would move toward the sole radio station of the country, where it would announce the victory of the revolt. At the same time, a select group would head toward the government house in the company of Crispin Reynolds, while Robert Bradshaw and Paul Southwell would be arrested in their respective homes. Before the break of dawn the entire country would be secured, and a new administration would be in place—one that would look at the idea of secession for Anguilla from the tri-island state with sympathetic eyes.

Deep into the night did Crispin Reynolds and Alwyn Cooke sit by the light powered by the small diesel generator at the back of the house, carving the details of an intricate plan to invade the island of St. Kitts and topple its government, to finally seal the triumph of the revolution and install Dr. Reynolds in power. Alwyn Cooke would not get another minute's rest for many days to follow, and it became his wife's job to see to him lying down for half an hour here, a full hour there, to keep him from collapsing from exhaustion. That morning Ylaria force-fed her husband fish and cakes before he announced gravely, *Gotta go, nuh—don' wait for me for dinner*. He had not yet made a decision about the sinister plan that Crispin Reynolds had laid before him just hours before; indeed, he had cut short his prayers that morning and asked only for *clarity of vision, My Lord, da' I may distinguish de right pat' from de wrong for my people*.

But even with divine assistance, Alwyn Cooke felt this was just a tad too much for him to handle on his own. Despite the unspoken pledge to secrecy with which he had comforted Dr. Reynolds, Alwyn felt the need to consult, if not with the peacekeeping committee, at least with someone whose judgment would be sufficiently cool to consider the option with an open mind. Alwyn didn't think twice: it was still early in the morning when he parked his white 1962 4x4 Ford pickup truck just outside Solomon Carter's residence.

Sol's only comment when he heard the plan was: *Who else you tell 'bout dis?*

Nobody.

You make sure you keep it dat way. If we go do dis, we mus' do it hush-hush.

To an extent, Alwyn agreed with Sol, although he knew the secret could not be absolute. While it would be reckless to bring this up with the entire peacekeeping committee, he still felt it was necessary to get the approval of someone within it. That's when he brought Rude Thompson, the most hotheaded person on the committee, into the equation. He was certain Rude would find the idea appealing, and somewhere in between Sol's sobriety, Rude's volatility, and his own instinct could lie the answer to Anguilla's problems.

Then came the call to Harry González, from a public phone in a bistro in French St. Martin. *We need t' talk. No—I wan' do dis face to face.* Then came the next trip to St. Thomas, the rendezvous with Harry González, and a hasty deal—*With this short notice I can only get you four machine guns and a whole bunch of automatic pistols.*

Wha' 'bout men? We need trainin', an' a helpin' han'.

Ten thousand dollars in advance, plus ten thousand more when it's done. I'll bring two soldiers. Come pick us up tomorrow, first thing in the morning—and bring some money with you.

When Alwyn Cooke landed, first thing in the morning on June 6, 1967, at the Harry S. Truman Airport of St. Thomas, Harry González,

Mario Gómez, and Titus Brown were already waiting near the runway, on the outside of the fence that encircled the airfield. Alwyn's nerves showed, despite his most deliberate effort to look cool.

Ready?

The men didn't move, they didn't speak, they looked like mannequins discarded against the fence. Then Harry González bounced himself gently against the wire and approached Alwyn Cooke, whispering to his ear, *Got the money?* A moment of inspiration led to Alwyn answering with a relevant question: *How you goin' get dem bags past customs?* Harry González smiled. *That's where your money comes to play. Gimme three hundred bucks over the ten grand, and customs will never see the bags.* Candidly, Alwyn gestured toward the right pocket of his pressed gray trousers. *Not here—let's go somewhere safe.*

Despite Alwyn's inexperience in the underworld of criminal activity, he had enough sense in him not to trust three mercenaries for company in a "safe place" when he had ten thousand dollars in his pocket. *You gettin' de money when we in de plane. I have a t'ousand dollars wit' me, to avoid complications.* His right hand finally landed in his right pocket, he counted three hundred dollars and handed it to Harry González. Only then did Alwyn notice that one of the men was missing most of his left arm. *Wha's dis s'posed t' mean? When you say two soldiers, I t'ought you mean two* whole *soldiers.*

Leaning against the fence, Titus Brown's size was disguised. As soon as he heard Alwyn Cooke's derisive comment he lifted his big round face and gave him a fierce look. Erect, Titus Brown towered well over six feet high. His shoulders were wide as a wall, his biceps bulged out in all directions, and his square torso seemed taken out of a comic book. *Just a souvenir from the war, brother.*

Titus Brown was a man of few, very few, words. He was neither good at nor fond of talking. Titus held too much rage, too much anger, too much frustration inside to vent it out in words. His natural form of expression was through actions—generally violent actions. So when Alwyn Cooke, somewhat intimidated, let out a pitiful *You mean Vietnam?* Titus Brown felt a burning urge to hurt him badly. But this was a professional job, and it was well paid, and Titus Brown could certainly use the dough, so he made one, and only one, exception, and his deep, grave voice came out loaded with so much aggression it was clear he would not explain again that *I been places you don't even wanna know about, bitch. I been to hell, and guess what: they wouldn't have me there.* His arms opened wide, as if to showcase his maimed body, but in the absence of symmetry the gesture got lost somewhere between horror and ridicule. *It couldn't kill me, brother. You want help, or you think you can lead a revolution just by asking stupid questions?* Before Alwyn Cooke had a chance to answer, Harry González stepped up to calm the tempers and explain, *If any of your men in Anguilla was half the shot my brother Titus here is, you wouldn't have asked me for training. Let's cut the crap and get going.*

Then came three days of training at a makeshift shooting range by Junks Hole Beach, on the uninhabited eastern point of Anguilla, where bottles survived far too long as targets and blasts got lost in the roar of the ocean. Then came *The Rambler*, drifting off the coast of Tintamarre, "The Lord Is My Shepherd," and, finally, *Too many people goin' dead.*

CHAPTER I REVISITED

THE BITTER ARGUMENT

PUT DA' AWAY AN' SAVE YOUR AGGRESSION FOR DE **B**RADSHERS. Alwyn Cooke spoke authoritatively, full of confidence, to the man whom, just a week before, he had not known how to address. In the previous ten days he had gone from being a charismatic rich man to becoming an efficient leader. He walked into the scene and, without making a big fuss, defused the situation. *We all tense, nuh, but we mus' take it easy. Gaynor—watcha doin' shouting nonsense like dat for?* And Gaynor, half ashamed but steadfast in his resolve not to yield, almost got started again. And Harry González, *Think very well what you're gonna say*, the hammer of his gun still cocked, no longer looking into Gaynor Henderson's nose but directed at the stars.

Yet at this point, it wasn't only Gaynor Henderson who had to choose his words carefully, because all of a sudden just about every person on *The Rambler*, except for Sol and Rude, had something to say about the plan. All of a sudden it was as if the words that had not been spoken had to be retrieved, rescued, from the previous silence. All at once, unsuspecting friends and family members faced the imminent danger of a blaze of fire spreading uncontrolled through the slums of Baseterre, which was all one big slum. Meanwhile, others who until now had seemed too neutral or perplexed to make any kind of statement displayed a vicious vein and condemned to death by fire all of those who had conspired against the rightful development of their homeland, even if it was only by omission. And then there were those standing between the rifles and the dynamite who claimed they had not come along to send anybody to the stake, for it was no one's business other than God Almighty's to decide who's to live and who's to die, and when and how, and there is no greater sin than to play God, and *there ain' no cause, no matter how righteous, wort' da soul of a single one of God's children. Amen!* And in no time at all the back of *The Rambler* became a franchise of Babel, where nothing was being erected and no languages were being spoken, other than English, but where everyone addressed everyone else, and no one addressed anyone in particular, and consequently no one heard what anyone said, and words came and went and mixed and jumbled and rose over, above, on top of one another, forming this unintelligible gobble that got lost in the endless darkness of the sea.

Fellows, stop it already. Leave it alone! But the words had taken their toll, and this bedlam was not about to be sorted out by the sober, understated reprimands of Alwyn Cooke. *Leave it alone, I say!* And he turned to the man whom he thought was stirring all the trouble, but he found Harry González sitting back in his place, hammer uncocked, gun back in its holster, head in both hands, looking at the floor, thinking, *What the hell have I got myself into?* and most likely making calculations, trying to figure out whether twenty grand split between three would be enough to account for all this shit.

Out of nowhere, Solomon Carter suddenly roared with intimidating vigor over the yapping crowd, *Yo Rude! If dem lights to de west Statia and dem lights dead ahead St. Kitts, you wanna tell me wha' dem lights over dere be?* As soon as he rose to his feet, it seemed like Sol stood on higher ground, and everyone aboard *The Rambler* fell silent. *You go tell me is Barbuda, nuh?* The question was rhetorical, but Sol Carter had been insulted, and he felt aggrieved, and he would not stop until Rude Thompson knew exactly what he thought of him. Because it was one thing to be inexperienced—none of the men aboard *The Rambler*, at least none of the ones who mattered, the Anguillians, were used to sailing between the islands; none of them had ever taken part in a rebellion, organized a revolution, or been in a military operation. But it was altogether a different thing to be proud—so proud that you would not see, would not accept, your mistakes, putting in jeopardy the success of an operation in which every single man was risking his life. *Or you t'ink you de only one riskin' somet'in' tonight? Tell me, nuh—wha dat light yonder be, if it ain' St. Kitts?*

As soon as Rude Thompson spotted the lights he pulled back the handles of the throttle, letting the engines idle. For a moment, all that could be heard was the empty thump of a wayward wave or ripple crashing against the underside of the hull, as the calm Caribbean waters rocked the boat melodiously, intensely, in the middle of the night. *The Rambler* drifted helplessly in no particular direction and Rude Thompson had the perfect chance to acknowledge his mistake, to humbly concede Sol's point, to steer the boat in the right direction and get on with it. He had the chance—Sol had purposely played his cards that way. Except, if Rude had been the kind of fellow with the temperment necessary to take such option, then he wouldn't have been called Rude: then his nickname would have been Rudy, or Rat, or he would have had no nickname and been plain Rudolf. But he wasn't; he was called Rude Thompson and he was called Rude Thompson for a reason. So when Sol Carter talked up Rude Thompson's mistake and made him look like a fool, he didn't take to it nicely. *Who you t'ink you be, Sol? You t'ink you de boss? You t'ink you de leader? You ain' not'in'—not'in' but a drunk-*

ard, a t'ief, and a failure. They were the first words that came to Rude's mind—he might have called him anything else he could think of, had he been able to think of anything at all. As he pronounced the words he approached with his fists balled shut, thumbs outside his fingers, ready to pounce on the fifty-year-old man who had spotted his shortcomings as captain and made him lose his cool.

Alwyn Cooke recognized this as the perfect opportunity to assert himself as the natural, undisputed leader of the revolution. Without thinking, he stepped between the two men and instructed Rude to *Go back to your post, captain.* In an instant, Alwyn had elevated himself to a rank superior to that of the captain of a boat at sea. Alwyn became the moral, the spiritual, the intellectual leader of a motley bunch with one dubious, unprepared gesture. *Who the hell you two t'ink you be?* And that was the very first time most of the men aboard *The Rambler* ever heard Alwyn speak about hell. *Wha' you t'ink you doin'?* Another mention of hell might have rendered the first one banal, so Alwyn stopped himself short of stepping too far into the realm of the common. His mien was severe, and all of a sudden renewed confidence could be seen in the way he carried himself. *Dis ain' no joke, gentlemen—dis serious, serious business.* But Alwyn knew nobody on that boat was really in the mood for scolding, so he did not remind anyone that they had all come along on this adventure willingly, and they had all known well in advance what the plan was. Instead, he turned toward the bridge of *The Rambler* to study the situation with his captain.

It was well past eleven p.m. when the resolution was made to keep heading toward St. Eustatius, to pass it on its western side and then tack toward the southeast, thus taking a safer route into Sandy Hill Point, avoiding the channel between St. Kitts and St. Eustatius for the most part.

When you t'ink we reach Sandy Hill Point?

Is still awhile was not exactly what Alwyn Cooke wanted to hear from Rude Thompson at that point.

Full t'rottle all de way, nuh.

With the logistical problems surrounding the arrival in St. Kitts having been discussed and resolved, Alwyn now had to address the more pressing question of how to handle things once they landed at Half Way Tree. Gaynor Henderson had raised an issue out of turn, but the reaction Alwyn Cooke had witnessed in the men aboard *The Rambler* told him that the matter was more troubling than anyone organizing the coup would have liked to think. So Alwyn approached Solomon Carter and, without any discernible trace of alarm or panic, *Wha' we goin' do, Sol?*

Solomon Carter might have sulked at this point. He could have made yet another scene, forced a power struggle, disturbed the morale of the group further; he might even have sought to put his name forward on the list of popular leaders of a revolution that was just ten days old. But Solomon Carter was not Rude Thompson—that was not his temperament, nor was it his ambition. When Alwyn Cooke approached him, looking for advice, Solomon Carter did not turn around and walk away, he did not rub his anger in Alwyn's face, he did nothing other than provide his sober point of view. *I ain' like it.*

Solomon was a pacifist. He was as unlikely a protagonist of a revolution as anyone could have found in the annals of Caribbean history, and yet he was wholeheartedly committed to the cause by a curious sense of fate that made him believe there was a particular purpose to his life, that God had placed him at a particular juncture in time, in a particular place, all for a good reason. *I ain' like it from de start,* yet his voice was low and discrete, and his muttering was less conclusive than the words he spoke. *If we do our job wit' de Defence Force, we no need to blow up no fuel depot or not'in'.* A long silence ensued, before: *You don' t'ink?*

Alwyn Cooke was thinking, all right—he was thinking about the people-goin'-dead nonsense which Gaynor had started, and he was thinking whether it really was nonsense, or if, indeed, too many people were going to die in vain. But Solomon Carter's question gave back perspective to his wandering thoughts, and helped him to focus again on the real question, which was not how many people would die in the exercise, but what was required for the operation to be a success. Could an army of a hundred-odd people take Baseterre by storm and depose the tyrannical government of Robert Bradshaw without creating the havoc that would follow the explosion of the fuel depot, right there on the edge of the urban area?

The sad reality of the affair, however, was that, posed with the million-dollar question, Alwyn Cooke could not provide an educated guess as to whether or not Baseterre could be taken without blowing up the fuel depot. The only man vaguely qualified to make an assessment on that situation was Harry González, and Alwyn Cooke had seen enough of his temper already to understand that he was not the right person to turn to at that moment. Alwyn Cooke sat in silence next to Solomon Carter for a long time. Not a word came from either of the two, as they both considered what was best for the day, what was best for the country. Then the next crisis arrived.

Walter Stewart, still sitting at the back of the boat, had paid little attention to the line of water that wet the soles of his boots a few minutes after *The Rambler* had retaken its adjusted course en route to St. Kitts. But now, some half hour later, the waterline was substantially higher, so much so that the fifteen-year-old felt it was time to speak up. Water had been leaking into the boat from the moment Alwyn had ordered to go at full speed. It came in through the rudder case as the backwash of the engines increased, and it collected in the aft of the boat due to its inclination. By the time Walter Stewart drew Alwyn Cooke's attention to the situation, the water had already reached the bags with the guns and ammunition. *The Rambler* had to slow down by a couple of inches and the men got together to bail out the boat. Of course, if there was one thing in abundance in *The Rambler*, it was hands to deal with the problem.

What there wasn't, however, was much confidence. All the excitement of some hours earlier had dissipated, or had turned into fear and anxiety. There was an air of restlessness, which grew with every mile that took them closer to St. Kitts. This anxiety reflected not an eagerness to get on with the task at hand, but rather a muted regret for having taken part in a senseless operation, a desire to turn right back and be homeward bound. Alwyn Cooke could feel the reservation of his men, even if none of them dared speak it—he could hear it in their slow speech, he could see it in their downcast eyes.

The Rambler reached the lights of St. Eustatius round about midnight, more than an hour behind schedule. This was the time when they were supposed to reach Half Way Tree; instead, they made their way at full-speed-minus-a-couple-of-inches to the shores of Sandy Hill Point. The final leg of the journey would be done in total darkness, with all the lights of *The Rambler* switched off to avoid St. Kitts's revenue cutter from spotting the rogue boat. So, as soon as they reached St. Eustatius, Alwyn Cooke summoned Gaynor Henderson, Harry González, Solomon Carter, and Rude Thompson to the bridge of the vessel. What he had to say, he knew, would incense Harry and undermine Gaynor, so he said it quickly, yet in stages: *Gaynor here, he right, you know. Ain' no sense in blowin' up de fuel depot if we don' need to*, and before Harry

González could utter a word, *We mus' leave de Kittitians do dey dirty job, if dey wan' do it.*

Despite the time of night, Alwyn Cooke still believed blindly in the figures that Dr. Crispin Reynolds had shown him six nights before in his residence at Island Harbour, still expected to find no less than one hundred supporters of Dr. Reynolds's cause who would constitute the bulk of the force making their way through the streets of Baseterre. Alwyn Cooke was happy to distribute the spare guns between them, he was happy to appoint them with explosives, with instructions, and with plenty of courage. But Alwyn had decided that God had not intended him and his people to kick out the police task force from Anguilla, to declare independence and call the attention of the entire world, only to land in St. Kitts ten days later to murder a whole bunch of innocent people in an attempt to put another, more sympathetic autocrat in power. So, Alwyn Cooke called off the attack on the fuel depot, cut down to ten the number of men who would go into Baseterre, reduced the squads from three to two, with him leading the group that would head toward the police station, while Rude and the three American mercenaries attacked the Defence Force camp.

So where you wan' me?

But Alwyn Cooke didn't think it was appropriate to let Gaynor Henderson know yet that he would be left to protect the boat with some of the youngest members, awaiting the return of the troopers. *I tell you later.* That was as far as this first stage of reorganization would take him. He was prepared to face the exasperation of Harry González, but not the brutish temper of Gaynor Henderson.

His strategy worked perfectly, as Gaynor, still too embarrassed about his recent outburst to be excessively forceful, accepted Alwyn's deferral without complaint. Meanwhile, Harry González, too far from hope to harbor any, simply delivered a tirade of insults that finished with: *Twenny minutes before landing you decide to alter the whole plan? You're all a bunch of morons.* To which Alwyn Cooke simply reminded him, *You job will soon be done, Mr. González.*

The meeting was already over when Rude Thompson announced, *Dem de last lights of Oranjestad. We soon be in de channel,* meaning the short strait between St. Eustatius and St. Kitts. Alwyn Cooke ordered the lights of *The Rambler*, including the navigation lights, to be switched off, and he told the men to take their positions. *An' be quiet, nuh.* It would be at least another half hour before they reached Sandy Hill Point, but given that they were over an hour late, there was no telling where the escorting boat might be at this stage, or whether the St. Kitts revenue cutter was on the lookout for them.

So *The Rambler* darted through the channel at full speed, cutting across the darkness of the night, while sixteen men, caught between whispers and mutterings, waited for a signal—any signal, from friend or foe—to put them out of their misery.

CHAPTER II

THE RENDEZVOUS

ONCE AGAIN *THE RAMBLER* DRIFTED IDLY on the calm Caribbean waters, this time off the northwestern coast of St. Kitts. Not a word was spoken as every one of the men aboard looked out in the distance, trying to spot the signal from the escort that was supposed to meet them at Sandy Hill Point. The atmosphere was tense and the nerves could be measured by the ticking of seconds in Solomon Carter's wristwatch. *The Rambler* had been waiting for close to thirty minutes, sporadically sending out the coded flickering of a flashlight in the hope that the signal would reach friendly shores before it was intercepted by the local authorities. Despite the slight delay they had encountered in the journey south from Anguilla, there was an air of disbelief among the militiamen at the silent vacuum that welcomed their arrival in St. Kitts. And yet, there was a limit to the discretion that could be expected from them—a limit that shared its boundaries with the sound of teeth being sucked.

On average, the common Anguillian man is likely to suck his teeth somewhere between 150 and 200 times a day. These suckings can vary in length and tone and will inevitably have a wide variety of meanings, most of which display a degree of disapproval. Frustration, fear, and anger are all most efficiently expressed through teeth suckings, which also play a role when entertaining a crowd or even wooing a woman. In the wee-wee hours of the morning of June 10, 1967, though, teeth were being sucked in *The Rambler* with a heightened level of anxiety and even a degree of desperation. Until one particularly long-drawn brood was cut short when, in the distance, a bright light flashed intermittently. It was hard to tell whether the sequence in fact corresponded with the previously agreed code, but the expectation inside *The Rambler* had grown to such extent that as soon as anything at all emerged from the flat darkness ahead, the boat tilted sideways.

Easy, fellas, easy. Alwyn Cooke tried to cool down the spirits of his men. *Hol' on tight, gentlemen—dere kyan be more excitement still.* And he instructed Gaynor, Glenallen, Dwight O'Farrell, and Walter Stewart to each pick up a bag and stand by on the port side, ready to throw them overboard upon his call. And then to Rude: *Stop signalin'—le' we jus' approach an' see wha' happen'.*

What happened was that as soon as Rude put the flashlight away, the other boat stopped sending signals, triggering fear among the Anguillians that, indeed, they had been picked out by the revenue cutter. Rude slowed down considerably, so as to have enough power left in the throttle to try to make a quick escape if needed, and Alwyn, on the same page, *Be ready for a sharp turn to de nort' side.* The final word of advice to the four men holding the bags was to make it as obvious as possible that they were dropping something—*Is we only hope if dem stop 'n' fish out dem packages, while we race away to Statia. So long we kyan get dere before dem, we safe.*

Suddenly, Rude Thompson, dismayed, *We lose 'em. Long time already dey should have come cross we pat'. Dey lose we.*

Alwyn's reaction was emblematic, countering Rude's consternation with immediate action, retrieving the flashlight and once again sending out the coded message into the night in all directions. And again. And again. Nothing.

Until the grave sound of another boat's engines emerged above *The Rambler*'s own 115hp diesel motor. Which meant it was too late to run. The other boat was just a few yards away, although the moonless night was too dark for anything to be made out in the mist. So Alwyn, terrified about the outcome of his move, switched all lights on and identified himself to the oncoming boat.

Whaddahell yer doin' wit' yer lights on? Turn 'em off! came right back from the silhouette of the escorting boat, and the scold was greeted with a deep sigh of relief that was only interrupted by the metal sound from the hammers and safeties of the guns of the three American mercenaries, whose immediate instincts had been not to run away, but to take care of the men aboard the revenue cutter. Nobody had noticed, but Titus Brown had stood firm, his one arm outstretched, his hand turned sideways, pointing his automatic handgun toward the port side of the boat, where he imagined the revenue cutter would appear, while Mario Gómez, right knee on the wet floor of the boat, covered him from a different angle and Harry González held a loaded M16 in his right hand.

Now that the situation had been defused, Titus Brown uncocked the hammer of his gun, slipped it back in its holster, and paced about *The Rambler* with a contemptuous sneer that gave away exactly what he thought about his Anguillian partners. Harry González threw his machine gun on top of a bag just as Gaynor Henderson placed it back on the ground. *I thought we were here to fight.* But no one really heard what Harry González had to say, or if they did, they paid no attention, because the friendly red hull of the escorting boat could finally be seen as it approached *The Rambler* from its starboard side. *Where di hell yer been?* was the warm welcome extended by the Kittitian contingent to their Anguillian counterparts. In typically understated fashion, Alwyn simply replied, *We here—we here waitin' long time.* A cackle from both sides sealed the peace, and the journey reached its next stage.

Twenty minutes later, the two boats arrived in Half Way Tree—a dormant little fishing village that for one day was supposed to become the headquarters of an insurrection. Except, to the men aboard *The Rambler,* it seemed like the beach of Half Way Tree, running parallel to a small road and a row of darkened houses, was far too dormant to be the hub of anything. Alwyn Cooke chose to ignore the *Where everyone be?* that revealed the prevalent anxiety, and set out to restore normality—*Bring de boat closer to shore before we drop anchor.* There was no pier to dock at Half Way Tree, so the landing would have to be made on the beach—not that this posed any difficulty to a people who lived on an island where no piers were built at all, not even for the import of food, medicine, and petrol.

As *The Rambler* neared the beach, Alwyn broke the news to Gaynor Henderson that he was to stay with the younger guys, looking after the boat.

Wha'? Who you go send in my place?

And Alwyn, not so much answering Gaynor's petulant question as issuing the final instructions: *Rude, you take Harry, Titus, Mario, and Glen to de Defence Force camp; I take Sol, Dwight, Desmond, and Whitford to de police station. Be careful wit' dem bags, nuh.*

As the men jumped into the sea and carried the heavy loads to safety on their heads and shoulders, Gaynor was caught between two minds, at once relieved about not having to face the prospect of killing anyone and aggrieved at being relegated to a peripheral role in the important mission. But before he could settle his thoughts, it was Alwyn's turn to jump into the night.

Remember, if you ain' hear not'in' by five a.m., leave to Statia. May de Lord be wit' us, may He guide we steps tonight and shed His light on our pat's to help us achieve de freedom of our country and de blessing of our Lord. Amen. Okay, le's see where all dem Kittitian people be.

It had not yet dawned on Alwyn Cooke that no one was hiding anywhere, because there were no other people than the ten, twelve lost souls sitting between the beach and the roadside. It had not yet dawned on Alwyn Cooke that Dr. Reynolds's folder full of numbers contained not so much an optimistic overcalculation but rather a vulgar lie based on nothing other than speculation. It had not dawned on Alwyn Cooke that Dr. Reynolds had come to his house six nights before much like a moribund Christian visits a shrine, seeking more a miracle than a cure. Dr. Reynolds had left Alwyn Cooke's house early that very same morning and gone straight to his office, where he had worked most of the day, manipulating the numbers inside his folder in order to make them look consistent, plausible, and, above all, encouraging. But fixed numbers on a sheet of paper have no resonance anywhere other than in a man's imagination. So, when Alwyn Cooke reached Half Way Tree imagining he would find one hundred or so incensed, brave, grateful Kittitians, ready to kill and to die for the future of their country, he was confronted with the cruel reality of a situation which had been quite deliberately misrepresented.

Alwyn Cooke, half-incredulous, half-enraged, walked up to one of the pockets of people visible on the beach. It was a group of four young men caught up in a game of dominoes that was prolonged by fumes of rum clouding the reasoning of the players. When Alwyn Cooke explained who he was, one of the young men turned, as if to make sure there really was someone there speaking the words he heard, and with a dismissive chuckle, *Wha'? Dis time at night yer come to cause trouble?* and the hard sucking of his teeth echoed in the night.

Not one to indulge in heavy drinking or even condone it, Alwyn Cooke was discouraged by the sight of an empty demijohn of rum toppled underneath the table where the domino stones lay. But before he could say anything, Rude Thompson stepped forward and vented the frustration that had built inside him ever since the lights of St. Kitts emerged far to the east of their course with a kick that sent the table flying while he grabbed one of the drunkards by the collar of his T-shirt. *You better show some respect to a brother come from far away to help you ass, nuh.* The racket shattered the silence of the night. *Where you leader be?* But the question landed on deaf ears, not so much because all four young men were numb from the rum and the violence, but simply because there was no leader at all. Between giggles and cackles, a mocking *Leader who?* was followed by, *We all free men in St. Kitts, yer know.*

Alwyn had already turned away in the direction of another group of people assembled farther up along the beach. Four young boys and a middle-aged man looked toward him, startled by Rude Thompson's burst of anger. *Yer guys wanna get caught before yer start?* This time the interaction followed more commonly accepted rules of courtesy. The middle-aged man called himself Ronnie. He might have been in his fifties, though it was hard to tell in the darkness of the night. His skin was particularly dark, and the features of his face—his bulging cheekbones, the creviced lines around his mouth, his large nostrils—carved a map of shadows that sharpened the roughness of his physiognomy. His voice was grave but soft, his demeanor reserved and collected, and his hands, uncannily large, gave away a history of hard labor, either out at sea or in the cane fields.

Ronnie explained how a larger crowd had gathered earlier that night, but they had expected the Anguillian contingent to arrive by midnight, so when nothing had happened by one o'clock most of them had dispersed, lured by the call of rum or women. As for the four rowdy men on the other end of the beach, *Dem a bunch of no-goods yer no wanna deal wit'*. What Alwyn needed, Ronnie explained as he waved the bright white palm of his hand, was brave young men such as these fellows here. Alwyn looked at the tired faces of the four boys. The oldest of them might have been fifteen. Their countenances were fixed by fatigue halfway between fear and excitement. They might have been brothers, half brothers, or just cousins, though they were certainly related to Ronnie, all strongly built. But *Dem too young to come along*, and while Ronnie expressed his indignation and explained how at their age he was already a grown man, working at the sugar fields, earning his own living, and soon to be a father, Alwyn considered the consequences of their delay on the subsequent execution of the original plan.

Ronnie didn't know it, but he had sealed the course of the evening with his vague description of the scene a few hours earlier: he had confirmed a bigger crowd had assembled, and Alwyn Cooke had immediately imagined the hundred-odd people Dr. Reynolds had promised, even though Ronnie was referring to nothing other than a motley crew of forty to fifty people, including women and children. People in St. Kitts had come to see the Anguillian forces with the same curiosity that other people in other places go to the circus to see the cannonball man or the glass-eating giant. But in Alwyn Cooke's mind, Dr. Reynolds had kept his end of the deal; in fact, in Alwyn Cooke's mind, Dr. Reynolds had put his reputation at stake for the good of the Anguillian people. Therefore, in Alwyn Cooke's mind, it seemed increasingly difficult to get out of the situation without going ahead as planned.

The voices of another group of people could soon be heard farther back along the beach, somewhere between the collapsed domino table and the four children. It was the crew of the red escort boat who had come ashore and convened with two other men who awaited their arrival by the beach. Alwyn Cooke made his way to the group, and walked into a conversation about how late *The Rambler* had arrived in St. Kitts. Alwyn immediately snapped, *Boy, da' de way it is, man—how many cars there be t' take we to Baseterre?* He then saw the rest of his men approaching. Harry González, typically cynically, *Not quite the army you were expecting, huh?* To which Rude Thompson, *Who say we need more men?*

This was the cue for Desmond O'Farrell, an eighteen-year-old kid, to deliver a speech he had not prepared, to try to talk some sense into a bunch of old men who seemed to have lost perspective. *I ain' wan' soun' like no coward, but we come help dem people an' dere ain' a soul to be helped. Seem to me we messin' wit' a problem that ain' ours to mess wit'.* But before he could finish his metaphor about eating from someoone else's plate, he was interrupted by Alwyn Cooke, who explained that St. Kitts was a problem that had very much to do with Anguilla's reality, that Anguilla wouldn't have a plate at all if Bradshaw had his way, and that whether or not there were any people to welcome their expedition had nothing to do with what they had come to do in St. Kitts, nor with the reasons why they had come to do it.

Desmond O'Farrell had already been comprehensively shut up when fate produced the trump card Ronnie still had to play, because it transpired that there were only two cars to take ten armed men and four large bags full of guns, ammo, and explosives into Baseterre. But Ronnie owned a small pickup truck, which was precisely what the group needed, so all of a sudden his posture on the dark sand of Half Way Tree became haughtier, and his attitude turned more relaxed—even aloof— and his position became unequivocal: either the kids go along, or there would be no using his truck.

Alwyn Cooke was growing unnerved by the whole situation, but there was no time to waste, least of all negotiating trivial matters, so he agreed to take one boy, the oldest, so long as he kept quiet, did exactly as he was told, and stayed right next to his father, who would have to take part in the attack. *Deal!* And as the cars were assembled to set out toward the capital, a dose of sense seeped into Solomon Carter's mind. He approached Alwyn Cooke and took him aside for a word. There, five yards away from the others, he explained how *Dis too dangerous, Al. We ain' need you here; we need you good an' healt'y at home.*

Solomon Carter was concerned about the future of the revolution if the present mission proved to be a failure. He recognized in Alwyn Cooke the undisputed leader of the people, the father of the nation, and he worried that, despite the best efforts of the peacekeeping committee, everything would spiral into havoc and ultimate submission, should anything happen to Alwyn that night. Alwyn, flattered as he might have been, was adamant about not staying behind—*We already too few, Sol*—and before he could say that they needed every man they could get, Sol disarmed his argument with the most powerful of remarks: *Dat why you leave six ah we behind?*

Naturally, this had not been the reason. In fact, the only consideration that had played a role in that decision had been the safety of his people. The excitement of the struggle for freedom had infected vast portions of the population in Anguilla—particularly the younger and the poorer on an island where poverty was the rule and infancy prevailed. But there had been too many adolescents too keen to fight a battle that was plagued with uncertainties. Alwyn himself might not have felt so strongly about it had Gaynor not uttered his shattering too-many-people-goin'-dead nonsense, although it had always been part of the plan to leave at least three people looking after *The Rambler* as a

decoy in case the authorities spotted the alien boat. Yet it was true that
even if the danger of getting caught or killed had not increased substantially, their awareness of it had certainly grown dramatically since their
departure from Island Harbour, eleven hours earlier.

If you no wan' sen' no kid, sen' Gaynor instead. Sol's insistence made
Alwyn angry, just as much as it made him realize how serious Sol was
about the issue.

*You really wan' a man next to you who get col' feet already an' might run
away any time?* and the *Better he dan you* came at the exact moment that
the three cars pulled up together on the roadside by the beach.

It was well after two in the morning, and the army of one hundred
men had been reduced to a single scared adolescent—but the operation was underway as three crowded vehicles raced out of Half Way
Tree and headed in the direction of Baseterre. Sol Carter looked over
his shoulder and saw the faint silhouette of a man disappear into the
night as they drove off toward the sites where the hits were to be carried
out. Once in town, the freedom fighters would be on their own—once
there, it would be their task, and their task alone, to succeed, or to find
a way back to *The Rambler*.

PART II

CHAPTER I

TINTAMARRE AND THE IMPLAUSIBLE TWIST OF ALWYN'S FATE

ROMANCE IS SO INTRINSIC TO TINTAMARRE that the two have been inextricably linked since the island first received its name. A word so typically French it bears no translation, like *bougainvillea* or *papillon* (could any language, ever, be so destructive as to turn the charming diction of the latter into the sordid sound of "butterfly"?). A word from the New World, the Wiki(pedia), in its commendable effort to make things simpler, affirms it stems from Acadian French. Itself the paroxysm of romance, Acadia, a linguistic corruption or evolution from the prior Arcadia, seemed so beautiful to the Italian explorer Giovanni da Verrazzano, so perfect, that it evoked in him the idyllic state of perpetual happiness associated with the pastoral dream. Not that this bore any relevance a few hundred years later when Acadia was ceded to the British together with the rest of the French territories in modern Canada, in exchange for Martinique and Guadeloupe, as part of the peace that put an end to that regrettable chapter of eighteenth-century European history: the Seven-Year War.

Tintamarre, pure cacophony at its best, has a confused origin (but what doesn't?). Three syllables that, pronounced (in French) like the first half of "Tintin," followed by the muted passage of the middle vowel, and the long, vibrating effect of the final sound (something along the lines of *mah-rr*), allude to the distant mystery of the new territories, to the muddled hierarchies of unknown lands, to the rattling noise of romance in the distance.

Let's go back to *The Rambler*, drifting idly by Flat Island, a.k.a., Tintamarre, and to Glenallen Rawlingson's tale about a certain Mr. D.C., an eccentric Dutch heir who had come to this far corner of the earth to dissociate himself from the civilized world and who had decided to set up his kingdom in Tintamarre, where he built a luxurious palace and raised cattle and grew cotton and, implausibly, became a major purchaser of Anguilla's one and only export: labor.

Fourth-generation Antillean, Degendarus Clement van Ruijtenbeek's great-grandfather, Degendarus Iustus, had escaped the weather, his parents, the impending war, and the taxman in Amsterdam round about the year 1800, when things in Europe got so heated that the newly elected Pope Pius VII opted against celebrating the traditional Jubilee. Not that Degendarus Iustus cared too much, because he was no papist; he was a disciplined, determined Methodist, and as such he excelled in Dutch Sint Maarten, where he furthered both his cause and that of his church, until the day, twenty years later, when he became governor, and Methodism became the leading cleric force on the island.

As it turns out, the fruit of young Degendarus Clement remained pretty close to the tree of his immigrant great-grandfather, as he too fled the taxman, this time escaping the remote colony of Sint Maarten to settle in the even remoter island of Tintamarre, in order to avoid having to pay the use tax on "Lover's Leap," his large estate on Dutch Cul-de-Sac. At the turn of the twentieth century, D.C. van Ruijtenbeek boarded up the property he had inherited a few years back in his natal Sint Maarten, stored his furniture, emptied his kitchen, dismissed his servants, and headed toward the flat desert island that lay across the channel roughly two nautical miles away, to start a new, secluded life. Maybe he sensed something about the twentieth century. Or maybe he was just particular about his tax, who knows?

Whatever the case, D.C. van Ruijtenbeek built himself a manor house in Tintamarre—a palace, some called it, mostly because the people engaged in its construction were predominantly Anguillians, and in Anguilla there were no plantations that required manor houses; in fact, in Anguilla there were no plantations at all, there hadn't been for centuries, nor were there any houses, any buildings, of the size or style of D.C. van Ruijtenbeek's new home. And the manor house was surrounded by a vast wall, and both the house and the wall were built in local stone, a beautiful hybrid between limestone and flint. And once the residence was ready, D.C. van Ruijtenbeek had his cattle, all thirty heads of it, imported to Tintamarre, and he tended to the goats, and had the local population replenished with some hundred heads from his farm at Dutch Cul-de-Sac, and he set aside a large piece of ground, around which another wall was built, for the growth of the only produce ever to be profitable in the triangle of islands formed by Anguilla, St. Martin, and St. Barths: sea island cotton.

D.C. van Ruijtenbeek set up his own little industry, with its own little gin, its own little dairy, its very own self-sustained economy in what wittingly or not became his own little Arcadia. It was not uncommon for him to spend a year or so without coming "ashore"; he would spend ten, fifteen, twenty months at a time away from Sint Maarten; he would distribute his produce around the Caribbean, gaining a reputation for the quality of his milk—and store this in your memory; this is more than just a passing comment, more than just a trivial fact—as well as for the extent of his extravagance.

But extravagance can sometimes be fashionable, especially in criti-cal times, and at some point during the summer of 1913, when Europe was well on its course to battle it all out in a war to end all wars, some-body finally noticed, and a trendy Parisian publication, not just one of those *petite journeaux*, included a full-blown feature about "The King of Tintamarre," a title that D.C. van Ruijtenbeek would always claim, even many years later, when he was long back in his estate in Dutch Cul-de-Sac (and, yes, there is a French Cul-de-Sac in St. Martin—located a few miles away from the Dutch one, ironically, just across the island).

But back in 1913, D.C. van Ruijtenbeek became a bright, though absent, star in the constellation of celebrities that formed the upper tiers of European society. Out of the blue, he received letters addressed to him in German, in Swedish, in Italian, in French, all from women far, far away who had read about his kingdom, or who had heard about his passion, and who dreamt of becoming his companion in this fairy tale, the queen consort of a distant, romantic, clamorous place called *Tintamarre*. Meanwhile, D.C. van Ruijtenbeek simply read in silence all these words he could not understand, but guessed, assumed (fantasized about) their meaning.

And tens, dozens, scores of Anguillians worked in the Kingdom of Tintamarre, which grew to have one hundred heads of cattle and five hundred goats, and a reputation that stretched across the Caribbean for the best milk, the best butter, the best cheese this side of France. But despite his name, the color of his skin, and the nature of his ex-travagance, D.C. van Ruijtenbeek was as Antillean as anyone could be, and he wanted no Swedish, no Danish, no German queen, because he preferred the figure, the temperament, the disposition of Antillean women, so he read his letters and he fed his ego, but he employed An-guillians and S'matiners, and nationals from a host of other islands, and he feasted himself in the world of curves and dialects that populated his little kingdom on a daily basis.

You digress, I hear you say. *What the hell does this have to do with anything? With* The Rambler, *with the revolution, with Anguilla?* But bear with me, for in the stars are written unfathomable fates, and one of them will prove to be fundamentally linked to the van Ruijtenbeek family saga—one that will reveal itself as pivotal in the development of our story. Just a little patience while D.C. van Ruijtenbeek, in one of his sporadic visits to Sint Maarten, meets a lady from St. Kitts, a British subject whose enslaved grandfather had been liberated in 1834. Yes, a love story—but one so intense, so passionate, so important to this tale that it simply cannot be ignored.

Elaine Nesbit was one of those Nesbits whose name had come linked to ownership in prior times. Indeed, Master Nesbit might or might not have exercised his rights over Elaine's grandmother beyond the limits stipulated by decorum. But regardless of her genealogical tree, Elaine Nesbit was cut from a mold that made her infinitely more appropriate to become queen of Tintamarre than any courtesan from Friesland or any pretender from Hanover. At least so it seemed, to go by the reaction of D.C. van Ruijtenbeek when he first saw her, one Sunday morning at church. Clad in her best clothes to pay her respects to the Lord, she looked at the same time elegant and comfortable, demure and experienced. Her long white dress clung to her bust suggestively, only to widen dramatically below her waist. The drapes of her skirt hung loosely from her hips, a fold of cloth catching over her buttocks, revealing the mounting heights of her glutei and the narrow bridge formed by her Achilles tendon, held firmly by the leather straps of her (very) high-heeled boots.

Sheltered by a tradition that placed him in the top echelon of Sint Maarten's society, D.C. van Ruijtenbeek should have felt confident enough to stop her as she passed in front of him, once the service was over. However, he found himself muted, paralyzed almost, by the extent of her beauty, as well as somewhat offended by her poise as she walked right past him without so much as a nod of her head. That same day, D.C. van Ruijtenbeek made inquiries as to who this stranger was who had left him with this longing in his heart, and the whereabouts of her lodgings on the island. That same day, D.C. van Ruijtenbeek was standing before the doorway of Elaine Nesbit's modest little house by the Great Salt Pond on the rear end of Philipsburg, offering his assistance in any aspect whatsoever that she might find wanting during the period of transition while she settled in Sint Maarten. D.C. van Ruijtenbeek was further baffled when Elaine Nesbit thanked him for his interest and indeed his generosity, but explained that she found herself very much at ease on the island, having spent the best part of the past year there. Only then did D.C. van Ruijtenbeek realize that he had been locked away in Tintamarre for the past nine and a half months. *Of course*, and he began a slow turn away from the untidy veranda of Elaine Nesbit's home before pausing to take a long, brazen look at the merchandise on display. A tilt of his white hat and yet another *Of course* put an end to their very first personal exchange. This was in the summer of 1931. Twenty-five years later, on his deathbed, he would still describe it as the happiest day of his life, while she held his hand to ease his negotiation with Death.

Instead of remaining at Lover's Leap for a few weeks, like he had during most of his prior visits over the past twenty-five years, D.C. van Ruijtenbeek decided to extend his stay at least another month. He spent this time developing a careful plan for the siege of the wonderful boon he had recently discovered near the marshlands adjoining the Great Salt Pond behind Philipsburg. His tread at the initial stages was delicate and discreet. He would make up pretexts to travel up to town, where in the past he would not have been seen other than for the weekly celebration of Eucharist at the Methodist church. But these days D.C. would spend long afternoons wandering from one end of Front Street to the other, inventing meetings to attend at conveniently disparate times, lingering in his passage from his brother's import business to his cousin's ocean liner ticketing agency, waving at unrecognized island-ers who called his name first in half-mockery, aware that some serious matter—a woman, no doubt—had to be the reason why, all of a sud-den, the king spent so much time in these precincts.

But Elaine Nesbit was not precisely high class, which was all with which Degendarus Clement had ever been acquainted, and Elaine Nes-bit did not spend too much time in the elite end of Front Street, be-tween the bank and the church. She tended to carry out her business toward the opposite end of Back Street, where the shops were messier but the products cheaper. Therefore, despite D.C. van Ruijtenbeek's best efforts, he never bumped into Elaine Nesbit on the street—not once in three weeks—and he would only get to see her at her very best during service on Sundays. Too proud to be seen in public addressing a common girl who had not shown the slightest interest in him, he took his regular place and sat throughout the Mass waiting only for the mo-ment when the natural flow of the traffic out of the monumental build-ing would land him a privileged view of that involuntary fold which would reveal to him the promising shape of those godly ankles, and the ecstatic proportions of Elaine Nesbit's otherworldly rump.

For three consecutive Sundays, D.C. van Ruijtenbeek would have been incapable of regurgitating even the most obvious points in the preacher's sermon, because for three consecutive Sundays all his thoughts, his energy, his attention was focused on the exact moment when his imagination would be fueled with new material, the moment when his memory would be refreshed with additional images, which would confirm, enhance, highlight the prowess of a body he had already enshrined. So, before the fourth Sunday arrived, D.C. van Ruijtenbeek devised a plan that gave him hope, that filled him with courage, and that led him through the mudded roads by the Great Salt Pond to the end of Philipsburg where the marshes adjoined the city.

Elaine Nesbit knew exactly who was calling when she heard the bell by her front door. She was startled by the sound, although she had been expecting her visitor for many days. Elaine knew too much about men and power to be fooled into thinking that a king would allow her to live her life unmolested, once he had set his eyes on her. And the first time Elaine had walked past Degendarus Clement van Ruijtenbeek, on the atrium of the church, below the square bell tower and the cozy façade covered in wooden shingles, she sensed in the rarefied air, scented by his lustful sweat, that she had mesmerized him.

D.C. van Ruijtenbeek had been memorizing his lines all day, but somehow, just a few yards before reaching Elaine Nesbit's home, they vanished from his mind. She attended to his call in a long, loose dark gown. He stuttered. But despite the opening false start, D.C. profited from his temporary amnesia, because like this he came across much calmer, more natural than he would have, had his absurd plan been put to action. Except, once the dreaded question had to be answered, D.C. explained that what brought him there was his curiosity as to whether Miss Nesbit drank milk. *Milk.* Elaine could not hold back the burst of laughter that escaped her teeth. Degendarus Clement desperately tried to save the situation, explaining that he owned the largest dairy on the island—well, not on this island, in Tintamarre, off the northeastern tip of . . . *I know who you are, Mr. van Ruijtenbeek, and yes, I do drink milk.*

She had regained her composure, and looked more beautiful in the evening sun than he had ever imagined her. *Good. Because I like to keep a close eye on quality control, and it would be so helpful if I could get your feedback every so often, to make certain all is how it should be.*

D.C. van Ruijtenbeek departed the marshlands that day with a lot less grace than he expected. But he did so with Elaine Nesbit's postal address (not that he needed it) and her permission to write to her every now and then, exclusively in relation to the quality of his products, of course. *If you like milk so much, you should come and visit my farm one day.* Her refusal was firm, but the smile she let out together with it lit up D.C.'s world and made him think it had all been worth his while.

He wrote to her every week for the following three years, without fail. As was to be expected, the content of his letters quickly transgressed the limits of what they had agreed initially, but she was flattered by his gallantry, and comforted by the harmless format of his courtship, and he was encouraged by the fact that she did not mention his transgressions, and indeed, sometimes she even fed them with a loose comment here, a careless one there that merited an answer. Until the time came when their correspondence made no mention whatsoever of milk or dairy products, becoming instead an affable conversation between two mutual admirers.

Then, one Sunday, D.C. van Ruijtenbeek showed up at church unexpectedly. He had been away in Tintamarre for a few months and nobody anticipated him back for some time. Only Elaine Nesbit knew what had brought him back to Sint Maarten so soon, and the truth was that by this point he had been so successful in his task of romancing her that she, too, felt anxiety overtake her bosom when she saw him. For the first time he acknowledged her presence in public. For the first time she was not certain of how to handle him. They walked along the promenade, between Front Street and the beach, beneath the scrutinizing eyes of the curious and the vile. Sitting by the beach, looking out over the sea, D.C. van Ruijtenbeek asked her to join him in Tintamarre. Suddenly, the fiery yearning Elaine Nesbit felt to allow him into her life turned into a shivering emptiness. She couldn't explain why, but she just felt revulsion inside her. It was the second time she had rejected him, *And I don't often ask anything three times*. Instincts overtook her and, without thinking, *I will not be no pawn in you kingdom, Mr. van Ruijtenbeek, or you queen.*

The following day D.C. van Ruijtenbeek had Lover's Leap cleaned up and prepared for a great occasion. Throughout the morning and well into the afternoon women cleaned windows, dusted tables, brushed floors, hung carpets, patted cushions, made beds, cleaned china, polished silver, unstained crystal glasses, and conditioned rooms for no apparent reason. Then, toward the end of the afternoon, D.C. had Elaine picked up in a horse-drawn carriage. He believed his efforts had seduced her into accepting his offer. The truth was, she had never thought of denying him the pleasure of her intimacy. Even the day before, after she had showed herself so adamant in her resolution not to leave Sint Maarten, she would gladly have accepted the invitation to Lover's Leap that D.C. van Ruijtenbeek had felt was not appropriate—nor had he had the courage—to make. Naked, in bed, exhausted by their shared exploits, in the shadows of an early sunrise, he promised her he would finish every letter he'd ever write to her in the future with an exhortation to come join him in Tintamarre. She pretended to be asleep.

Three years later, Elaine Nesbit still lived in her small, modest house by the marshlands, toward the Great Salt Pond in Philipsburg, while D.C. van Ruijtenbeek remained the only member of the aristocracy of the Kingdom of Tintamarre. On one night of peculiar discomfort, D.C. jumped on his sailboat and cut across the two-mile channel onto the bay at French Cul-de-Sac. He had been drinking copiously at his farm, perhaps to forget the extent of his solitude, and he had taken a demijohn of rum along with him for the evening. Once at Lover's Leap, he procured himself a horse, and made his way from Dutch Cul-de-Sac to Philipsburg. That he did not hurt himself on the way was a sign that fate still had a role for him to play. He reached Elaine Nisbet's house right at the stroke of midnight, amidst the darkest dark of night. Elaine could hear him coming long before he reached the steps that led him to her untidy veranda. When he saw her on the threshold of her doorway, barely covered in the thin nightgown she used more to protect herself from the mosquitoes than from anyone's sight, he felt an intense anger grow inside his chest. He garnered the last bit of sobriety he could find in his consciousness and breathed in with intent, meaning to strike Elaine with a thunderous roar that could, perhaps, express the extent of his frustration. She stopped him in the middle of his gesture, grabbing the collar of his shirt with both hands and shoving him inside her house with more violence than he could have mustered.

She ravaged him repeatedly that night while he, caught between nightmares, thought he merely dreamt of her. The following morning, hungover and disoriented, D.C. van Ruijtenbeek understood there was nothing he could do to break this woman's will. *What do you want me to do?* he asked himself, more than her.

I wasn' born to be no queen. The silence that ensued might have lasted a few centuries.

Fine—you win. But tonight you'll leave this house for the last time: from now on we'll live together in Lover's Leap.

Elaine Nesbit and Degendarus Clement van Ruijtenbeek lived in his estate for over twenty years. They ran a farm that prided itself on producing the best milk, butter, and cheese this side of France. The sea island cotton business was liquidated and Tintamarre sold to a merchant from the French side of St. Martin. Consequently, the need for labor was dramatically reduced and a substantial amount of jobs had to be cut. Nevertheless, Lover's Leap remained a steady source of income for a considerable amount of Anguillians and S'matiners during the years when, in the northeastern Caribbean, there was simply no work to be found. At any one point the farm was likely to have as many as twenty workers, and even in the direst of times there were at least twelve to fourteen people—mainly women—employed there.

One of them was a young Anguillian who had arrived to the farm as a twelve-year-old boy in 1938, having secretly escaped his home in order to look for means to help his mother maintain a family of thirteen children and no fathers. D.C. van Ruijtenbeek hardly needed another burden to his payroll at a time when the Great Depression was striking the Caribbean at its hardest: 1938 saw the wave of social unrest that swept through the British West Indies from the beginning of 1935 reach its peak with the Jamaican labor strikes, spearheaded by the cane-cutters who refused to continue to work for less than one dollar per day. Not that this had any relevance in Anguilla—just like the prior rebellion of the oil workers in Trinidad had had no relevance, or that of the workers in Barbados, of the coal loaders in St. Lucia, or the working class in St. Vincent; in fact, even the 1935 riots led by the cane-cutters of St. Kitts, nominally part of the same administrative entity as Nevis and Anguilla, had had little repercussion in the latter, because the realities of the two islands were so disparate that they could have been in opposite corners of the world. So, while Robert Bradshaw and the rest of the Workers' League in St. Kitts strived to secure more humane conditions for the working class in their homeland, people in Anguilla emigrated to St.

Thomas, to Santo Domingo, to St. Martin, desperately seeking the minor privilege of belonging to any working class at all.

As luck would have it, D.C. van Ruijtenbeek's workforce happened
to be short a man—by illness or drunkenness—on the very May Day
when the young Anguillian knocked on his door. *Can you milk a cow?*
The young Anguillian would have claimed to have direct communication with God if that would have earned him a job. *You can stay for the
day—that'll give you enough money to pay your way back home tomorrow
morning.* Eighteen years later, the young Anguillian had gone through
every possible position on the farm, learning every aspect of the trade
and excelling, above all, at milking cows and delivering fresh milk to
customers all around the island.

Then, one mysterious day in November 1956, D.C. van Ruijtenbeek came back from the farm feeling particularly tired. He told Elaine
Nesbit he would skip dinner and go straight to sleep. The following day
his tiredness was accentuated and his mood gloomy. He never got out of
bed again, as his condition deteriorated rapidly. The doctors could find
nothing wrong with his body but he insisted he felt tired and weak. He
was diagnosed with acute depression and advised to leave the island for
a change of atmosphere. Upon the slightest suggestion that she might
be the cause of his illness, Elaine Nesbit discharged the family doctor,
never to speak to him again. She sat by the side of D.C. van Ruijtenbeek's bed, holding his right hand day and night. He died later that
same week, on November 29, 1956, roughly at the time when a group
of eighty-two young enthusiasts aboard the sixty-foot cruiser *Granma*
realized that rough seas and navigational blunders had made them lose
their course on their journey from Mexico to the southern coast of Ni-
quero in Cuba, where they intended to topple the puppet government
of Rubén "Fulgencio" Batista.

Elaine Nesbit was determined to continue the legacy of her husband in all but legal terms for over twenty-five years. She chose the
two longest-standing workers of the farm as her right and left hands in
the day-to-day running of commercial affairs. But fate was reluctant
to have Lover's Leap outlive its extravagant master for too long, and
Elaine missed her Degendarus more deeply, more profusely, than she
ever thought she could miss anything, and although she was considerably younger than him, every year she spent without him felt like a
decade to her spirit and her body. So, finally, on New Year's Day 1959,
Elaine Nesbit said her prayers before going to sleep for the final time,
and even as Rubén "Fulgencio" Batista was fleeing from La Habana to
Ciudad Trujillo in the Dominican Republic, granting full control of his
country to the revolutionary forces that included the surviving core
of the naive fighters who twenty-six months earlier had landed on the
southwestern shores of Cuba, she met the love of her life after a wait
that felt longer than the twenty-five years they had spent together.

As a reward for their devotion, for their professionalism, for their
loyalty, she left her entire estate to her left and right hands. One of them
was, of course, the Anguillian milk boy who had first arrived in 1938. His
name was Alwyn Cooke, and in 1959 fortune once again turned his way,
this time in the shape of a piece of land worth over one million dollars.

CHAPTER II

RUDE THOMPSON
AND THE ARUBAN CONNECTION

W HATEVER WAY YOU LOOK AT IT, DE WHOLE T'ING TWISTED. *Dey go say everyt'in' change when we go vote, now we vote second time and still all de same.* The men sat around a precarious table late one night toward the end of December 1957. The general elections for the islands of St. Kitts-Nevis-Anguilla had taken place six weeks earlier, resulting in an overwhelming victory for the representatives of the Labour Party of St. Kitts, including Robert Bradshaw and Paul Southwell, despite an increase in the popularity of independent candidates on the islands of Nevis and Anguilla. But the constitution of the islands stipulated a ten-member parliament, or legislature, and seven of its ten seats were appointed to the electorate of St. Kitts, and Robert Bradshaw had spent the past twenty years of his political career galvanizing his position as organizer of the masses, benefactor of the poor, activist for the cane-cutter, and altogether indisputable leader of his people. So, when the Anguillian men sitting around a wonky table made of dry old wood said *de same*, this might well have been another way of saying *screwed up*, because a lot had changed throughout the British Caribbean between the day in 1952 when adult suffrage had been introduced in St. Kitts-Nevis-Anguilla and the afternoon of November 6, 1957, when new elections took place to shape the political landscape of the three-island presidency, in the wake of the formation of one integrated Federation of the West Indies.

Indeed, for some, these had been years defined by the sweeping changes that shook the legal ground of the colonies, whereby the ancient administrative conglomerates—the Federal Colony of the Leeward Islands and the Colony of the Windward Islands—had been dismantled and integrated into one comprehensive state that was ostensibly being lined up by the British government to achieve full independence in the near future. For some, I say, because for others, parliamentary acts of dissolution and association meant nothing, or close to nothing, as their pragmatic minds focused only on the palpable consequences of this shuffling and reshuffling of power which politicians in a faraway country seemed so fond of enacting.

It was to them, to the pragmatic ones, that, despite the reams and reams of official paperwork involved in the political reorganizations, things seemed frustratingly unchanged. Unchanged not only in that Anguilla remained quite a desolate place, completely isolated from the rest of the world—there were no telephones, no telegraph, no radio station, not even a pier, and just a barely functional dust airstrip. Unchanged not so much in that Anguilla remained hopelessly poor, incapable of feeding its own people—jobs an unthinkable commodity in a land where no commodities existed: no electricity, no running water, no paved roads, nothing. Unchanged, and quite tellingly so, in that there was no hope ahead—damn, not even a trace of accountability—despite the fact that the popular vote had shifted dramatically in the opposite direction, lifting its support from the Labour Party's administration and backing overwhelmingly an independent candidate. And yet, all Anguilla could expect in the years to come were new tirades of insults from the likes of Robert Bradshaw, who would vent his anger at the people of Nevis following their sovereign decision to vote against him with a threat that he would spike their soup with pepper and their rice with bones, and who would react much in the same fashion after discovering the fate his party had suffered at the hand of the Anguillian voters, vowing to turn the place into a desert. Which suggests his knowledge of the island and its situation was probably sparse.

But that wasn't even the worst part—the worst part was that *nobody hear wha' Anguilla say, becausin' Anguilla part of St. Kitts, an' to de world dem one an' de same t'ing.* When Anguilla spoke, Anguilla spoke to St. Kitts, which is to say it spoke to deaf ears. *Dat why we mus' aks England for direct administration, man,* insisted Rude Thompson, who sat around the rickety table, made of a combination of driftwood, excess building material, and an old collapsed table.

Rude Thompson was a man of action. He was a man to whom words meant nothing unless they were backed by real facts. That is why, as soon as he returned to Anguilla, Rude Thompson went from home to home, from bar to bar, from shop to shop, raising a question that, he now knew, was also troubling the rest of the population. *Is a double-colony we livin' in—but why mus' dis be so?* And Rude's fist slammed against the domino table, disrupting the game; against the shop counter, making the cans jump; against the dining table, startling the children outside. Rude Thompson was no politician—his manner was brusque, his words ill-chosen—but this was not so much a debate as a sing-along, because if there was one thing on which Anguillians agreed, and there weren't many, it was that the island's relation to St. Kitts had brought more harm than good. But agreeing in conversation was not enough—what Rude Thompson demanded was action.

He had not taken part in the elections of November 6, 1957 because he had been away, like so many Anguillian men, earning his living abroad

and sending money home on a monthly basis through the only means
of communication with the outside world there was on the island: the
postal service. Faced with the millenary challenge of survival which
all of his ancestors had encountered before him, Rude Thompson had
chosen to sidestep the option of subsistence farming and fishing, setting his sight instead on achieving a higher level of respectability—of
comfort, even—by venturing offshore, by relocating somewhere else on
a temporary basis, somewhere more conducive to that which Anguilla
wanted most: employment.

Cursed as the Caribbean might be by a fate whose highs and lows
entwine with perverse celerity in a historical roller coaster, it remains
an unlikely fact that for every bit that circumstance takes away from a
specific island in the Caribbean, some sort of cosmic retribution is put
in place elsewhere. There is no other way to explain the emergence of
the southern islands—the very first, or very last ones: Aruba, Curaçao,
and Trinidad—as regional centers of employment, as the providers of
the Caribbean, precisely at the time when the conditions of the international market and increased competition had dethroned King Sugar
from its privileged position as the driver of the regional economy.

In 1922, a subsidiary company of Royal Dutch Shell essentially
stumbled upon by far the largest known oil well in Venezuela, at the
farm of Mene Grande by Lake Maracaibo. The well was so big, legend
has it, that locals thought the gringos had found a Black Lake, as large
as Maracaibo, underground. For nine consecutive days the geyser shot
up one hundred thousand barrels of the dark stuff, preempting by over
forty years the advice Mick Jagger and Keith Richards would give to the
world, and painting everything, absolutely everything in sight, black.
Just like that, with one fortuitous find, Venezuela had made a giant leap
on the charts of oil producers of the world.

Alongside Royal Dutch Shell, Standard Oil owned the concessions to drill for crude in Venezuelan territory. The eagerness of the corporations competing to exploit the resources of the land, together with the desperate financial situation in which Venezuela had found itself since the days of the populist dictator Cipriano Castro, complemented each other perfectly in a multilateral effort to quickly develop a sophisticated oil industry in the country. By 1930, Venezuela was producing around three hundred thousand barrels of crude daily, allowing the president of the republic, General (and, of course, dictator) Juan Vicente Gómez, to make a final payment of US $3.1 million to put an end to the country's foreign debt. Right at the peak of a Great Depression that was deemed to be global, a delegation of Venezuelan diplomats traveled from one side of the Atlantic to the other to settle a large debt in solid gold, and to commemorate the hundredth anniversary of the death of Simón Bolivar, "the Liberator." Now, there's extravagance for you.

Be that as it may, while Standard Oil and Royal Dutch Shell milked the ground surrounding Lake Maracaibo at full speed, they were faced with a geographical challenge that could not easily be avoided. As far as lakes go, Maracaibo is vast, but it is also uncommon in that it is not completely surrounded by land, but rather feeds into the Caribbean waters of the Gulf of Venezuela through a narrow strait. This sounds like excellent news if you are a multinational oil giant seeking to transport three hundred thousand barrels of crude every day out of the basin. Not so excellent news, however, is the matter that the strait is not only narrow, but also seriously shallow. Indeed, too shallow to allow the passage of large tankers bound to the coasts of Europe and North America.

Consequently, transshipment facilities had to be built in the neighboring islands of Aruba and Curaçao, where flexible fiscal arrangements for the import and export of crude were sufficient incentive for both companies to build storage bases. Soon enough, Standard Oil began erecting the Lago storage station and refinery in Aruba, completed between 1924 and 1929, while Royal Dutch Shell developed the Isla complex in Curaçao as early as 1924 and the Eagle refinery in Aruba by 1928. In this same period, two decades of tentative explorations in and around the town of Pointe-à-Pierre in Trinidad bore fruit as well, placing the island at the top of the list of oil producers in the British Empire.

Imperceptibly, the scene had been set for the paradigm shift to take place in the economy of the West Indies, as the brutal consequences of the 1929 market crash were evident in the price of sugar, which was far too low to warrant the cost of labor of the thousands of workers required to cut the cane. And while, yes, the price of oil was also affected by the global crisis, the rate of recovery was far quicker for an industry that was to power every war in the bloodiest century in the history of mankind. Thus started the black-gold rush in the Caribbean; thus emerged a new industry, which took over as the main provider in a region that was desperate for provision.

Aruba's Lago refinery went on to become the largest in the world, employing more than seven thousand people during World War II and processing most of the crude extracted from Venezuela. Strategically, it became such an important site that the German navy sought to test the effectiveness of its U-boat force by sending a mission to the shores of South America. The big hit was to take place in the early hours of the morning of February 16, 1942. U-boat 156, stationed off the coast of St. Nicolaas Bay in Aruba, had successfully torpedoed a number of tankers moored nearby, setting them ablaze. Lago refinery glowed in the darkness of the night, not so much due to the fires burning offshore, but because during the war it was operated 24/7, and it had not occurred to anyone in charge that this could be done equally efficiently and sub-stantially more safely if the compound remained unlit.

So the bulbs that hugged the contours of the refinery also marked the target against which the able seaman aboard U-156 aligned his 10.5 cm gun to launch a good proportion of the 110 shells he had available. However, just as Lieutenant Commander Werner Hartenstein gave the order to *Feuer!* the seaman proved to be less able than expected, as he overlooked the essential task of removing the gun cap from the end of the barrel, provoking an explosion that took his life, ruined the gun, and sent U-156 with its tail between its legs back to an R&R station in, not Tintamarre, but Martinique. Uncannily, Lago and the quarter of a million barrels of crude it processed daily for the duration of the war were saved from extinction. For good measure, though, the refinery worked in complete darkness from that night onward.

At the time of the attack, Rude Thompson was but a four-year-old toddler with no knowledge of where or what Aruba was. However, within ten years the refineries in the south, be it Lago, Isla, or anywhere else, represented a very distinct way out of the misery in which Rude, his five siblings, and his single mother were immersed. Struggling to make a living, he did whatever he could to help his mother. But there simply wasn't all that much to do in Anguilla in the early 1950s—shops were attended by their owners, the civil service comprised about fif-teen people, there was no industry on the island, not even tourism, and construction was largely a private affair handled by the landowners and their families during their free time. So, on the warm afternoons when the yard needed looking after, Rude Thompson would till his family's land to grow the eggplants, the yams, the ginger, and the sweet potatoes they would later trade for flour, tomatoes, and corn, while standing in the relentless sun, wearing his tired hat and his long trousers, pick and

rake in hand, and would dream about the possibility of making the journey to Aruba, to Curaçao, to Trinidad, to work hard and earn his right
to dream a proper dream.

And so, before the oil companies discovered the benefits of au-
tomation, Rude Thompson heard from his best friend since primary
school, Gaynor Henderson, that the brother of a cousin's friend worked
in a refinery, and that the work was easy, although the hours were long,
and that the company provided for anything you needed, or pretty close
to anything, anyway—they had large housing complexes, with their
own schools and their own hospitals, and they had vast dining rooms
where you could purchase a meal with coupons that worked out to be
real cheap, and the best thing was the pay—a check so large that this
brother of Gaynor's cousin's friend could afford to send more money
home than you've ever seen all at once, and he could still afford to pay
for his life out there, and *Hell, for da' kinda money, I go do twice so many
hours dan he.* Except, of course, that Rude Thompson couldn't have
done a single minute of work, because he was just fourteen years old,
and none of the refineries down south would allow him or anyone else
below the mandatory age of sixteen to come anywhere near a job.

For two years Rude Thompson was left to hear the scolding mutterings of his overworked mother, while he dreamt of what might be. But
while he worked and dreamt, his purpose became stronger and, coinci-
dentally, his path became clearer, as the steps removing him from being
an employee at Lago refinery in Aruba became progressively fewer. One
day Rude met Gaynor's cousin, and then he met his brother, whose
friend worked at the refinery, and all of a sudden this friend gained a
name, Wilbur, and the refinery wasn't just any refinery, it wasn't an
indeterminate place, it became Lago, which meant *lake* in Spanish, in
reference to the lake from where all the oil originated, and it was lo-

cated in a specific place, not just in Aruba, a specific island, in the bay of St. Nicolaas, right on the southern end. In the blink of an eye, everything turned so much more real, so much more plausible. Rude was so excited, so pleased, he felt like he wanted more than anything else to befriend Wilbur, the brother of the friend of Gaynor's cousin, who was away, stationed in Aruba, providing for the family.

So Rude tried everything not to be his usual self, he tried to be cordial and witty and quick with his cousin and his friend, and he tried to disguise the rude attitude that defined his character and gave him his name. But he tried too hard, and it was all so unnatural, and he came across as an annoying teenager in search of attention, and eventually, *Boy, give it a rest wit' de questions* was followed by *Wha' wrong wit' you friend, boy? He a battyman, or wha'?* And now humiliation was inevitable, because once a scapegoat is found among a crowd of mocking men there is no stopping the insinuations and laughter. But it had all been worth it, because Rude Thompson had gained bucket-loads of information that he could attach to his fantasy.

Rude didn't hear from Gaynor or from anyone else that Wilbur had come to Anguilla that year, to spend a few days with his family during the Christmas period, until he had already left. As soon as he found out he was overcome by disappointment, but the pain inside was immediately replaced with a sense of expectation that grew at a disproportionate rate, as he envisaged a clear and resolute plan that would get him out of Anguilla this very same time the following year. Rude Thompson told nobody, but throughout the year of 1953 he did not spend one cent above what was absolutely necessary. He rationed his food, eating only when his body couldn't live without, and even then only taking the least attractive items—the ones that could not be traded—out of the crops from his mother's yard or the catch from the sea. He would collect whatever loose coins he found on the floor of the shop, on the road, outside the bar he no longer frequented. He mended his clothes however many times he needed to mend them and used one single pair of trousers all year long. In fact, he mended everything from gardening tools to plumbing fittings to save every piece of copper that went into his pocket.

Come Christmastime 1953, Rude made certain he was ready to meet Wilbur. For weeks in advance he asked friends about Wilbur, he became acquainted with the house where he lived, he introduced himself whenever there was a chance to meet a member of his family. Soon the battyman jokes reemerged, but this time Rude Thompson was more amused than infuriated by them, to the point where whenever he heard, *Boy! You aks 'bout Wilbur more dan he wife—what business you have to do wit' de man?* he would simply answer right back, *How come you care wha' my business wit' Wilbur be? You wanna become battyman too?*

But all the preparation in the world would not have been enough for Rude to keep calm the day he was told Wilbur had arrived on the island. He went straight back home to count the money he had managed to save; he took a shower; he put on his best trousers—the other ones, the ones he had not used during the year. He combed his hair, he shaved the beard that still didn't grow, and he left his house, heading for the home of a total stranger to welcome him back, as if he were his best friend. When his mother saw him leave the grounds she was exhilarated, thinking that he could only be on his way to meet a girl, which made her immensely happy, because she had never seen her oldest son waste his time with girls before, and while earlier on she had taken much pride in this accomplishment of the education she had imparted him, by now even she had heard the nasty talk about Rude being a battyman, and she had heard so much about it she was beginning to believe it.

So you de boy spreadin' round rumors 'bout me being battyman!

Wilbur's face looked rougher, more labored, than he had expected. In fact, the whole meeting was nothing like Rude had pictured it in his mind so many times before. Wilbur's distance pointed not so much at a reticence to be forthcoming with Rude, but rather at an active resentment toward the liberties the young man had taken so unabashedly. But Rude had learned his lesson, and this time he didn't try to be friendly or personable or even likeable, this time he just tried to be himself: straightforward, frank, and unequivocal. *I wan' get job in Lago*, to which the automatic *I kyan't help you*, followed by a blank gaze, gave neither hope nor ground for expectation. *Bu' you does wok dere*, and again all hope was shattered by: *So do seven t'ousan' other people*.

Bu' you mus' know . . .

I ain' know not'in'. Now, stop vexin' me and go back to you mamma.

This was enough for Rude to be Rude again, to make it clear that *I ain' aksin' not'in' from you, mister. I goin' Aruba wit' or wit'out you help. I just t'ought—I ain' even know wha' I t'ought I get from a bitter ol' man like youself.* But Rude didn't turn around; he didn't storm out of the room; he didn't slam any doors; he didn't break down and cry. Instead, he stood motionless, quiet, looking straight into Wilbur's eyes.

How ol' you be? and his lie *(eighteen)* was both obvious and expected. *So if you t'ink me a fool, how come you aks me for help?*

Rude Thompson understood that pretending was going to lead him nowhere, so he acknowledged that he would turn sixteen the following March. Wilbur explained how he was too young for the contractual policy at Lago, but halfway through he seemed to bore himself with his explanation and cut it off with an, *Oh, wha' do I care if dey go give you no job.*

The next matter, however, was somewhat more critical: *You have some money?*

Rude Thompson's young face lit up with pride when he said, *One hundred and seventy-two dollars Bee-wee, t'irteen dollars and eight cents US, and seven guineas, four shilling, and five pence.*

Wilbur was impressed, but he didn't care to show it. He tried to dissuade the young man one last time, explaining how many people came to Aruba every day.

I ain' sayin' you have to open de door for me, mister. I jus' need you to show me where de door be.

Wilbur rolled his eyes and sucked his teeth. *I leavin' from S'maaten dis Monday comin'. Plane leaves at six.*

The following Monday at six o'clock in the morning began the new life of Rude Thompson—a life that almost came to an end a few days later, as he made his way to the door at which Wilbur pointed on his behalf. There he stood, erect but humble, wearing his best trousers, but still looking shabby and, most importantly, exceedingly young. The negative response was to be expected—after all, his age provided the perfect excuse not to hire him. But Wilbur Hopkins had worked harder for Rude Thompson than either of them would admit, because Wilbur Hopkins had felt aggrieved—annoyed, even—at the nerve of the young man to stalk him the way he had, and yet one conversation had been enough to make him understand that behind so much determination lay an unusual amount of willpower, and a particularly large dose of necessity. So Wilbur dug a little bit deeper down the structure of the company to make certain that when he provided Rude Thompson with the opportunity he so desperately craved, he gave the young fellow islander at least the faintest chance of making the best out of the occasion. If Wilbur Hopkins had introduced Rude Thompson to a minor executive at Lago—to one of the middlemen—then his new life would not have lasted as long as a week. Instead, Wilbur pointed Rude in the right direction, told him when and where to go, and gave him one long shot at the head of production of the refinery.

Therefore, when Rude Thompson took the initiative and dared address the man who held the key to all his dreams with the frankness, the directness, that had earned him his nickname, his words did not land on deaf ears, and when Rude Thompson closed his argument affirming that, *If dere be a law dat stop a man from makin' a livin' jus' becausin' he mother decide to push he out to de world on Shrove Tuesday an' no before, den, I tell you, dat law wrong*, his boldness reached the desk of a person who wouldn't, really, have to make any excuses for taking him onboard. *Dat law wrong*, Rude Thompson had said. Not something more conciliatory such as, "That law I don't understand," or even something more pleading, such as, "That law must have an exception." There was an air of righteousness in Rude's choice of words that stopped short of deriding the policy of the company (he hadn't, after all, said, "I don't want to be involved with a company with such law"), but that, at the same time, demanded the right to attain something deserved, something for which sacrifices had been made. Rude Thompson wanted to say that he had saved for a whole year to pay for the journey to Aruba, and that he had spent every shilling in his pocket to secure this meeting, but he knew the minute he opened his mouth tears would come to his eyes, and he would not ever be seen crying before another man. Rude Thompson never knew it, but it was his initial choice of words, together with the numbness that froze him up inside as the head of production walked past him to escort him to the door while he excused himself (*I have business to attend to*), which, mistaken for a mature resolve not to yield, led the American executive to ask his secretary, *Will you show this young man to the diner? I think they're short of a dishwasher.*

Four years later, Rude Thompson had worked his way from dishwasher to kitchen cleaner, to assistant cook, to porter, running boy, forklifter, and truck loader, until he finally made the big leap to gauger. For the first time in all these years—hell, perhaps for the first time in his life—he felt like he belonged to something, like he belonged to something *special*, when he received a promotion that was compensated in so much more than just cash, because for the first time since he had made the journey to Aruba, guided by the reluctant hand of Wilbur Hopkins, Rude Thompson had actually joined the select few who not only lived from the refinery, and made its existence possible, and provided whatever was needed for it to run smoothly, for the first time since the day when he debuted as a migrant worker, Rude Thompson was engaged to do that which he had dreamt about all along: to operate an aspect, however small, of the actual refining process.

This is where fate and history entwine in the tale of Rude Thompson, where circumstances made him understand the meaning—the relevance—of politics, where he learned to be the leader, the agent for change, he would later become. But let's go back to Venezuela for a moment and look at the state of its oil industry, which, come 1945, was so prosperous and developed it was deemed exemplary. Except that, strange though this might seem, the leadership of the country had failed to realize the importance of the refining business. Consequently, up until end of the 1940s, the full extent of the production of Venezuelan crude was transported in small tankers across to Aruba or Curaçao for refining. It was not before the mid-1940s that provisions were made to force the existing oil companies in Venezuela to develop the infrastructure necessary for at least a portion of the refining to be carried out domestically. And the practical effects of these provisions only became obvious between 1949 and 1954, when several major complexes were opened along the country's coastline, triggering a second, brand-new oil rush a full generation after the first one.

Initially, these refineries were almost exclusively operated by foreign executives imported by the companies who owned the concessions, but soon enough the first batch of graduates from the newly formed Oil Engineering Faculty of the Central University of Venezuela competed for a flurry of new jobs. These students were expected to train in large refineries to familiarize themselves with the practicalities of every aspect of the process, from distillation to desulfurization, from alkylation to catalytic cracking, before returning to Venezuela to provide a local face to an eminently foreign industry.

Precisely the large "cat-cracking" unit, where high-octane gasoline was produced, had become the defining symbol of the Lago refinery, as it dominated the skyline with its huge cylindrical plant rising monumentally above the rest of the complex. Rude Thompson had been working for less than six months as a gauger at the cat cracker when a new pump system operator was incorporated into the team. His name was Ignacio Ojeda, and he was a Venezuelan graduate carrying out his period of apprenticeship.

Ignacio Ojeda had the confidence of someone who knows that if the shit hits the fan, he can call upon someone else to open an umbrella and keep him from getting stained, though his attitude fell short of arrogance, and his demeanor was always gregarious, and he just had a way about him that made you want to be friends with him. He had a natural inclination to speak, regardless of the situation, and yet he avoided causing annoyance by virtue of an innate rhythm that kept his stories poised at all times between the implausible and the enchanting. Ignacio had finished his degree almost a year before, but he was so up-to-date with the activities of his faculty, so engaged in the day-to-day happenings of his native Caracas, that he seemed to live with one foot in Aruba and the other in Venezuela.

Because, of course, Ignacio Ojeda was a staunch detractor of the military dictatorship of General Marcos Pérez Jiménez, who, following rigged elections, had been declared president of the republic in 1953. While a student, Ignacio Ojeda had seen his country go from one constitutional crisis to the next, as a provisional junta took as many steps to negotiate the turbulent waters of political unrest as it did to add further trouble into the mix. Pérez Jiménez, a member of the junta, had been the absolute victor in the power struggle, landing sole control of the country's government. His first resolution was to reduce the autonomy of the universities, as he feared students were his most dangerous enemies. Three years into his degree, Ignacio Ojeda saw his faculty disappear into thin air. He was forced to switch from oil engineering to mechanical engineering, as the structure of the institution was streamlined and its student base reduced. From that moment, in the summer of 1953, until late 1957, when it was announced that the elections, scheduled for December that year, would be replaced by a referendum to determine by popular vote whether Pérez Jiménez should remain in power, militant factions within the Central University of Venezuela actively demanded the dissolution of government, the resignation of Pérez Jiménez, and the democratic election of a new president. Suddenly, a society used to being led by the whims of the elite and the backing of the military forces was struck by the destabilizing effect of an informed and committed youth, a gadfly in the government's face, a vibrating quantum string in the staid Newtonian universe.

Ignacio Ojeda, pump system operator at Lago's cat cracker in Aruba from June to December 1957, somehow managed to remain a part of this dissenting force, of this discerning voice that called for an end to the days of nepotism and abuse, of suppression of liberties and in-timidation in one of the fastest-developing countries in South America. Therefore, every time a friend or comrade was captured, every time a meeting was organized or a resolution was taken, Ignacio Ojeda arrived in the morning overcome by excitement, indignation, or exultation. Then he would explain how *It cannot be, my friend, that in this day and age a citizen of an independent country should be put in prison for expressing his opinions about the policies of his government,* or he would predict the end of all dictatorial rule in Latin America through the integration of the people in search for one common goal, or he would plot the demise of the tyrannical government through the incorporation of all strata of Venezuelan society in a combined initiative that would restore the most elementary of rights in the country: freedom of speech.

On paper, Ignacio Ojeda was just one tier above Rude Thompson in the company's pecking order, but, ironically, it was Ignacio's knowledge of the fast rise through the ranks of the refinery which his future had in store for him that allowed him to develop a natural relationship with Rude, unhindered by the nuances that shape the dynamics of direct competitors on the same career path. Because Ignacio was at the cat cracker to learn the practical side of the refining process he had so clev-erly dissected during his years at university—he was there to experience and learn to cope with the intense boredom that came with the routine of constantly monitoring temperature and pressure readings, to partake in the feeling, be it pride, or occasionally even antipathy, that came with the sense that, somehow, by opening a valve wide or slamming one shut, by shifting the flow, by altering the mix, this huge concrete and iron beast could be tamed. But, in addition to all of that, Ignacio Ojeda was taking advantage of the opportunity to understand the mentality of the proletariat, to exchange views on an equal footing with members of the working class.

Now, it might seem like nothing could glue together the realities of a neglected little island in the Caribbean atoll with those of a developing industrial country of millions of people in the South American mainland, the realities of a middle-class Latino graduate and those of a poor Antillean migrant worker. But at a time when Venezuelans longed most for universal suffrage, Anguillians had already gained the right to vote—had gained the nominal power to express their opinions about who should represent them in government and how they should act. And so, implausibly, Ignacio Ojeda and Rude Thompson, joined through circumstance by their shared condition as foreigners in this Dutch colony, compared the evils of having no discernible popular voice—strangled by the brute force of a repressive government—with having a voice that was loud and clear but that remained impotent because of the way power had been distributed among the islands forming the territory.

That was how, in the days and weeks leading up to the general elections of November 6 in the presidency of St. Kitts-Nevis-Anguilla, which also happened to be the weeks and months preceding the general elections of December 15 in Venezuela, the cat cracker at the Lago refinery in Aruba's St. Nicolaas Bay became a grand forum for political debate. Every morning when Ignacio arrived in the plant bouncing his revolutionary jargon and his socialistic attitude from wall to wall, Rude Thompson would engage him in conversation and question him, ask him to elaborate his point, to explain himself, *becausin' de man does have a big passion, but he does forget wha' he passionate 'bout.* And so, a simple *How you mean people go jail for sitting in de same room?* would lead to a heated presentation of the legal framework that authorized the police to break up social gatherings and arrest the participants as troublemakers, which would lead to the usual teeth sucking, followed by an exasperated *But dat law stupid, man!*

Yet during the previous five years many West Indian islands, from Trinidad to Anguilla, had gone to the polls for the first time, and many were the voices that, washed in coffee or distorted by a mouthful of rice and peas, emerged to discredit Ignacio Ojeda's idealistic expectations about a functioning democratic society by spewing bluntly, *In me country I know only two parties: dey who can afford me vote, and dey who kyan't*; or, *So much votes be bought in di bar I nuh understan' why politicians even waste dey time wit' public meetings.* And yet, despite the inauspicious landscape of experimental democracies where ethnic backgrounds had far more relevance than governmental policies when it came to supporting a candidate, where party politics were shadowed by personal allegiances, and where corruption was not only rampant but indiscreet, Ignacio Ojeda continued to display an enviable—almost candid— resolve in his apology for the most precious right and most pressing duty of any citizen in the civilized world: the opportunity to make a contribution to the decision-making process that would determine the course of the country's policies.

So, when Ignacio Ojeda found out that Rude Thompson would not be returning to Anguilla for the general elections of November 6, he simply could not understand it: he could not understand how anyone would squander the chance to actively influence the destiny of his country, and he couldn't understand how anyone would let down his fellow citizens by not taking part in the selection process at all; but what he really could not understand was how financial considerations could stand between a man and his civic responsibility, how they could play any sort of role in a decision that was, ultimately, moral, not rational. Therefore, when Rude Thompson let out one day, *No, man—I cannot afford to cast my vote dis time,* Ignacio Ojeda read into that particular use of the word "afford" all kinds of connotations; and, later on, when it

became official that the Venezuelan dictator, General Marcos Pérez Jiménez, would not allow any opposition candidate to run for the election
of December 15, but instead would take the opportunity to consult the
electorate in a countrywide referendum on whether he should extend
his mandate for another five years, Ignacio Ojeda could not fathom
what had ever taken hold of his good friend Rude Thompson when he
said, *Da' exactly wha' Anguilla need: we no need no election—we need only
a referendum to aks us wha' we wan'.*

Of course, it would have been easier for Ignacio Ojeda to understand had he noticed the results of the November 6 elections in St.
Kitts-Nevis-Anguilla, where independent candidates swept the floor in
the small islands of Nevis and Anguilla, to absolutely no avail, as the
men from the Labour Party, including Robert Bradshaw, took the seats
up for grabs in the larger island of St. Kitts, gaining an overwhelming
majority in the presidency's legislature in the process. But during the
days following those general elections, Ignacio Ojeda was far too busy
liaising with his militant comrades in Caracas, organizing the logistics of
a new plan to openly challenge the authority of the Venezuelan government and demonstrate publicly.

So, between Xeroxing thousands of subversive fliers and coordinating the timing of the operation, Ignacio remained a stranger to the
predicament that assailed Rude Thompson and the rest of his fellow
islanders. Two weeks later, however, Rude became more than aware of
the exact activity that Ignacio Ojeda and his accomplices were planning in Venezuela, as the streets were swarmed with students from all
the universities in the country. Violent confrontations between the riot-
ers and military forces led to huge numbers of students being detained
and tortured. But a government that remained in place by virtue of
intimidation had lost its most precious weapon: fear. And soon enough

the protests would turn into a general strike that flipped the country on its head and forced General Marcos Pérez Jiménez to flee to Ciudad Trujillo in the Dominican Republic.

Come Christmas 1957, Rude Thompson had spent every single day of the past four years in the settlement located just to the north of the refinery, where most of the migrant workers from all over the Caribbean dwelled when they were not at work. He had been there, on his own, on March 1, 1954, when his sixteenth birthday brought him the best gift he had ever received—legitimacy at his post; he sat there too, no longer by himself, during the Christmas and New Year's celebrations, the very first ones he had ever attended outside his family circle in Anguilla; unaware or uninterested, he had also sat at his home in the settlement near St. Nicolaas Bay during those heady days of 1956—on August 2, when the British Caribbean Federation Act received royal assent, on November 29, when D.C. van Ruijtenbeek exhaled his last breath, on December 2, when sixty of the eighty-two gullible recruits who had traveled aboard the *Granma* were ambushed and killed by the armed forces loyal to President Rubén "Fulgencio" Batista in Cuba; through the general elections of November 6, 1957 in St. Kitts-Nevis-Anguilla he had sat too, this time more informed than before, but still not fully certain of how he felt about it—or about anything else.

The village near St. Nicolaas Bay had not been built by the Lago corporation for the benefit of its employees, unlike the more exclusive colony to the southeast, which had been designed to house all the executive personnel of the industry—most of whom were American citizens. Consequently, the settlement to the north of the refinery was shabbier, more crowded, but also much more natural in the way it had grown and developed. Over the past four years, Rude Thompson had been too fascinated by the mixture of cultures and traditions he'd found in this place to think much about what he had left behind in Anguilla. Here he had learned the painful inflection of the Aruban *Papiamento*, as well as the extravagant excesses of the Trinidadian *mas*, the musical luridness of the Dominican *bachata*, the wretchedness of the Colombian *vallenato*, the theatricality of the Panamanian *murga*, the sweetness of Grenadian nutmeg, and the reason why Jamaicans call their hot sauce *jerk*. For four years running, Rude Thompson had religiously sent exactly half of what he earned in Aruba back to his family in Anguilla, and for four years running Rude Thompson had worked every day except Sundays, without ever missing his home island.

Until he met Ignacio Ojeda, that is. Because Ignacio Ojeda, with his crazy talk about choice and change, about people power and integration, struck a distant note that at first inspired nothing but ridicule in his Caribbean coworkers. But little by little, one argument at a time, Ignacio Ojeda managed, perhaps not to convince anyone, but to make them understand that there was, if nothing else, conviction in his speech, and that such conviction made him a stronger, more resolute man. And so, one day, out of nowhere, Rude Thompson awoke feeling the kind of patriotism he had never felt before—the kind that goes beyond the blind pride for belonging to a given piece of land, to a given rock, the kind that makes you take a step back and look at things from a distance and wonder what can be done to improve the island, the country, the situation of the people—of *my* people.

By this time, Rude Thompson was hooked on the saga that Ignacio Ojeda recreated every morning as he walked into the cat cracker at Lago, he arriving from the colony, Rude approaching from the settlement, both eager to tell and to hear respectively the torrid, dreadful, distressing news of what had happened the day before, or the one before that, in the city of Caracas, where schools and universities had become the laboratories where recipes for change were tried and tested, while on the outside an eerie calm, a tense stalemate, oozed an air of normality that created a false sense of security, occasionally disturbed by a vicious rumor here, by a violent outburst there, all immediately discredited or crushed by the military units deployed all over the city for the safekeeping of peace and quiet in the run-up to the referendum of December 15—which, inexplicably, Marcos Pérez Jiménez claimed to win by an overwhelming majority of over 70 percent of the population.

Thus, round about Christmastime 1957, Rude Thompson made a resolution, and he approached his supervisor at the Lago refinery and requested to have all the days of holiday he had not taken in the past four years put together to allow him to spend some time in his home this season. The head of gauging posed the question to the head of the monitoring process, who subsequently asked the vice president of pump operations, until the request finally landed on the desk of the head of production. In only his second interview with this high executive in the hierarchy of the Lago corporation, Rude Thompson used as excuse the fact that his island would be incorporated into a new administrative entity that required him to travel personally to St. Kitts to get his new documents. At the same time, Ignacio Ojeda decided he would go back to Venezuela and fight the fight that had not yet been taken to the streets, but that he knew would soon erupt. Rude Thompson and Ignacio Ojeda departed Aruba on the same day, the last of 1957. Three days later, on January 3, 1958, as the Federation of the West Indies officially came to exist, Ignacio Ojeda narrowly escaped prison after taking part in a failed coup against President Pérez Jiménez.

Rude Thompson set out to work as soon as he landed on Sandy Ground on the very first day of 1958, going from home to home, from bar to bar, from shop to shop, raising a question that, he soon learned, was also troubling the rest of the population. But Rude Thompson was a man of action, and all he found in Anguilla as he pounded his fist against domino tables, shop counters, and dining tables was agreement about how sour the association with St. Kitts had turned. Nevertheless, there seemed to be not one single proposal, not even a rudimentary plan, to do anything to address the situation. So Rude Thompson came up with a simple idea—a peaceful first step—and he gathered a group of friends who would be willing to ignore the lessons of history, and together they tried, just like the members of the vestry of Anguilla had done in 1825 and again in 1873, to appeal to the British Crown to find an immediate and satisfactory solution to the neglectful running of Anguillian affairs by the central administrative body located in St. Kitts.

Hence, Rude Thompson was not looking when the opinion of the vast majority of Venezuelans suddenly switched against the despotic rule of General Marcos Pérez Jiménez on the morning of January 21, 1958; nor was he aware of the general strike that quite literally paralyzed his friend's country for the following seventy-two hours; nor did he learn until many months later that on the morning of January 23, 1958, Ignacio Ojeda and the rest of his gang had finally succeeded in making Pérez Jiménez understand that he was not wanted—that he was not safe—in his own country. Because Rude Thompson was far too busy drafting the memo that turned into the plea that finally contained the threat that was passed from hand to hand and spoken from mouth to mouth for months in Anguilla, for everyone to know and for everyone to sign, so that when the governor of the Leeward Islands received it, he would not have the slightest doubt that this request to *Make every exertion which lies within your power to bring about the dissolution of the present political and administrative association of Anguilla with St. Kitts* was not only shared by the vast majority of the population of the island—two thousand signatures, or about 70 percent of the electorate—but was also urgent. In a passing moment of inspiration, it occurred to Rude Thompson that it would be pertinent to place the particulars of Anguilla's situation within the larger context of the social unrest that, from Cuba to Venezuela, was sweeping through the region by explaining how *A people cannot live without hope for long without erupting socially; and it is because the people of Anguilla prefer petition to eruption that we implore Your Excellency to use your best endeavours to have Anguilla emancipated from the dead hand of the political leaders of St. Kitts.*

No response was ever received.

(A FEW WORDS ON THE TIMES AND THEIR *GEIST*)

O N THE SECOND DAY OF AUGUST **1956,** the British Caribbean Federation Act received royal assent, setting in motion the legislative machinery that would eventually see the official establishment of the Federation of the West Indies, on January 3, 1958. The ten-presidency state was dominated by the overbearing presence of its two most important players: Jamaica and Trinidad. But the feeling in Jamaica was that federation was a burden to the coffers of the country that would bring little benefit in return; and the feeling in Trinidad was that they would not be pushed into playing second fiddle to Jamaica, or to any other country in the federation; and, ultimately, the generalized feeling of mistrust was so prevalent among the members of the new political entity that, when a referendum was called in Jamaica in September 1961 to decide upon the question of secession from the federation, the matter was already settled. The victory by the separatist faction of the population was a mere formality, the raising of an official certificate of death that was finally signed off when Trinidad's prime minister, Eric Williams, used basic arithmetic to illustrate the future of the state and made it clear that "one from ten leaves naught."

Between the first days of 1958, when the Federation of the West Indies came to be, and the middle point of 1961, when Jamaica's disenchantment with the enterprise led to its imminent demise, the Caribbean was a hotbed of insurrections and revolts. First came the popular uprisings that on January 23, 1958 signaled the end of Marcos Pérez Jiménez's tenure as the head honcho at the helm of Venezuela's volatile political establishment and forced him to seek shelter in the fatherly bosom of the Dominican Republic's fellow nationalistic scourge, Rafael Leónidas Trujillo Molina. Less than a year later, the Cuban revolutionary forces led by the collective hands of Fidel and Raúl Castro, Camilo Cienfuegos, Ernesto Guevara, Juan Manuel Márquez, and Juan Almeida Bosque entered La Habana, putting an end to a highly romanticized but ultimately filthy war, which had been waged since the landing of the sixty-foot cruiser *Granma* on the southeastern coast of Cuba on December 2, 1956, just a few days after the death of D.C. van Ruijtenbeek.

On New Year's Day 1959, Rubén "Fulgencio" Batista, the deposed dictator of Cuba, also fled in the direction of the Dominican Republic, although, as fate would have it, the colorful meeting of all three tyrants under the same roof never quite took place, since Marcos Pérez Jiménez had already relocated to the friendlier shores of the United States. Batista himself would move to the island of Madeira eight months after landing in the Dominican Republic, where he would live under the auspices of fellow Fascist leader António de Oliveira Salazar. Indeed, it seems as though Trujillo was not the most magnanimous of hosts, if you go by the time both his peers spent in his country, or by the five million dollars Batista is said to have off-loaded during his stay. The greatest plantation owner of all time, Trujillo governed the Dominican Republic like it was his own hacienda from the time he first came to power in 1930 to the time he was forced out of the realm of this world in 1961. Alas, he never had the chance to taste from the cup of exile, as he suffered in full the outrage of his subjects on the night of May 30, 1961, when a couple dozen bullets from, take note, .32-caliber pistols and

.30-caliber M1 semiautomatic carbines put an end to one of the most sinister tales of the twentieth century.

May 30: a date that might bear no more significance than pure stellar coincidence—lightning striking twice—but a date, nonetheless, which still today is celebrated in Anguilla with as much fervor as Bastille Day in France, or July 4 in the United States, because on May 30, 1967—six years to the day of the assassination of Rafael Trujillo—Alwyn Cooke, Rude Thompson, and the rest of a crowd of three thousand Anguillians marched up to the police station in The Valley to the infectious tune of a common *Kick 'em out! Kick 'em out!* and made it absolutely clear to Inspector Edmonton, head of the police task force, that enough was enough, that the time had come for Anguillians to take care of their matters by themselves, and that he and his thirteen policemen should leave the island in one piece while they still could, which was not going to be very long.

But way before that, Anguilla's fate was again being determined by another people's will, as the Jamaican electorate set in motion the dissolution of the Federation of the West Indies. Following the withdrawal of both Jamaica and Trinidad & Tobago from the federation, new elections were called in each of the presidencies and a last-ditch attempt was made to save the pieces of the failure by reorganizing the remaining group into a new entity, which came to be known as the Little Eight. Predictably, the bureaucratic machinery set in motion by such a move meant that it took four years to come to the obvious conclusion that the rift between Barbados and Antigua was no more bridgeable than that between Kingston and Port of Spain.

Come 1966, all prospects of integration in the English-speaking Caribbean were abandoned in favor of internal self-governance for each presidency. A brief stepping-stone in their journey toward full-fledged independence, the former presidencies would become "associated states" of the United Kingdom, whereby the British would be responsible for representing each of the islands abroad and for safeguarding their sovereignty in case of an outside threat. That was the carrot the British chose to brandish before their Caribbean colonies in their initiative to dismantle the empire. That was the momentous affair Anguillians were supposed to celebrate during the Statehood Queen Show that on February 4, 1967 turned into a street riot.

Because Anguillians saw this less as an opportunity to reach for their inalienable right to dictate their own destiny, and more as the final nail in the legal coffin that was their association with St. Kitts—a relation that was as lopsided as it was fruitless and unwanted. Because in the ten years of political experimentation that elapsed between the general elections of 1957, immediately prior to the establishment of the Federation of the West Indies, and those of July 1966, just eight months before receiving statehood from the United Kingdom, the only phenomenon that managed to leave any kind of mark, be it in the landscape of Anguilla or in the psyche of its people, was the disastrous passage of Hurricane Donna on September 4, 1960, whose damage was still there to be seen six years later: a callous reminder of both the size of the storm and that of the government's neglect, a clear sign that things needed to change.

CHAPTER III

THE INGREDIENTS OF CHANGE

T HE INGREDIENTS NECESSARY FOR CHANGE were not particularly evident at first sight, but they were present nonetheless: present in the shape of Rude Thompson, who went back to Lago in 1958 to learn that his friend's struggle in Venezuela had been successful—as successful, too, had been the experiments carried out by the oil company a few months earlier to delegate some of the more basic tasks in the refinery to appropriately conditioned mechanical controllers that would not suffer the effects of boredom, that would perform identically throughout the working day, that would save the company millions over the course of a year and cost it half its workforce.

Elaine Nesbit had passed away and Fidel was already in power, although the place occupied by Cuba in the jigsaw puzzle that was world politics in the Cold War era was yet to be clearly established, when Rude Thompson became the helpless victim of technology as yet another batch of workers was laid off by Lago. When he returned to his island, only for the second time since his initial departure early in 1954, he felt as if he had never left. It had been an intense five and a half years for everyone—he knew—but to him it seemed as if Anguilla was simply immune to whatever happened around it, immune to change.

The ingredients necessary for change might not have been terribly evident, but they included the presence of Alwyn Cooke, whose sudden wealth had left him dumbfounded and confused, and had triggered in him an urge to work harder than ever before, which he did for a while, perhaps as a way to justify his own luck, or perhaps as a gesture toward the dead—as a ritual of mourning that he wore on his sleeve instead of a lugubrious countenance or a black suit—before he let himself go entirely, as if one morning he had woken up to this dream and finally realized that it was true, that it was all his, that he really didn't need to work another day in his life.

Then came Hurricane Donna, bringing along misery's cruelest face. For once, however, history was on Anguilla's side, as the island's demographic distribution—sparsely populated and lacking any urban center whatsoever—meant that the storm claimed only one human life. But at every other level, the destruction it left behind had never been witnessed by any of the living—some said a similar monster had raced past the island back in the 1880s, others claimed God sent a purge to rid the island of all sins every hundred years, but no one had ever seen anything quite like this: not a single roof remained intact—although the wind had been so violent it had uprooted whole houses and transplanted them to the other side of the island, it had lifted ceilings and wedged them so hard against alien structures that, as you walked around (no cars survived), you could see small concrete houses with roofs that were too large, too wide, sitting firmly above their new base, as if they had always belonged together.

Upon sight of this mayhem, of this indiscriminate slaughter of beasts—all kinds of them: goats and cattle, birds and lizards—of this torrential rain that caused everything to flood, of this ferocious unearthing of trees and plants, of crops and roots, Alwyn Cooke understood that Donna had been sent by God as a sign for him, as a despotic

call for him to do something—to do something *good*—with the golden
gift He had bestowed on him. Thus, despite the fact that death and destruction were even more dramatically present in the relatively developed island of St. Martin, Alwyn knew that the governments of France
and Holland would be more forthcoming in their contingency plans to
rescue their respective portions of the island than the central administration of St. Kitts would be in helping his homeland. So, Alwyn Cooke
took it upon himself to do all he could to ease the suffering of his fellow
islanders, and he pledged to himself and to God Almighty that with
His help and support, he would not reduce his efforts to the manage-
ment of this crisis, but would persevere until his people were treated as
children of God and citizens of the free world, with all the rights such
thing entailed.

Nevertheless, among the ingredients necessary for change on those
uncertain days prior to the general elections of July 1966, the most determining factor was a widespread discontent among the vast majority
of Anguillians. Maybe they weren't all as vociferous as Rude Thompson,
but they knew exactly what he meant when he scorned the candidates
and dismissed their attempts to win his vote by making it absolutely
clear that *I ain' wastin' my precious time in no more elections*; and when his
reticence was met with indignation, he would come back with a violent
*For wha'? Vote, for wha'? If we be no better dan slaves to Bradshaw, den I
go behave jus' like dat: like a mad slave*; and here the argument turned
heated, because nobody wanted to be called a slave by anybody else.
And, for all the animosity inspired by the Labour Party and its government in Anguilla, there were still a good few hundred—the teachers, the
civil servants, those related to somebody who was well-connected in
St. Kitts, even the few fools who still believed in the promises made
by Bradshaw himself—whose point of view was neither as radical nor

as negative as Rude's and who still saw the possibility of improvement within the present administrative arrangement as the most viable solution to Anguilla's problems.

But Rude Thompson was not a man of reasonable views or temperate solutions, so when he heard anyone expressing opinions that were less than resolute in their condemnation of the behavior of the Kittitians, or the British, or anybody else even remotely related to the present reality of the Anguillian people, his instant reaction was to make everyone around him understand that *You all waste you time talkin' pointless t'ings. You t'ink we have choice? You t'ink somebody care wha' we say? We ain' got no voice, we ain' got no right to have no opinion, an' most of all, we ain' got no vote at all, at all.*

Rude Thompson's thunderous voice broke out like a heavy burden which settled on the air, making everything seem more serious—critical, even—and suffocating the merest intention to try to make a joke out of this. *You t'ink you have vote? Tell me—wha' happen las' time, when dat fat fool run for Labour an' got jus' a few votes? Wha' happen? I tell you wha' happen: not'in' happen, becausin' our man who beat him sit every day in Baseterre listenin' to oders take decisions when it no matter if he say yes or no, becausin' Labour have the majority, anyway, so dem kyan sit all day an' make faces to our man, an' if he say yes, no one listen, an' if he say no, no one listen still. Dat you call a vote? Liberty, you call dat? Slaves, I tell you— not'in' more dan slaves.* And the sound of that word spoken again echoed in the collective memories of the growing crowd, sending insults flying from side to side.

Nothing productive could be derived from this spontaneous meeting-turned-screaming-contest, but Alwyn Cooke had stood by the side of the road long enough to notice the passion, to see the commitment, and to want to hear more of what this fellow had to say, so he went back to his green Ford Anglia, and he pulled up right next to Rude Thompson, and opening the door and ordering him to *Get inside an' shut de door*, all was one and the same action, and in the blink of an eye, two of the most important ingredients necessary for change blended into one.

Late into the afternoon Rude and Alwyn sat on the back porch of Alwyn's house in Island Harbour by the diesel generator, discussing the maladies that had befallen Anguilla just because it had occurred to some ignorant bureaucrat somewhere in the empire that it would be a good idea to consolidate the governments of two distant and fully unrelated islands, when Rude snapped out of the conversation and aggressively asked—*So wha' you say we do 'bout it?*

It had not quite crossed Alwyn Cooke's mind that anything at all could be done, other than negotiate with the British until they agreed to untie the bond that kept Anguilla and St. Kitts joined, but *We done dat already—I myself wrote de letter dat two t'ousand people sign in '57. But so long Bradshaw in power, we ain' go see no British politician talk to us straight to de eye.* Alwyn was reminded of the letter he himself had not signed, not because he was against it, nor because he didn't care, but simply because that had been in another time—another lifetime—the one he had lived in St. Martin at Lover's Leap, during the doubly demanding days when D.C. van Ruijtenbeek had already died and Elaine Nesbit struggled to decide whether to continue living his life—his legacy— without him or give up all will to carry on and take a huge gamble in the hope that—somehow, somewhere—she would be reunited with the love of her life.

Alwyn Cooke liked what he saw in Rude Thompson but could not see a way to marry the two arguments his interlocutor put forward. *You keep sayin' we mus' do somet'in' but den you say dere ain' not'in' we kyan do so long as Bradshaw in power. What kinda foolish talk is dat?* Rude Thompson was not the type of guy who would let a question—an affront—like that pass, but neither was he a political or military strategist, so his answer was both fiery and vague, simultaneously infectious and disappointing. *Bottom line, Al, bot' you an' me know Anguilla need change but no soul ain' goin' hear not'in' we says, only if we go make one big mess dem go hear us, you know.*

Rude Thompson might not even have known it himself, but the words he spoke came straight from the mind—from the mouth—of Ignacio Ojeda and those long conversations at the cat cracker almost ten years before, where he had learned everything—the little—he knew about world affairs. And Alwyn Cooke heard the words of one activist filtered through the shape, the tone, the attitude of another, but despite his willingness to understand, despite his eagerness to act, he simply had no idea of how to turn all this talk into practical measures, how to effect the change both he and Rude Thompson knew was critical for the future development, or even the most elementary conditioning, of the island.

From that point onward they sat together frequently on Al's back porch in Island Harbour or in Rude's front yard in East End, trying to elucidate a way to catch the attention of some—any—world player, to turn their eyes in the direction of a small, underdeveloped, unproductive, and scarcely populated island in the Caribbean. There they met the news, Al full of expectation, Rude rather cynically, that the opposition candidate, Aaron Lowell, had won the elections in Anguilla by a landslide, while the Labour Party candidate had fared no better than his counterpart five years before. *So wha'? Dem guys in St. Kitts go ignore him jus' so like dey be doin' for de last ten years.* And even though the newly formed opposition party had swept the two seats granted to

Nevis, it soon became obvious that Rude Thompson was right, that with a majority of seven seats to three, the Labour Party would pay no more attention to the representatives of Anguilla and Nevis than they had ever done, and that *Ain' not'in' goin' change, Al—not'in' at all: until we go break up good wit' dem despots in St. Kitts.*

There, too, they sat, still looking for the plans they could not find, when an idea found them, traveling sixty-five miles over the Caribbean Sea on middle-frequency waves to smack them right between the eyes, as they heard the news broadcasted by ZIZ Radio St. Kitts that Robert Bradshaw, recently elected chief minister of St. Kitts-Nevis-Anguilla, would travel together with his right hand, Fitzroy Bryant, to the island of Anguilla during the New Year on a date soon to be announced, on a trip that was meant to promote the notion of statehood among the local electorate and dispel any doubts or concerns that the people of the island might have harbored over the years about it. To Rude Thompson nothing could have been more obvious: *Dis wha' we be lookin' for all along, you know. Dis we only chance.* It took Alwyn Cooke just a tad longer to understand, but soon enough he, too, was convinced that the first step in their struggle not only to be rid of the unjust and neglectful central administration of St. Kitts, but, first of all, to be heard, to be noticed by the world outside the imaginary entity that was St. Kitts-Nevis-Anguilla, would be to create an alarming situation when Robert Bradshaw visited the island.

And so the brainstorming continued—evolved, really—and moved on from the general question of what to do, to the particulars that entailed creating a situation that was alarming without becoming threatening, because Anguillians were fed up with this artificial association into which they had been born, and Anguillians craved more than anything else in the world a chance to build a future for themselves, and

Anguillians were determined to put the time and effort required for change to come about. But the rod would still have to bend a lot further before it snapped, and Anguillians were God-fearing people, principled in their actions and peaceful in their manners, and the mere suggestion of using violence to intimidate Bradshaw—to make him understand the gravity of the matter—would have been enough to split the public opinion in two and give more strength to the pro-government minority. Therefore, as soon as Rude Thompson noted, *We bot' have shotgun in we trucks*, Alwyn Cooke looked at him straight in the eye and with a final, curt tone, *Don' even t'ink about it.*

So he didn't. That was that as far as guns and violence were concerned—but more than stones and bullets can be used to turn a crowd hostile. There would be no stone throwing when Bradshaw and Bryant showed up in Anguilla, but Rude Thompson and Alwyn Cooke made certain there would be a suitable reception to make the foreigners realize that they were unpopular and unwanted, and that what had transpired in the recent elections was an accurate representation of the opinion of the vast majority of Anguillians, and that the most the two of them would be able to achieve in their visit would be to get out of the island in one piece.

Rude Thompson and Alwyn Cooke spent days preparing for the occasion—organizing meeting points, coordinating means of transport to mobilize the crowds, devising slogans, producing banners, riling the people, and making completely and definitely sure that the message would be one and the same wherever Bradshaw went, whoever he asked. When the date of the planned trip was announced, Alwyn Cooke went to the small haberdashery by the tamarind tree at the heart of The Valley and bought four brushes and two gallons of black paint. That was the final touch—a touch of spontaneity—missing in the plan.

Everything else was set in place and ready for the big day—the day the world would hear, perhaps for the first time, about the hardship, the neglect, that was inflicted upon Anguilla on a daily basis.

CHAPTER IV

THE SPEECH THAT NEVER CAME TO BE

AS SOON AS THE SLENDER DARK FIGURE of Robert Bradshaw emerged from inside the de Havilland Twin Otter operated by the Leeward Islands Air Transport (LIAT), a deep, loud jeer erupted from the back of the crowd awaiting his arrival at the precarious wooden "terminal" of Wallblake Airport in Anguilla. Indeed, the cloud of smoke lifted by the contact of the aircraft's fixed wheels with the dirt strip had barely settled when a group of protesters pulled out large banners and wooden boards demanding the expulsion of Bradshaw, the dissociation of Anguilla from St. Kitts, and the direct mandate of Britain on the island.

The first thing Bradshaw could see when his hunched frame, humbled by the small dimensions of the only commercial aircraft capable of landing on the short runway at Wallblake, finally found the space, beyond the threshold of the plane, to rise erect, was a minor brawl that ensued when a young man produced a placard that read, *Bradshaw NO—Britain YES*, next to a middle-aged Bradshaw supporter. The older gentleman, a square, dark fellow with thick hands and a smooth, round face, grabbed the wooden pole from which the young man held the placard and, fueled by an overwhelming indignation, screamed, *Boy, wha' kinda manners dem teach you at home?* as he smashed the wooden board against the floor and the boy's head alternately.

The second thing Bradshaw could see as his body straightened up on the steps of the Twin Otter, left hand in the air, greeting the crowd with a wave of his wide-brimmed slouch hat to go with his khaki field uniform and his Sam Browne belt, was a message which had been delivered overnight in thick black letters painted on the façade of the building that stood directly behind the ramshackle terminal: *ST. KITTS + ANGUILLA = UNHOLY UNION*. The tone had been set for Chief Minister Bradshaw's visit.

In January 1967, when Robert Llewellyn Bradshaw visited Anguilla, he was fifty years old. He had been actively involved in politics for more than twenty-five years, had been part of the St. Kitts Workers' League and later the Trades and Labour Union since its creation in 1932, and had served the island's legislature for twenty years, emerging victorious every single time the people of St. Kitts-Nevis-Anguilla had been summoned to the polls after the introduction of universal suffrage in 1952. Bradshaw had been elected to the legislature in 1952 and had joined the Leeward Islands Executive Council in 1955; he had figured as minister of finance in the Federation of the West Indies and had been an outspoken advocate of the union even as it faced fierce criticism from within during the months leading up to its disintegration; he had been an important part—pivotal, some would say—of the legislature of St. Kitts-Nevis-Anguilla under the government of Chief Minister Paul Southwell between 1961 and 1966, before being elected himself as chief minister. Now, as he was poised to become the first premier of the self-governing "associated state" of the tri-island entity, he approached all Anguillians in an effort to advertise the concept of statehood, to make certain everyone understood that this was the most effective way to move forward—forward toward the future, forward toward progress, forward toward complete independence.

In short, in January 1967, when Robert Llewellyn Bradshaw visited Anguilla, he was already a successful politician, experienced beyond his age, self-confident and self-assured, assertive in his manners, unbending in his convictions, unaccustomed to opposition, and intolerant of dissent. Hence, when Robert Llewellyn Bradshaw emerged from the constrained space inside the de Havilland Twin Otter that had taken him and his right hand, Fitzroy Bryant, over the sixty-five-mile strait that separated Anguilla from St. Kitts, he was not in the least bit amused by what he saw first. What he saw next simply sent his temper through the roof and ensured that this would not be a successful visit. Even before Bradshaw had set his right foot on the dirt strip at Wallblake Airport, it was already evident that the purpose of his journey would not be achieved. In fact, had he turned around then, taken his seat, and ordered the pilot to hop back to St. Kitts, he would have made a more favorable impression than he did by touring the island. Then again, hindsight is both precious and free.

Determined to show these people what was right for them and their country, Bradshaw descended upon the crowd with restrained anger and moved composedly toward the front, where he intended to deliver the first and shortest of his speeches that day. Little did he know how short his foes would force all of the speeches to be. Think about it, the setting strikingly poor, with a small, rundown plane on a dust strip; cows would have been grazing all around him, had there been any cattle on the island. But Anguilla is sparse and dry and arid, and there's hardly any grass at all—let alone anything but goats to eat it. And this imposing, successful, father-like figure approaches untroubled by the barrenness of the environment, willing to offer a (strong) hand, to give (unquestionable, inexorable) advice, to reassure the people—his people—that everything will be all right. And how do his people respond? Like rebellious teenagers, like spoiled brats, waving placards, vandalizing buildings, hurling insults, and dissenting without even listening.

Toward the front, some fifty or so Anguillians were there to welcome Chief Minister Bradshaw with their worries, their concerns, their petitions, because the situation on the island really was alarming, but how could Robert Bradshaw, or anybody else for that matter, know exactly how bad things were in Anguilla, when nobody had visited the island in so long? And, besides, there was no point in all that foolish talk about separation and all the rest. What was a poor, small island like Anguilla going to do on its own, when much bigger places like Jamaica, like Trinidad, were having hell at being independent? Toward the back, however, gathered a substantially less understanding bunch of dissenters who had come to take a look, face-to-face, at the character they had learned to dislike so much. Among those, spread out in pockets of three or four, were the men and women whom Alwyn Cooke and Rude Thompson had mobilized to create a discernibly hostile environment for Bradshaw and Bryant. And in the middle, caught out of place, a bit too far toward the front in the heat of the moment by a burst of excessive enthusiasm, was Walter Stewart, whose placard had been smashed to pieces by an older supporter of the regime.

Bradshaw, enraged by the embarrassing scene, turned a short arrival speech into a piercing threat: *I see already some of di Anguillian people have no respect at all. Is good t'ing yer always have St. Kitts to lead yer by di hand!* And the resentment could be sensed on both ends of the mob.

Alwyn Cooke's signal wasn't necessary for the crowd of dissenters to start heckling Bradshaw as he spoke.

So you t'ink dis a bunch of children you speakin' to?

But Bradshaw simply ignored the question and kept on with his warning message: *Di future for St. Kitts looms bright and fair. T'rough short, certain steps we soon be able to call dis we land, we nation, we country.*

The next interruption came from a woman who had not been involved with, or even aware of, Alwyn Cooke's gang: *So you t'ink dis St. Kitts where you be?*

And Bradshaw, as if answering the question he never heard: *Together, as brothers*—and here the left fist was raised to the heavens in a signal of unity—*we go make Anguilla share from our future.*

T'ief!

Statehood is jus' di beginning.

Liar!

Today statehood, tomorrow independence, and all of a sudden a widespread *Boooo* erupted at Wallblake Airport.

Aaron Lowell, representative of Anguilla in the legislature of St. Kitts-Nevis-Anguilla, approached Robert Bradshaw solemnly to bring across a point the Kittitian had been too blind (deaf and dumb) to see. Escorted by Lowell, Bryant and Bradshaw headed toward the maroon Morris Minor that would take them through their planned tour of the island. On its way from the airport, along the dust road that joined George Hill and The Valley, the Minor was greeted by vociferous Anguillians who shouted and gesticulated at the men inside, as they went past the grandiose façade of the Wallblake House to their left, one of the very few plantation manors left standing on the island, past the emblematic stone tower that crowned the top of the road by St. Mary's Anglican church to their right, before arriving at the central point of the political life of the island: Burrowes Park.

The meeting at the park—*park* as in a sports venue, not its metropolitan usage as in Central, or Hyde—had been called well in advance, and the speech Bradshaw would deliver was expected to contain the kernel of whatever it was that he (personally) wanted to say to the people of East and West End, respectively, so from the moment LIAT's de Havilland Twin Otter could be heard in the distance, people started heading toward the center of town. Unlike the one gathered at the airport, however, this crowd seemed far more restless, far less awed by the figure of the chief minister, and far less evenly split between sympathizers and detractors of government. The Morris Minor carrying Aaron Lowell, Fitzroy Bryant, and Robert Bradshaw had to crawl behind a procession of anxious Anguillians who only made way for the vehicle to pass after they had jeered at the passengers, waving their index fingers, sucking their teeth in anger. Once the car reached the grounds of the Anglican church, the concentration of people was such that there was no way to go through. At the merest sight of an opportunity to dissociate himself from the foreigners, Aaron Lowell jumped from the vehicle and walked the final three or four hundred yards of the way ahead of it, his short, stocky legs pumping, his small hunched torso further dwarfed by the occasion, his thick, gigantic hands awkwardly bulging out of his gray flannel suit to pull the crowd apart and allow the passage of the Minor.

By the time Bradshaw managed to step onto the small stage (more a speaker's box than anything else), Alwyn Cooke and Rude Thompson had already taken their positions. At their positions, too, were Walter Stewart, the fifteen-year-old grandson of Connor Stewart from Island Harbour, and Gaynor Henderson, Rude Thompson's childhood friend from East End. Infiltrated among the crowd was also Bernice Cooke, one of Alwyn's twelve siblings, as well as her pal and confidant Maude Sullivan, a heavyset young girl from Island Harbour. Indeed, among the twenty or so conscripts Alwyn Cooke and Rude Thompson had managed to gather expressly to create the tense atmosphere within which they hoped the people of the island would fail to be intimidated by

Bradshaw's presence and would feel confident or angry enough to voice their true opinion, there were at least eight or nine women.

Some of them were young women, frustrated by the state of Anguillian affairs and enthusiastic about change—any change. Others were already grown women, wives or sisters of fellow troublemakers (quite literally) who would (unequivocally) not allow their men to get involved in something like this unless they were nearby to protect them. Much to the surprise of Alwyn and Rude, but not at all to the women they had brought along with them, more than half of the crowd awaiting Robert Bradshaw at Burrowes Park that day was female.

When Robert Bradshaw took to the stage that was nothing more than a speaker's box, he was filled with a warm sense of security, with a comforting coziness that obeyed his impression that he addressed nothing more than a harmless group of housewives. But nothing could have been further from the truth, because all the women gathered at Burrowes Park that day—young and old, big and small, fat and thin, all of them without exception—were there for a very serious, a very troubling, and a most uncomfortable reason. They were there because they were not only deeply aware of but also deeply dissatisfied with the neglect in which Anguilla was mired; they were there because they worried about the well-being of their families, and whatever they would have to do next to secure it; they were there because they feared for their children, for their future, and for their country. Thus, even before Robert Bradshaw was given the opportunity to introduce himself and his right hand, Fitzroy Bryant, the women, much more vociferous— ferocious even—than the men present at the park, asked the Kittitian politicians, *Why you starve me child? Why you kill me family?*

This time Bradshaw could not ignore the question—the accusation, really—of the crowd of listeners, not least because only ten yards away from him stood Euralia Lannock, a teenage mother of three boys from The Valley, whose youth had been sapped by the complications of her third pregnancy, and who tirelessly asked the same question repeatedly, the rollers on her head slowly coming undone with every one of her angry jolts, her thunderous voice quashing every other muttering around.

Woman! Stop aksin' dat same question over an' over. I ain' know why yer child dead but it ain' got not'in' to do wit' we. We here to protect people like yer, we here to offer one hope for di future, we here to make yer be part of dat future. Bradshaw stopped short of explaining that what he really meant was St. Kitts's (bright) future. Instead, he turned this into the perfect platform to make his speech—affected with the diction of the populace, speaking like one of "them"—to return to its agenda, to labor on the concept of statehood, to stress the temporary nature of such status, to build toward the climactic end and the ultimate goal: independence.

But Euralia Lannock had managed to interrupt Chief Minister Bradshaw. Indeed, she had forced him to engage directly with her, directly with the people, in an exchange, rather than just a one-way communication. So, as soon as Bradshaw stopped to acknowledge Euralia and her calls, the whole crowd erupted in a multitudinous voice that corroborated her position, that questioned his response (*What?* asked a man toward the back, lingering with indignation on the vocalization of the "w" and dropping all the weight of his anger on an abrupt and violent "t"), that built on the point she had just made, or that simply added further questions to the equation, such that Bradshaw's voice became indistinguishable, lost within the common roar, just like that of Euralia, who continued to express herself effusively, hitting her bosom with her closed right fist, grabbing her breasts in desperation, holding her head in agony, tearing her rolled hair from her scalp, as if she had truly lost her family, her children, as if it were not all an apt, yet radical, metaphor.

Bradshaw's anger grew (visibly) by the minute, but he was unable to overcome the tumultuous clamor. He gesticulated frantically, pointing with his left hand toward members of the audience to the left, toward a woman out there to the right, but all to no avail: no one was listening anymore, because nobody had come to listen in the first place. Exasperated, Bradshaw made one final attempt to control the mob. He stood erect, looking out in the distance, in total silence. But there was no room for silence in Burrowes Park that day, and no one really noticed Bradshaw as he, á la Caesar, once again lifted his left hand, arm outstretched, then lowered it again, slowly, as if to instruct the crowd to be quiet. Three times his left hand rose up in the air, and three times it came down, progressively more manically, more frustrated, more disgustedly, until, at last, an instinct led him to open both arms wide and to direct a gruesome *SILENCE!* at the crowd.

There it was, the unfamiliar stump at the end of his right arm, a hand still vaguely recognizable, if clearly deformed, turned inward at the wrist, fingers atrophied, too small, too thin, not quite capable of making a fist because of the machine shop at the sugar refinery, which, more than thirty years before, when he was just a teenager, had endowed him with a humiliating legacy. Right-handed at everything— hell, even at onanism—up until that point, Robert Bradshaw had had to learn how to live all over again. But his reinvention as a left-handed unionist had been a successful one, and from very early on—when the pain was still sufficiently fresh in his brain to remind him that there was no shame to be had in the measure of ill fortune that had been allocated to him—Bradshaw had learned to turn the tragedy of an accident into an inevitable act of fate—of a higher being, a larger consciousness—to keep him away from the physical travails of cutting and processing the cane, and to land him closer to the organizing ranks at the helm of St. Kitts's Workers' League, where, by the gracious will of God Almighty, it had all started.

Now, it might not have been thirty years since Fitzroy Bryant had seen that stump in public, but it certainly had been a good while—so when he saw his friend and colleague open his arms wide at the crowd, he understood (perfectly, immediately) that it was time to move on to the next venue. Aaron Lowell, on the other hand, had not been serving as representative of Anguilla in the legislature of St. Kitts-Nevis-Anguilla long enough to have been confronted with the real shape of Bradshaw's right hand. Indeed, all along what had seemed more conspicuous to Aaron Lowell had been, rather, how seldom Bradshaw used his right arm, overcompensating to a degree that made the lack of symmetry in his body become more accentuated. Hence, Aaron Lowell had to be shaken out of his stupor by physical means before he caught up with the revised agenda and joined Fitzroy Bryant and Robert Bradshaw on their way to the Morris Minor that would take them out to the West End.

The abrupt close to a meeting that had brought to surface such delicate issues without proposing anything even remotely resembling a solution would generally have bred so much bad blood it seems difficult to imagine how Bradshaw, Bryant, and Lowell made it out of the park unscathed, but such was the effect of the unexpected apparition of that right stump, such was the extent of the surprise it spread among the crowd that, while everyone questioned everybody else, rubbing their eyes, shouting to the heavens, *Boy, you see de dead stick Bradshaw carry for a right hand?* the politicians were able to make a mute, though not so secret, escape.

Back in the safe haven of the maroon Morris Minor silence reigned. Aaron Lowell sat incredulous, hunching his frame as low as possible, hiding his small, round head between the lapels of his suit and the narrow brim of his understated trilby (to match the gray flannel), avoiding by whatever means available the sight of Bradshaw for fear he might not be able to govern his eyes away from his right arm. The police officer at the wheel of the Minor had already driven past the Anglican church in The Valley and the Wallblake House, he had left behind the airport to the left and Wallace Rey's shop to the right (flying a banner that read, *BRADSHAW NO*), he had gone up and down George Hill and found himself by the dangerous intersection with the downhill road toward Sandy Ground, when he mentioned nonchalantly, *Dem coming wit' us to West End*, as he pointed with his chin at the image of the green Ford Anglia that grew larger in his rearview mirror. *Bastards*, was all that Aaron Lowell could discern from the mumblings Bradshaw let out as response.

The road got considerably worse after the Sandy Ground junction, as the Minor made its way through the bushland of South Hill until it reached the massive stone structure of the Methodist church, overlooking the fishing village of Sandy Ground from above, with its large pile of salt reaped from the adjacent pond, the narrow stretch of land (where the Road lay) that separated the pond from the sea, the turquoise, unspoiled waters of Road Bay and its tropical tilde off the coast, and the minute Sandy Island, a sandbank high enough to host a nest of palm trees. Robert Bradshaw's fit of anger was appeased by the natural beauty of the scenery, or maybe it was by the irrefutable evidence of the total abjection in which the island was immersed, perfectly portrayed in the tiny two-toned fishing boats, direct heirs of the indigenous canoe, anchored along the bay, without so much as a pier to load and unload them. Perhaps Robert Bradshaw was struck by an instant of compassionate lucidity, as he understood the recalcitrant—plain rude, actually—behavior of the crowds at Wallblake Airport and Burrowes Park when he was confronted firsthand with the size of the potholes on the dust road that took him, Fitzroy Bryant, and Aaron Lowell from The Valley to West End at a speed more befitting a mule than an automobile, simply because by every inch that the right foot of the police officer behind the wheel approached the floor of the car, the possibilities of a blown tire were increased exponentially. Or perhaps Robert Bradshaw was simply reassured—comforted—by the levels of despondency that the insolent Anguillians who had just dared address him with such disrespect had to withstand day in, day out, throughout the course of their pitiful, miserable lives.

Whatever the case, as the maroon Morris Minor cruised through South Hill and penetrated farther west, beyond the junction that led toward the southern coast—Blowing Point, Rendezvous Bay, and the only hotel on the island—and downhill again past the marshland next to Maid's Bay Pond, where the island narrowed visibly, Bradshaw's countenance shed its load of languor, of anger, and regained its usual composure. By the time the three men had reached the low hill that rises just beyond Maunday's Bay, Bradshaw was already harassing Aaron Lowell again, asking, *Wha' coin we expect from dis bunch, here? Will yer be able to restrain yer own people?* Lowell didn't even know whether the question was addressed to him, let alone how to answer, so he kept his eyes low (away from that cursed right arm) and his mouth shut. *Hey! He speak, or he dumb like all Bobo Johnnys?*

Nobody really knows where the term "Bobo Johnny" actually came from, nor, in fact, what it means, beyond it being a derogatory appellative used by Kittitians to refer to Anguillians. Some adduce, with the blessing of common sense, that the "Johnny" element stemmed from Anguillian laborers working in the cane fields in St. Kitts, who all, without fault, would take a johnnycake to munch on their way to work. The "Bobo" aspect has a more obscure origin but it would not be inconceivable to link it to an identical Spanish word, which means fool or dupe, and which might have entered the Kittitian dialect as an influence from the Dominican Republic, where many West Indians worked as cane-cutters until the second half of the 1930s, when a combination of the low price of sugar in the world markets together with Rafael Trujillo's sudden craze to moderate the country's largely African heritage meant that black migrant workers were no longer either terribly welcome or particularly willing to make the journey to Santo Domingo.

Either way, regardless of whether or not, etymologically speaking, "Bobo Johnny" originally meant "the fool with the cake for the journey," in 1966 the expression certainly had been ascribed a negative connotation. So why would Robert Bradshaw, an accomplished politician soon to become the leader of an autonomous state, use such an unfortunate choice of words when addressing his Anguillian colleague? The answer to this question might be as simple, as blunt, as "Because he could." Although he had collected himself, Bradshaw was still angry, and when people are prone to being contemptuous, one thing that is sure to trigger it is anger. The chief minister had come to Anguilla as a gesture of good faith—not to actually consult the people about anything, but to reassure them that things would be fine. He could understand there were concerns, and he could just about tolerate people burdening him with their petty problems, but there was unequivocally no room for anyone to question his words, his judgment, his decision. In other words, Robert Bradshaw had come to Anguilla like a stern father to inform his children about, rather than to discuss with them, the next move, in full confidence that his way was not only the best, but actually the only way.

So, when Robert Bradshaw called Aaron Lowell a Bobo Johnny, when he said all Anguillians were dumb, he did so in relatively good spirits—as good a spirit as he was capable of displaying. Because to him the question of superiority of Kittitians over Anguillians would have appeared no different that the question of whether turtles are better equipped to live on land or sea. After all, St. Kitts had enjoyed progress and prominence and riches for centuries, while Anguilla coped with famine and droughts and extreme poverty. And, after all, St. Kitts had produced a character such as his, whereas Anguilla would always foster weaklings like Aaron Lowell, who refrained from answering even as they were being insulted to their face. And, moreover, Anguilla had accomplished nothing throughout its history, which was precisely all to what they could ever aspire without an association with St. Kitts.

Aaron Lowell stopped himself from falling into Bradshaw's game for as long as he could. For as long as he could, Aaron Lowell kept quiet in his seat, avoiding direct eye contact with Robert Bradshaw and fearing more than anything the force of that limp right hand. But as the maroon Morris Minor came closer to West End Pond, and it neared the stage at the West End village, where Bradshaw would deliver the third of his speeches that day, he built up his confidence, disguised his temper, and refashioned himself into the persona he had developed over so many public appearances in the previous three decades. *If di man don' answer my questions, I will have to give orders instead: Lowell, make sure yer control yer people dis time.*

Upon the second mention of this whole "your people" nonsense, Aaron Lowell could no longer hold back. *I from The Valley, I ain' from Wes' End, an' dem people no more mine dan yours.*

Bradshaw could sense the defiance in Aaron Lowell's words, but the stage was too close to allow anger to filter into his demeanor again, so he simply explained, *Dey Anguillians, dey di electorate, and dey choose yer as representative. Dey yer people, Lowell—jus' keep 'em under control.*

Aaron Lowell played no role whatsoever in keeping the people from the West End under control, but the crowd was considerably smaller than it had been at Burrowes Park and, somehow, they seemed less passionate, less interested, less bothered by the whole issue of state-hood, by the association with St. Kitts, by anything, in fact, that was not immediately related to their fishing, and even as Alwyn Cooke, Rude Thompson, Gaynor Henderson, Walter Stewart, and a number of men and women intent on disrupting the proceedings joined the crowd and purposely twisted every one of Bradshaw's statements and launched tirades of insults, of accusations, at the politician, their words seemed not to find interest, quorum, or even favor among the others assembled, and Bradshaw, his confidence restored by the presence of a reasonable, if not terribly engaging group of people, remained calm and collected about the imported troublemakers.

But this was the only point Bradshaw would score on his visit to Anguilla. The meeting on West End was short and swift, and the chief minister even displayed some sort of a sense of humor as he scornfully made fun of the men and women following the maroon Morris Minor: *Boy, dey mus' be grateful for we visit, Fitz.* To which Fitzroy Bryant, abject and disturbed by the terrible conditions of the road, simply retorted with a forestalled smile that awaited the punch line, *How else dey will know the geography of dey island? Look at dem—is a field trip dey having.*

When Robert Bradshaw finally ventured to ask, *Who dem hell-raisers be?* Aaron Lowell, desperately clinging to the sight of anything, any-thing at all, except that dead right hand, simply disguised his ignorance by claiming, *Dey is jus' some ragamuffins from East End.* He had recog-

nized Alwyn's car, but he had not looked hard enough to get a clear
picture of the members of the organized dissent they had encountered
that day.

And yet, the worst was still to come. Indeed, it appeared as if Lowell's reply had acted as the perfect cue for more trouble to happen, but
the real determining factor had been where the party found itself,
because the Kittitian policeman—let's give him a name already—
Constable LaRue, had long left behind the Anglican church at The
Valley, and the Minor had turned to the right, and the road had taken
them to the tamarind tree by Albert Lake's shop, and the driver had
continued past Proctor's corner and taken Long Path out to the east.
And at this stage the green Ford Anglia had been joined by Wallace
Rey's red pickup truck, and from time to time the cars would meet a
group of people blowing their conch shells in disapproval, and as the
marshlands extended farther east, the potholes on the road began to
resemble lunar craters, and they multiplied by the second (or the me-
ter), and soon enough the Minor had to drive so slow the people outside didn't even have to run very fast to keep up. And the cars behind
blew their horns, and the crowd jeered and blew the conch shells, and
expressed in guttural, rather primeval fashion their animosity toward
the Kittitian delegation.

Inside, Bradshaw's mood transmuted once again as his temper got
the best of his humor. But he would not ask the driver to stop, and he
would not give the signal to turn around, until the situation reached
breaking point right by the Sandy Hill intersection. There, trailed by
dozens of people walking behind and beside the Minor, blowing into
their conch shells, Bradshaw was startled out of his skin when a cooking
pan hit the window on his side of the car. Ylaria Cooke had brought it
specifically for that purpose, though she never thought it would be as

effective as it proved to be. The crowd, gathered by the maroon Morris, felt invigorated by the rattle of the old metal, by the courage of her gesture, and suddenly they reached toward the car, first fearfully, but then progressively more confidently, slamming the bonnet, pounding the roof, shouting into the windows. Afraid, Bradshaw informed his driver of his sudden need to *Get back to di airport.*

The speech in the East End would never come to be. Alwyn Cooke, Rude Thompson, and their makeshift army had landed a blow that would certainly help their morale, if nothing else. In turn, Bradshaw produced enough bile during this one trip to harbor an intrinsic hatred of Anguilla for the rest of his life. For the time being, however, he could only drain his rage by harassing Constable LaRue to *Go faster—fast as yer coin*, to get to Wallblake Airport as soon as possible and end this nightmare.

As Fitzroy Bryant climbed the two steps leading to the de Havilland Twin Otter that would take him and his chief minister back home, his bottom ached from the indirect beating that, through the negligence of his own government, Anguillians and their terrible roads had delivered him.

CHAPTER V

THE UNDELIVERED MESSAGE

As the de Havilland Twin Otter that carried Robert Bradshaw and his right hand, Fitzroy Bryant, sped off the dust strip of Wallblake Airport and soared over the late-afternoon sky, it left behind a thick cloud of smoke and a general sense of vindication among the Anguillian population. Alwyn Cooke and Rude Thompson were beyond themselves with excitement—an excitement that was contagious as they playfully pushed and shoved each other. *We done it!* one would say to the other. *We teach 'em good!* the other would answer back, and their common cackle would only come to an end in order to begin the mirth again with a *Now wha' dey goin' say 'bout we people in Anguilla?* which would be rhetorically answered with *Now how dey go ignore us?*

Except the practicalities of ignoring the wishes—the actions—of the people from a small, anonymous rock in the Caribbean atoll were still far simpler than Rude and Alwyn imagined. As it turned out, ignoring the people of Anguilla was the easiest—the least embarrassing—thing Robert Bradshaw could do under the circumstances. Consequently, when small crowds of disgruntled Anguillians gathered around radio sets powered by batteries bought collectively by five or six people, or they tuned in, rather ambitiously, to the BBC with the help of the only generator in this particular area of the island, hopes and expectations were progressively traded for confusion, frustration, and, ultimately, anger, as no story—not one word—about Anguilla, Bradshaw, or his recent visit to the island made it to the regional news coverage.

And the dial rolled up and down, seeking ZIZ Radio St. Kitts, and eventually a familiar voice, a familiar accent, announced that it was time for the local news, and three reports of a missing old man, and dates for the upcoming season of cane cutting, and two buses that would be added to the public transport service, monopolized the program, and *Is only fifty-one days to statehood*, and not one word about Anguilla, or Bradshaw, or the visit he had just paid the island. Because nobody had informed ZIZ, the BBC, or anyone else about the incidents; because in Anguilla, just like there was no electricity, no running water, no telephone, no paved roads, there were also no news reporters, or news agencies, nor were there any means of sending out communication in any quick or effective form; and Bradshaw was certainly not the kind of man who would inform the world about his failure to appeal to a bunch of rowdy housewives. So, in the end, Bradshaw got back to St. Kitts and acted as if everything had gone according to plan, and he didn't even have to say, *Don' mention a word 'bout dis*, to Fitzroy Bryant, because Fitzroy Bryant was too intelligent to need telling and too loyal to want to smear Bradshaw's public image with such nonsense. And so, after the same scene was repeated the following day, and the day after that, and the day after that, Anguillians took a break from the evening news, because no one really expected to hear anything about themselves on the radio anymore.

Then it dawned on Alwyn Cooke, then it dawned on Rude Thompson, how lost—how forsaken—Anguilla really was. *I don' understan'— what we s'posed to do?* and the long-drawn silence that followed was the best—the most appropriate—answer Alwyn Cooke could muster. And then: *We already done wha' we s'posed to do. We already done it, an' is the same as before, becausin' nobody know we done it. Tell me somep'in', Al: wha's de difference between somep'in' happenin' an' de same t'ing not happenin' at all, when nobody know if it happen or not? You tell me—wha's de difference?*

And the difference, of course, was, *If Anguilla screwed an' nobody know, Rude, you an' me an' everybody else you know in dis island screwed jus' de same. Da's why it our job to get some people to know.* And the difference was the dismay in Rude Thompson's heart, the disappointment evident in Alwyn Cooke's countenance, after they had achieved what they thought had been the first victory in their fight for recognition.

I bet you anyt'in' de English don' even know 'bout we. And Rude would have lost anything Alwyn Cooke might have wanted to gamble, because the British did know, at least some of them did—after all, there was a ministry of foreign affairs and a whole department devoted to the Commonwealth. Aaron Lowell himself had exchanged some words with (minor) British officials, and in light of the overwhelming demonstration of animosity against Bradshaw, which the people of Anguilla had so civically displayed, he had promised, almost immediately, that he would arrange to go to London to hold talks with— and here his explanation fell short of the desired, because almost certainly he did not have a clue with whom he should speak—some *senior* official.

Naturally, no senior official wanted to discuss the question of Anguilla—least of all with the Anguillian delegate—and, indeed, Rude Thompson might have come close to the bull's-eye had he said that nobody *of importance* in England knew about Anguilla. But Rude was not in the mood for details, and matters of degrees had never been his strength, so he just continued his diatribe, as much to himself as to anyone else. *Nah, boy—we ain' not'in' to dem. Worse dan slaves, becausin' we be de slaves of de slaves. Not'in' at all, at all.*

For a few days it was evident that the population of the island was shell-shocked from the lack of news, but little by little things got back to normal, and soon thereafter you could see the children walking from school to their homes, the taxis taking the occasional passenger from George Hill to Blowing Point, the de Havilland Twin Otter from LIAT landing on the dust strip from time to time. Until the stillness brought about by the lack of news was broken—smashed, obliterated— by the emergence of another, quite different piece of news: it was announced that a member of the British government would be traveling to Anguilla prior to the declaration of statehood for St. Kitts-Nevis-Anguilla. Statehood was scheduled for February 27; this was January 15. There were still six weeks to build hope, along with a plan of action, and to do something about it. And in the middle of it all, the British were finally coming.

Thus, in the middle of winter 1967, to the fine tune of the cool breeze and the short days laden with unpredictable showers that came and went, Rude Thompson and Alwyn Cooke picked up the pieces— whatever was left—of the plan they had prepared two months earlier, prior to Robert Bradshaw's visit, and worked together to forge a way out of the voiceless anonymity in which Anguilla found itself. But Rude Thompson and Alwyn Cooke had already explored many avenues, and the alternatives which emerged were alternatives that either one or the other was unwilling to contemplate: *I say so already, Al, you have you shotgun, I have mine, an' we bot' know how to use it,* to which, *I t'oght I tell you already not to t'ink 'bout it. So wha' you doin' talkin' da' foolishness again?*; or, *Is a letter we need write to de British before dem sen' dis guy down, so he know wha' we need before he arrive,* to which, *Jus' becausin' you ain' sign de damn paper don' mean it don' exist, Al. We done dat too! Is goin' back ten years, goin' back to dat.*

For days Rude and Al went round and round in circles, discussing, proposing, studying, and dismissing theories, ideas, and plans to get the process of emancipation from St. Kitts off the ground. For days they argued heatedly outside, in the front yard of Rude Thompson's house in East End, on the back porch of Alwyn Cooke's house in Island Harbour, in the ill-lit hall of the only bar on the eastern part of the island, the Banana Rod, where at the end of each conversation Rude would vent his frustration with an angry slamming of his empty beer bottle on the wooden table, which would send a heavy thump echoing through the darkness outside.

It was on one of those days, after Rude's thunderous outburst had startled the night, that the largely impotent enthusiasm of the two plotters was unexpectedly invigorated by the fresh thrust of a newcomer. Sol Carter was disgusted with the spectacle that Rude and Al provided on an almost nightly basis, the two of them imbued on a trip of self-importance that contributed more to the growth of their egos than to the improvement of Anguilla's situation. So one night, after Rude disturbed the peace with his beer bottle, Sol snapped, *Boy, why you slam you glass so? You t'ink the night you own? You talk an' talk an' talk an' ain' never not'in' useful comin' from you. Look wha' you do las' time when Bradsher come to Anguilla. Instead of talkin' to de man, you make him leave,* and so began the first of many bust-ups between Rude Thompson and Sol Carter.

Because if ever there were two characters who were not meant to be together, two personalities that were incompatible, they were Sol Carter and Rude Thompson. Because Rude Thompson was a man who simply could not sit and watch life pass by without doing something, but he was not necessarily the most efficient of persons, as his urge was to act, regardless of consequences, whereas Sol Carter, older, wiser, and more collected, was a man whose priority lay with results, and how those results could best be achieved. And, indeed, it was one of the early victories of the revolution to be able to pair poles as far apart as these two in the quest for a common goal. But before that, the first bust-up had to take place, and Sol Carter had to tell Rude Thompson how futile—how fruitless—his attitude, his endless talk, and his thoughtless actions had turned out to be, only for Rude to throw back at him what he threw back at anyone who dared recriminate him, *So you know whattodo? Why you don' do it already? Why Anguilla still de same?* while his arms flailed in the air—chest puffed out, head tilted upward—and his disposition was in place to settle the score with his fists.

Yet, at fifty-five, Sol Carter was still a mountain of a man, and he had lived too long, through too much, to be intimidated by a hotheaded idiot. Sol did not flinch, he did not take a step back, he didn't even blink—he just let out a sentence that would stay with Alwyn Cooke long after the scene was defused and the three sat down together working as a team: *Wha'ever I do, I do quiet, and I make for sure it work. If you knew wha's best for dis island, if you knew wha' you want, I tell you how t' get it—but I don' t'ink you even know dat.*

Whether or not Rude Thompson knew was unimportant, because Alwyn Cooke certainly did know what he wanted for the island, and faced with this degree of self-confidence he could not help his curiosity, so once tempers were calmed he opened up toward Sol Carter with candidness and, without getting ahead of himself, explained that all they wanted, as a starting point, was to find a way to let the people outside Anguilla know—understand, even—the conditions in which *you, you, he, she, an' me mus' meet every night: in darkness, in silence, to drink a drink that ain' even cold because de ice melt too fast.*

Sol Carter's expression changed as soon as he heard the explanation. It might have been that he did not expect as specific a response so quickly, or maybe he was surprised at how easily the problems of these rash youngsters could be solved—whatever the case, Sol's eyes grew larger in the darkness as he heard Alwyn describe what to him appeared to be the most immediate need to further Anguilla's case, and his cheekbones dropped, and his jaw was drawn outward, as if he could no longer hold back his words, and, *Boy—you see wha' happen when all you do is talk an' talk an' you don' boder looking roun' youself?* Neither Alwyn nor Rude knew where this was going, but they were willing to take one minute's scolding (no more than that, thought Rude) before Sol explained, *De stage you lookin' for exist already in St. Kitts, and de owner a man who would be willin' to let you speak.*

Solomon Carter had a knack for speaking in metaphorical terms, but eventually he would cut short his musings and call things by their name. So, eventually, Alwyn Cooke and Rude Thompson understood that the stage to which Solomon Carter referred was none other than the *Speaker* newspaper, established prior to the election of 1966 by the leader of the opposition party, Dr. Crispin Reynolds, to counteract what he denounced as censorship of the news on behalf of government, who controlled the only radio station on the island, ZIZ, and the only newspaper until that point, the *Labour Gazette*.

Crispin Reynolds own a house in Sout' Hill—he come to Anguilla all de time. When he next on de island, go speak to de man.

But this was not Rude's way. From that moment onward, not a day would go by when Rude would not write about the neglect in which Anguilla found itself, the reality it was forced to confront, and the absence of hope with which the people of Anguilla lived, oppressed by an institutional bully such as Robert Bradshaw.

As soon as Alwyn Cooke realized why he had suddenly seen so much less of Rude Thompson, he feared the worst: there was no telling what sort of nonsense his friend might be moved to narrate; moreover, there was no telling what the new paper would be rash enough to print, in its anxious determination to smear the name of the man who just a few months earlier had beaten its party to every single seat in the constituency of St. Kitts. Therefore, when Alwyn Cooke saw Rude Thompson's letter printed in the *Speaker*, he bought an extra copy and went straight to Rude's house in East End. There, neither angry nor enthused, he asked Rude how many of those he had sent.

One every day—dis de firs' dey print. But dere ain' no stoppin' us now.

Alwyn Cooke was not interested in stopping anything, but he was concerned about the effectiveness with which Rude would make use of this avenue, which, suddenly, had opened up for their purpose. *I notice some mistakes—da' comma after "abuse," wha' you put it dere for? Why you go use commas jus' like da', like it no matter where dey be? De people don' go believe you when you use big words like "negligence"—dey go t'ink you know 'bout dem big words so much like you know 'bout dem commas you use all over de place.*

There wasn't much wrong with the use of commas in the text, and if there had been, nobody in Anguilla or St. Kitts would really have cared (much), but Alwyn Cooke saw this as the subtlest way to propose to Rude Thompson to allow him to go through the text before he sent it to the *Speaker*, without making him feel censored, or even monitored. It worked perfectly, as Rude agreed to hand him the first draft of the letters before sending them on—*But you don' change not'in' before aksin' me firs'.*

The editing process of Rude's letters to the *Speaker* from that point forward consisted in him producing the first text and handing it over to

Alwyn, who would then visit Sol Carter behind Rude's back (no matter how subtly put, Rude would never have agreed to that) to discuss the content. Invariably, Sol would find fault in the aggressive tone of the prose, but he would not be allowed to make any changes—instead, he would have to suggest to Alwyn to alter a word here, to suppress a sentence there, which Alwyn would do diligently in his own handwriting, so that when he met Rude Thompson anew, he could claim the corrections were his own. Seldom were there any commas or semicolons to change, although Alwyn always made a point of adding or taking out three or four—not too many, lest Rude's feelings be hurt, but not too few, to emphasize the need to continue with the editing process.

Indeed, as the days went past and Rude detected the pattern of the commas and semicolons replaced by Alwyn, he adapted his writing style to avoid making the same "mistake." Alwyn, of course, didn't have much of a pattern—or, at least, he didn't think he did—and soon enough he was placing commas in Rude's texts in the exact same place where previously he had taken them out. Bitter arguments ensued between Alwyn and Rude as to where commas should be placed and why semicolons should be used, while the increasingly appropriating corrections made by Sol Carter through Alwyn Cooke's handwriting were approved almost without exception.

The first thing Alwyn did when he saw Rude Thompson's name in the *Speaker* was drive to his friend's house in East End to convince him that four eyes were sharper than two. The second, once Rude had agreed to show him the letters before submitting them, was visit Sol Carter in his home in Island Harbour. It was a Sunday afternoon and Sol was outside tending to his goats and planting some seeds in his small plot of land. Alywn approached with the *Speaker* opened on the relevant page. *I wan' you help me shape his letters wit' a clear message.* But

Sol was not in the mood to make things easy. *You say so youself—his letters. Wha' I got to do wit' it?* Alwyn took a conciliatory approach, explained how all of them were on the same side, claimed they needed Sol as much as he needed them—as much as all Anguillians needed each other in these difficult times. *We mus' stan' together, for only as one shall we succeed. Now, take me to Dr. Reynolds's home—I wan' speak to de man.*

Sol Carter hesitated for a moment. He stood erect in the afternoon sun, looking stronger, bigger than he was, by the size of his shadow. He took a few steps into the bush, tied the rope of his lead goat to a sturdy neem tree, and on his way into his house, almost brushing Alwyn Cooke, he just muttered, barely audibly, *Berightback*. Sol Carter washed his hands thoroughly, dried the sweat covering his chest, slipped a white cotton top on, and met Alwyn Cooke by his green Ford Anglia. The eight-mile ride between Island Harbour and South Hill, plagued with enormous potholes, took the best part of an hour.

Crispin Reynolds was neither tall nor imposing. Indeed, other than his corpulence, his physique seemed to lack the stature necessary to leave a lasting impression. At best Crispin Reynolds might have been described as the sketch of a man made only of different-sized circles: his head was small and his neck nonexistent; his torso was sizeable, if short of obese; his hind climbed all over his back; his legs were short, stocky, and powerful; his arms, less rotund than the rest of his body, fell limply on either side of his rib cage. Almost as if to confer an air of distinction to his presence, Dr. Reynolds was generally a tad overdressed, to the point where, even on a spontaneous visit such as this one, he was found wearing a light pair of gray trousers with a pleated white cotton shirt and a fedora. As soon as Sol Carter introduced Alwyn Cooke to him, his soothing voice, charged with the importance of someone who is used to being heard, addressed him with familiarity. *I t'ought to find a younger face to go wit' di name*, and with a touch of flattery, *Pleasure to meet yer, Mr. Cooke.*

But Alwyn Cooke was not in the mood for flattery. He was polite but unresponsive to Crispin Reynolds's sweet talk and, without much delay, went straight to the heart of the matter. *We in Anguilla very grateful in de last few mont's to find a different way to look at t'ings from St. Kitts,* and Alwyn Cooke produced the latest copy of the *Speaker.* To which Crispin Reynolds, allowing his credentials as a politician to shine at their brightest, *And yer expressed it overwhelmingly in yer support for Aaron Lowell in di last elections.*

Alwyn Cooke turned a deaf ear to Dr. Reynolds's complimentary tone and continued his progress toward the issue he really wanted to discuss: *Now we even have one of our own writin' in de paper,* and the rough creasing of the pages of the *Speaker* as Alwyn turned them, trying to find the right one, shook Dr. Reynolds out of his surprise at learning that an Anguillian—a Bobo Johnny—had been published in the paper. *But wha' we really like to see, an' I come to aks, is somet'in' even larger.* This time Dr. Reynolds failed to make a comment while he waited for Alwyn Cooke to explain that he had come to ask if Rude Thompson could have a regular space in the paper, where the news from Anguilla would be aired to fellow citizens in St. Kitts and the islands abroad.

Crispin Reynolds saw in the request a simple initiative to gain support among a people who were desperately looking for any kind of leadership to show them the path ahead. They had voted for his party in the previous elections, that much was true—but Aaron Lowell had been an independent candidate for much of the campaign, and it had been a wise move on his part to bet on the winning horse and bring Aaron Lowell into the fold. However, it was all but certain that Lowell would have won the election even without the party's support, and it was much less than evident that party politics would take root in Anguilla to an extent where they would determine who would be its representative. So, presented with this unexpected tool to increase his and the party's presence on the island, Crispin Reynolds appeased Alwyn Cooke: *Of course—we committed to improvin' di standards of life in di island an' makin' di union a uniform whole, where each part is as important as di oders, no matter how big or small.*

Alwyn, tired of political rhetoric, was at least relieved that he had chosen to visit Dr. Reynolds in the absence of Rude Thompson. But he also wondered why in the world, if the parts were supposed to be equally important, and the commitment was to improve the quality of life on the island, why, then, no one at the *Speaker* had so much as mentioned Bradshaw's embarrassing visit just a few weeks before.

Dr. Reynolds explained, typically elusively, that after Bradshaw's win in the recent elections and with the prospect of statehood ahead, he had really turned the heat on anyone who opposed him. *He feel invincible, an' anyone 'gainst he facin' trouble right now.* In view of this situation, it had become increasingly difficult to publish negative comments about the prime minister without being deemed defamatory by the government, and risking anything from closure to prison. For that very reason, the *Speaker* had recently adopted a strict editorial policy whereby they would only publish that which they could, immediately and unequivocally, verify. Often this meant publishing only that which the staff of the paper had witnessed and documented. *I di only person linked to di paper in Anguilla, an' I in a meetin' in St. Kitts when Bradsher visit di island, so nobody over here cover di event.*

Alwyn Cooke looked Crispin Reynolds in the eye with a trace of disbelief. *How you mean no one from de paper see de event? Why, Rude Thompson was dere—I see him wit' mine own eyes!*

Predictably, Crispin Reynolds didn't know who Rude Thompson was.

Well, de man be de paper contributor in Anguilla—you should know he!

And suddenly a glint of mischievousness caught Dr. Reynolds's eyes, as he recognized the cunning move Alwyn was proposing. *Suppose we get in trouble—how we back it up?*

But Alwyn had thought of that too, and the idea he had conceived was the sort that can only be conceived in a place immersed in another century, because in Anguilla there were no video recorders, no tapes, not even cameras. So, Alwyn's response—almost instinctively—was to offer as many signatures as were required to confirm that whatever was written in Rude Thompson's next—first official—"Letter from Anguilla" in the *Speaker* was all completely and incontrovertibly true. *I kyan even get you man, Aaron Lowell, to sign the paper. I kyan get twenty signatures in one hour, fifty in one morning, one hundred in a day—how many you need?*

Crispin Reynolds did not need any signatures just yet. All he needed was assurance that the article would be carefully worded and strictly bound to the truth. *Yer bring me a letter like dat nex' week an' I promise yer dis Rude Thompson will be published so long as he do de same t'ing week in, week out.*

For the next four months, until the expulsion of the police task force from Anguilla on May 30, 1967, "Letter from Anguilla" exposed the shortcomings of governance on the island on a weekly basis.

Rude Thompson and Alwyn Cooke, with Sol Carter in the background, worked on an article that would accurately describe the total failure of Robert Bradshaw's visit to the island in January 1967, trying to avoid the slip of the pen onto controversial, contentious, and slanderous statements against the prime minister, who always seemed most appropriately described with an insult. During that same week, Aaron Lowell came back to his constituency with what he considered to be good news. Instead of him traveling to the UK, the British had agreed to send over a local-government expert to look into the details of statehood with Lowell himself and a committee of advisors, who could then pass on the information to the population in general in a public meeting where all questions would be addressed.

The problem, of course, was that Aaron Lowell had promised to speak to a *senior* officer in the British government about Anguilla's situation, and no matter how you looked at it, Peter Johnstone, expert in local-government issues, was not only not senior, he was so far from the higher echelons of decision-making he didn't even qualify as a *minor* officer, because he was, really, nothing more than a powerless, if perhaps knowledgeable, advisor. But he was an advisor who could offer insights into a question that the vast majority of Anguillians considered unimportant, uninteresting, and, ultimately, irrelevant, because the only question that really troubled the Anguillian population had nothing to do with statehood as a system of government, with the possibilities established by the system, or the best way to procure effective representation within it. The only question that really troubled Anguillians led, in fact, to the immediate course of action to get the island out of the fold of St. Kitts, with or without statehood, be that through direct administration by the British or otherwise.

So, when Aaron Lowell announced, victoriously, that a local-government expert named Peter Johnstone would travel from the United Kingdom to Anguilla to discuss the ins and outs of statehood with a local committee on January 27, 1967, the general response was not so much lukewarm as angry. This was not what he had promised; this was not what the people wanted.

Rude Thompson, Alwyn Cooke, and, in the background, Solomon Carter finished their letter on January 26, 1967. As soon as Alwyn handed the first official installment of "Letter from Anguilla" to Crispin Reynolds, he went back to the eastern end of the island to work on the collective welcome the people of Anguilla would give to this Mr. Johnstone.

However, by the time Alwyn got back to the thick of things, everything was already in place. Banners had been made, posters, placards, all delivering one firm, uniform, and unmistakable message—*NO ASSOCIATION WITH ST KITTS*. More than three hundred people gathered at Wallblake Airport on Friday, January 27, 1967 to greet the de Havilland Twin Otter operated by LIAT which brought the British expert in local government to the island. Much to Aaron Lowell's embarrassment, the crowd was overwhelmingly opposed to the visit of this anything-but-senior official. Peter Johnstone was escorted through the shouting and fist-shaking multitude into an official vehicle—a taxi, accompanied by Constable LaRue—that would take him to the island's courthouse.

The drive from Wallblake to the heart of The Valley, where the single-story wooden building stood, between the police station and the government house, was about two-thirds of a mile. Nevertheless, the atrocious condition of the dust road, heavily scarred with potholes the size of tires, combined with the attentions paid to the visitor by a hostile crowd that ran to keep pace alongside the car, meant that the journey took a good ten, fifteen minutes. By the time Peter Johnstone faced the hand-painted board that in black lettering over a white background read, *Courthouse*, nailed to the side of a feeble wooden building, he was already frightened out of his skin. Then he encountered the blockade that a furious Anguillian mob, led by Rude Thompson and Alwyn Cooke, had mounted in the courtyard, intimidatingly demanding something that was out of his remit entirely, unwilling to listen to any alternatives, desperate to take a stance, to make a statement, to turn him into an example.

Peter Johnstone did not so much as take three full breaths of Anguilla's clean air: a few seconds were enough for him to understand he could not accomplish a thing through peaceful dialogue with these savages. Put to the test, his decision-making proved instantaneous, because his instincts told him his life might be at risk, and he knew when he was not welcome, and no mission was worth him sticking his neck out, so he turned on his heels and ordered the taxi driver to take him back to the airport, straightaway. Luckily, the de Havilland Twin Otter operated by LIAT that had brought him to this godforsaken place had not yet departed the island. By the time it did, Peter Johnstone was back in it, along with his undelivered message.

CHAPTER VI

THE STATEHOOD QUEEN SHOW

IF LEADERS CAN BE JUDGED BY THE MEASURE of their understanding of their people, then Robert Bradshaw was a most incompetent ruler for the Anguillians. In this respect, it's somewhat fitting that it was the British who indirectly made him their head of state. But Bradshaw's ignorance was such that, despite the fact that he could hardly have been more distant from the island's political pulse, he simply assumed that the havoc he had witnessed on his failed visit to Anguilla had been organized and orchestrated by a handful of troublemakers—*Dem rascals in di green Ford following us all roun' di place an' wexin' di crowds wit' dem nonsense*—and he was convinced beyond doubt that all the Anguillian people really wanted was—like the spoiled children they were—a bit of attention, and that this had been nothing if not the collective equivalent of a tantrum. Now, on the whole, Robert Bradshaw had, up to that point, carried himself with the authoritative air of a strict—severe, even—if benevolent father. (From Papa Doc to Papa Bradshaw to Uncle Gairy, what is it with Caribbean political leaders and the father syndrome?) Yet even the strictest parents allow, on occasion, some time for play. Perhaps as a strategy to gain popularity; perhaps as a means to keep the frustration that evidently assailed the people of Anguilla from escalating into full-fledged rage; or, perhaps, as a genuine measure to bring joy to the people of the island—who knows?—but after being forced to cut his visit short by one full speech, Robert Bradshaw decided that the best way to solve Anguilla's problems would be by staging some of the celebrations, scheduled for the days leading up to the final declaration of statehood, on the island.

The month of February was meant to be one of jubilation in St. Kitts, Nevis, and Anguilla; the month of February was supposed to bring the culmination of a long and painful process of regional integration and decolonization which Bradshaw had seen wither from the association of ten presidencies to the administrative union of merely three islands; but the month of February was sure to herald the dawn of a new era: an era of self-governing and responsibility, a political coming-of-age for the three neighboring islands and their populations that would set the example for the rest of the Caribbean to follow, that would vindicate the defeated but not-yet-forgotten cause of regional integration, that would make the whole wide world gasp in wonder and, even, envy. And so, still fresh from the anger that assaulted him inside the maroon Morris Minor that took him from his failed meeting at the park to his more successful meeting in West End, Robert Bradshaw spontaneously decided that a beauty pageant would be the perfect balm to soothe all tempers, and he decreed that nothing could be more fitting than to directly engage the capricious but ultimately beautiful children that Anguillians were in the statewide official party that would precede the declaration of statehood, and suddenly, without any sort of consultation or deliberation, the Statehood Queen Show was set to be held in Anguilla on February 4, 1967.

Which is to say that exactly eight days after the envoy from the British government, a local-government expert by the name of Peter Johnstone, had been expelled from the island, a big show, including

Jaycees from Nevis, musicians from St. Kitts, and contestants from Anguilla, was supposed to take place to celebrate the attainment of a status most Anguillians desperately sought to avoid. Understandably, no sooner was the de Havilland Twin Otter operated by the Leeward Islands Air Transport that carried Peter Johnstone back to whence he came from up in the air, than the de facto leaders of a revolution that had not yet started gathered to make a decision as to what would be the plan of action concerning the upcoming event. In the absence of any form of communication on the island, Alwyn Cooke, Rude Thompson, and everyone else knew that if the British were, finally, to show any sort of reaction, the Anguillians would not know about it until, at least, one or two days later. However, following the disappointment that had come after Anguillians had, effectively, kicked Bradshaw off their island, the sense of expectation was far less dramatic, far less pervasive, now that they had done the same with a perfect stranger sent for no reason from Mother England.

That Friday, the evening news carried no comment about the British local-government expert's inability to communicate with the people of Anguilla. Nothing in the BBC; nothing on ZIZ. Predictably. When the eight o'clock news shows again failed to mention the island the following day, no one was surprised. But Rude Thompson had already discovered the escape route represented by the *Speaker*, and he had spent the previous twenty-four hours reproducing the details of the events that took place the day before, trying his absolute best not to leave anything out—nothing at all—and still make it all fit on one page. It would be the only article Alwyn Cooke would ever let him publish without making a single amendment to it—other than a comma here, a semicolon there, not to allow Rude to feel he could dispense with his editorial advice at this early stage.

And yet, commas and semicolons weren't the only things about which Alwyn Cooke and Rude Thompson would disagree in the days to come: no sooner was Peter Johnstone off the island than the two sat together, discussing what to do if, indeed, the Statehood Queen Show went ahead as planned, the following Saturday, February 4, 1967. Rude Thompson's frustration grew as he became progressively more convinced that their present strategy was too passive—too impotent—to bear any palpable results. It didn't help matters that Alwyn's suggestion for the show on February 4 was to disable the airport and bar anyone outside Anguilla from entering the island.

Tell me somepin', Al: How dat goin' make any difference to us? How dat goin' change anyt'in' at all?

Alwyn didn't even have to ask to know that Rude was, again, thinking about violence; but the truth was that he himself wasn't sure whether, in fact, closing the airport would create any kind of impact.

We problem be nobody know the first t'ing 'bout Anguilla. Now you have a whole load a dem comin' over for somepin'—not to let dem come in would be stupid!

Alwyn was not convinced, but it seemed like this time nothing could persuade Rude against using brute force, not even *You fire one shot an' de British will be walkin' on our streets tomorrow.* Because to Rude that seemed like the perfect solution, to Rude *If de English come we win already. Dem people kyan't be so blind to come to Anguilla an' not see de problem we have wit' St. Kitts. Besides, who talkin' nonsense now? Who say not'in' 'bout guns? Dere be plenty ways to intimidate people dat ain' got not'in' to do wit' guns.*

To which Alwyn responded, *I ain' wanna know not'in' 'bout intimidation.*

And so, a few days before the biggest day yet in Anguilla's struggle against association with St. Kitts, the two leaders of a revolution that had not yet started went their separate ways, peacefully—not even acrimoniously—but individually. So it was that in the days leading up to the celebration of the Statehood Queen Show, two independent plans were organized uncoordinatedly to send a sharp message of dissent in the direction of anyone who cared to listen. So, too, it was that Rude Thompson never heard when Aaron Lowell came to Alwyn Cooke with news freshly arrived from London, where the British had learned in total bemusement about the hostile reception their advisor had received from a people who had been fully aware, they said, participatory and supportive of the political process for the past year or so. Alwyn looked as bemused as the British claimed to be, while Aaron Lowell read out loud the scolding and utterly misinformed piece of correspondence. *Participating? Supportive? How dey mean? Dem t'ings mean somet'in' else over dere?* Aaron Lowell was in no position to answer—not that Alwyn Cooke was expecting a response.

The travesty of the consultation process had reached its climax just before the turn of the New Year, when a meeting between British officials and representatives of the islands of St. Kitts, Nevis, and Anguilla had been called with late notice. By the time the summons reached Aaron Lowell, the meeting had already taken place. A few days later, however, he received a file with a detailed account of the minutes of the meeting, along with a request for formal agreement from Mr. Lowell to discuss these matters further at a later stage. Aaron Lowell's agreement was now being taken as proof of the participatory and, indeed, supportive attitude displayed by the Anguillian electorate toward the creation of an autonomous association with St. Kitts. Alwyn queried Aaron Lowell as to how they had gotten into this situation in the first place, and how he planned to get out of it, to which all Aaron Lowell could muster was, *I mus' get audience wit' a senior British official an' den I go make real clear wha' our position be.* For the first time, Alwyn Cooke understood the exasperation Rude Thompson felt toward his own peaceful methods.

But Alwyn Cooke would still not be convinced to use force against anybody—at least not yet. One point Rude had managed to drive home with Alwyn was the need to allow people—anybody—to come to Anguilla for whatever reason and see for themselves both the extent to which the island lived in neglect and the popular sentiment against the imposed union with St. Kitts. Alwyn had given up on his idea to block the airport and, while he still distanced himself from the aggression Rude was promoting, he trusted the man enough (just) to allow him to play his cards without intervening.

On the days leading up to Saturday, February 4, 1967, on the Monday and the Tuesday and the Wednesday of that very week, two parallel, uncoordinated schemes to foil the plans of the organizers of the celebrations—all *Bradshers* by conviction or association—were simultaneously developed on the back porch of Alwyn Cooke's home in Island Harbour and in the front yard of Rude Thompson's place in East End. One group scouted the most ragged areas of the island, looking for round stones the size of a cricket ball, or slightly smaller, but large enough to fit snugly in a man's palm for accuracy and power when it came to releasing it; the other sought cloths and sticks and paint to create banners that could be hung all around the school, the only venue that featured anything comparable to an auditorium, where the contest was meant to take place. Some looked at the old building—a building with which they had been familiar all their lives—with renewed interest, seeking new ways in and out that would provide escape routes, locating the generator that would offer a rare sight of electric lights for the evening; others surveyed the perimeter of the school, searching for the perfect place to stage their demonstration.

By Friday afternoon Rude Thompson had recruited about twenty young men who were ready to teach those Bradshers a lesson. Rude's crude plan was to place groups of four militants armed with pockets full of stones at opposite corners of the building, who would stage brief preliminary attacks upon the school, while two infiltrators smuggled into the auditorium created unrest from within. Once the initial supplies of stones were exhausted the whole gang was supposed to gather by Rude's green pickup truck, loaded with the rest of the stones, to continue the assault as a unified force. The operation would be coordinated through the disruption of electricity, which would come right at eight o'clock, the time when Dwight O'Farrell would sever the live high-voltage wires that emerged from the generator.

Dwight O'Farrell was the oldest son of an important cleric from East End—an Anglican canon whose close relation to the people had vastly increased the popularity of his creed in the past ten years. His name was John O'Farrell and he was as committed to the revolution as anybody in Anguilla. However, he was unaware of his son's involvement and would likely have smacked him in the head had he known Dwight's was the arm behind the machete that cut through the live high-voltage wires that emerged from the generator of the Comprehensive School on the night of the Statehood Queen Show.

But at twenty-one Dwight was old enough to decide what he should do, and he was definitely old enough to understand what was going on, and there was absolutely no way he would not take part in the single most important moment his country had ever lived. So Dwight O'Farrell defied the instructions of his father, the leading minister on the island, and actively engaged in the nitty-gritty of the revolution.

On Friday afternoon Rude Thompson himself went to the generator house, inspected the connections, and wedged a thick plank of wood between the cables and the wall, behind which he hid a machete. Then, the following day, as he dropped Dwight O'Farrell in town during one of his trips in and out of the East End, he instructed the young man to *le' go de machete*. Dwight O'Farrell didn't really understand what Rude meant, but he didn't have to ask either, because Rude just continued, *When you get to de generator house, you understan': before de blade hit dem cables, le' go de machete, boy*, and he slammed his door shut as he drove away.

Meanwhile, Alwyn Cooke had assembled an even larger group of some thirty or forty angry young men and women who would make certain they would let their Kittitian and Nevisian neighbors understand that things were neither joyful nor at all right in Anguilla. Rather than recycling old posters, Alwyn decided that a more striking, more hostile message had to be delivered. Therefore, he spent days devising powerful slogans, imprinting retailored pieces of cloth with texts that foretold the *Death of Anguilla*, that predicted *War* among the people, that claimed *Sooner Dead for Free than Alive for Shackles*.

Then, when the placards were ready and the banners too, when the people had been chosen who would attend the Statehood Queen Show not to be entertained but to make a political statement, when the best place for the demonstration had been agreed upon—before the very entrance of the school, right where everyone could see—Alwyn Cooke came up with the final touch, the coup de grâce that would really define this protest: he got hold of a handful of green-yellow-and-blue flags, the flag that was meant to represent the associated state of St. Kitts-Nevis-Anguilla from February 27, 1967 onward, and he soaked them in gasoline.

On Saturday, February 4, 1967, there was much activity on the eastern end of the island, long before anything was meant to happen at The Valley. Because the logistics involved in the transportation of twenty or thirty or forty people with hardly any vehicles was a matter that could not be accomplished inconspicuously. So, Rude Thompson and Alwyn Cooke crossed each other on the road several times that day, each looking at the other with more than just a bit of guile, and yet each playing along, waving as usual, blowing the horn as if one didn't know the other was plotting something sinister, something neither could prevent without jeopardizing his own individual plans.

The sun still hung up high, and the midday heat lingered in the yards, on the streets, inside the wooden homes of committed partisans and unaware bystanders alike, when Rude Thompson decided it was time to leave his green truck—white canvas covering its bed—parked in a hidden corner near The Valley, where it would remain until the signal had been given at eight o'clock sharp, until darkness had regained its supremacy on Anguilla and the real show could begin. Rude stepped outside his front yard and made the last preparations to take his final trip into The Valley for the day. He had already brought all the men into town where they would wait, with some friends, family, or simply at the bar, for the time to come when they would have to head toward the school.

As Rude made his way to the truck, he heard two young girls, maybe thirteen or fourteen years old, laughing and joking about how they would wear their hair that night, for the big occasion. *Wha' you two laughing for? Where you t'ink you goin'?* Rude Thompson's bark scared life out of the whole scene, left East End sunk in an uncanny and most unusual silence. *De mouse eat you two tongue, or wha'?* but the girls just looked at him with a blank stare, frozen halfway between surprise and horror. *You better stay outta town tonight, if you wanna stay outta trouble at all, you hear me?* And as he approached the girls, hands stretched out open, ready to clasp them, they ran toward their home. *Da's right, nuh—go home an' tell you mamma if I see any one of you two at de school tonight, she de one goin' get big trouble.* But the young mother of the young girls was already at the door of her house—mop in hand, sweat dripping down her loose colorful dress, sticking the cloth by her chest to her haughty breasts.

Watch your mout', Rudolf Thompson, man—ain' no one go tell me how to raise me choild, you know. Not even you rowdy piece of ass—I don' care wha' craziness you plottin' dis time.

Rude kept walking toward his truck as he roared, head tilted sideways, eyes partly turned away, *You right, Verlinda Blake, but I know you girls since dey be not'in' but a pea sittin' in you belly, an' like I know you a good mother I know you take good advice when it dere to take!* Rude was no longer speaking to Verlinda Blake, nor to anyone else. He had already picked up the pace of his stride and had shifted the focus of his mind completely, when he let the world know with a deafening howl, *Hell go burn in school tonight, you know!*

Alwyn Cooke never even tried to disguise his intention to stage a protest before the school on the day of the Statehood Queen Show, but he did fear the police would try to break up his concentration of people before the event, so he waited until sunset to come with his F-series pickup truck loaded to the rim with dissidents. He had already transported the placards, the banners, the posters, the flags soaked in gasoline, and the megaphone to Wallace Rey's shop in George Hill in the hours prior to this final mobilization. He knew Wallace to be a committed detractor of the association with St. Kitts and a trustworthy character who would not raise much suspicion. He had also taken a group of young men into The Valley some hours before, instructing them to keep a low profile until he arrived with the women from Island Harbour. In his mind, a truck full of women would hardly alert the policemen to his plot, even though the women who had requested—demanded—to take part in the protest were as fierce and less fearful than any of the men on the island.

Round about sunset Alwyn Cooke made his way from Island Harbour to The Valley. He dropped off the women near the entrance of the school, right next to the police security post, and continued along to pick up the subversive material at Wallace Rey's shop. On the short journey from the Comprehensive School to Wallblake Airport and up George Hill to Wallace's shop, he saw a good dozen of the guys who were supposed to drill the crowd attending the Queen Show that night with the simple message, *No to association with St. Kitts!* He gave them the signal to get the others and join the women at the agreed spot, where, he thought, they would be in full view of the authorities all night long and, consequently, safe from any involvement in whatever craziness Rude Thompson might be plotting.

By the time the sun set in Anguilla on Saturday, February 4, 1967, Whitford Howell and Gaynor Henderson were already causing trouble inside the auditorium of the Comprehensive School. Stripped of stones, bottles, and anything else that could be used as a projectile, the two bold men relied on their mouths to stir the crowd into action. No sooner was the jester from Nevis onstage than the two troublemakers were throwing all kinds of venomous hecklings to and fro. Whitford and Gaynor had been drinking much of the afternoon, and to them it seemed later than it really was, and they were convinced something had gone wrong with the generator plan, so they decided to take things in their own hands—which is to say that Gaynor Henderson and Whitford Howell did their utmost to disrupt the Nevisian performer, to move the crowd to anger, to break up the whole affair from the inside. In fact, had this been anywhere else in the world, under any other set of circumstances, Whitford and Gaynor would have been quickly escorted to the exit, long before the jester took the stage. But this was not anywhere else in the world, this was Anguilla, on the verge of being forced into an unwanted status with the enemy, so if Gaynor Henderson, deliberately incendiary in his comments about *dem people pulling de strings of dis show*, was, perhaps, overstepping a line, there were few, very few, members of the audience who could not, at least to a certain extent, relate to the issues he kept bringing up; and if Whitford Howell was perhaps a tad brutal in his depiction of the situation, it was only because he'd had one Guinness too many, but that did not mean the man had no truth in what he was telling. Hence, generally speaking, the Anguillians gathered at the auditorium of the Comprehensive School might not have been tremendously amused by the spectacle provided by Gaynor and Whitford, but at the same time there was no danger that any of them would force the issue and kick either of them out.

Until Gaynor Henderson grabbed a folding chair and answered one of the jester's jokes by throwing it with all his might right at the man's face.

Luckily for the jester, Gaynor was too far influenced by the drinks to aim properly or even measure his strength, so the chair flew right over the man's head, landing harmlessly at the back of the stage. Whitford Howell understood this was their last, their only, chance to create some sort of reaction, so he too grabbed a chair and threw it in the general direction of the jester. Alas, Whitford Howell did not have the strength to make the chair reach the stage, so it landed instead on the head of some member of the audience at the front. From the first row an angry Anguillian rose and with a wailing cry promised to *go bash he head in two*, as she split open the sea of people that separated her from the frail frame of Whitford Howell. Amused by the implausibility of it all, and not yet threatened by the flying tempers, the jester sought to win over a crowd that had been hostile—even if not *this* hostile—all along, but his *Yer ruinin' de show, nah; yer s'pose' to be all wex wit' me* fell on deaf ears, and he was halfway through telling the audience in the auditorium that *No matter wha' yer all crazy people do, show mus' go on,* when the flight of Dwight O'Farrell's arms took the machete to the live high-voltage wires that emerged from the generator, as if they were a coconut he had to split open for his survival. The sparks that flew from the severed cables as the machete slashed forward through the final six inches of space to the wooden plank, once Dwight O'Farrell had let go of it, were the last traces of light that could be seen on the night of February 4, 1967 in Anguilla. Inside the Comprehensive School the jester didn't quite finish his sentence, and if he did, nobody noticed, because nothing could be made out over the pure noise of arguments and threats on the one hand, and panicked screams on the other.

Outside, pellets were directed at all four corners of the school, with a particularly heavy assault being waged on the entrance, where the police had been carrying out the security checks. Alwyn Cooke had already heard some of the loud jeers, the noise coming from the auditorium, which had warned him that trouble was about to be sparked. However, as soon as he saw the lights go out all at once he let out a long, if restrained, *Shhhhhit.* Seconds later people were darting out of the school whichever way they could find. Alwyn seized his opportunity and in an instant of lucidity provided his people with the image that, many years later, would commemorate the birth of the revolution in a series of stamps: he moved instinctively to the back of his truck, reached for the soaked flags, and with a Zippo lighter set them ablaze. In the absolute darkness of the night, no one could see what it was that Alwyn Cooke was burning, but as havoc reigned in The Valley, the image of this freedom fighter hanging precariously from the edge of his truck holding a wild ball of fire in his right hand remained forever imprinted in the collective Anguillian unconscious as a symbol of the struggle against St. Kitts.

The gasoline burned violently, and in no time at all the cloth of the flags had been completely consumed and the flames were dangerously close to Alwyn's hands. He dropped the flags and, preempting further trouble, moved to assemble his group in an area from where he could lead them out of danger. But it was already too late; seeing fellow Anguillians throwing stones at the Kittitian police, and inspired by Alwyn's own heroic gesture, some of his most hotheaded recruits had run for cover, picking up bottles, cans, anything at all, to add to the arsenal and join the battlefield. Stray stones had landed near the demonstration too, prompting the more squeamish to dash away for safety. Alwyn would have given the order to head back toward the road, to start making way on foot while he took as many trips as were necessary to return everyone safe and sound, but suddenly his eyes welled up, his nose itched, and his breath felt like a fish bone tearing up the inside of his throat. When he looked up, all he could see was a thick cloud of yellow smoke blowing from the direction of the Comprehensive School, and people emerging from every corner like ants, coughing, gasping for air.

Meanwhile, Rude Thompson had moved to the truck loaded with stones where he awaited the arrival of his comrades. He knew from before the start of the evening there would be serious confrontations with the police—he had prepared for this both with his plan and with the mind-set he had installed in his recruits. But even Rude Thompson could not have guessed—he couldn't have even hoped for—the mayhem that ensued around the Comprehensive School on Saturday, February 4, 1967. Because, while Dwight O'Farrell dallied over the loose piece of wood and the live high-voltage wires he was supposed to sever with his machete, and Gaynor Henderson and Whitford Howell put to use the brazenness that a mouthful of rum and a head full of fumes had given them to cause havoc among the crowd inside the auditorium, and Alwyn Cooke and his lot verbally and psychologically abused the police, the stage was being set for the greatest success yet to take place in the history of a revolution that was about to start.

As soon as the fracas caused by the impudence of an inebriated Gaynor Henderson and Whitford Howell started inside the Comprehensive School, the police force outside had suspected foul play. Therefore, as soon as the first signs of trouble could be observed—loud screaming in the auditorium, members of the audience departing the school before the start of the show, neither injured nor ruffled but full of anger and indignation—Inspector Antwain Edmonton, chief of the police task force, had already evinced a plan to evacuate the building and break up the mob. The decision to fill the Comprehensive School with tear gas was reached at roughly the same time that the blade of Dwight O'Farrell's machete flew in the night and cut through the live high-voltage wires in the generator house. Then came the stones at all four corners of the school; then came the exodus, people like ants emerging from every possible escape route in the building; then came the yellow smoke, the coughing, the crying, the screaming, the itching, the sting in the throat, the gasping for air, the *Lord, wha' kinda curse You sen' we from de Heavens?* the chaos, the confusion, the shock, the terror, the desperation, the horror, and in the middle of it all Rude Thompson and some twenty young men entrenched behind a pickup truck, throwing stones blindly in the general direction of the police, hitting them with the same frequency as they struck random spectators, innocent bystanders, officials, cars, goats, chickens.

The whole affair lasted, altogether, some fifteen minutes. As soon as Inspector Edmonton realized the real threat came from outside the school, he ordered his men to launch the tear gas against any pocket of insurgents they could identify. Which, in the middle of the darkness brought on by the blade of Dwight O'Farrell's machete, was the closest you could get to a meaningless order. However, darkness or not, the police force had received so much abuse from Alwyn Cooke and his bunch of protesters that a canister was immediately launched in their direction. Alwyn Cooke, hanging precariously from the edge of his white Ford pickup truck, just barely visible through the light of the flaming flag burning on the ground, would have given the order to head back toward the road, but it was already too late for that, because now the thick cloud of yellow smoke coming from the Comprehensive School enveloped him, and the more hotheaded of his recruits had joined Rude Thompson to mount a new offensive against the established order, and the more squeamish had run away toward the relative safety of the East End.

If Alwyn Cooke had been able to see anything—had the tear gas not blinded him almost totally—he would have glimpsed the placards he and his colleagues had so conscientiously made for the occasion scattered all over the ground, illuminated by the one headlight left intact on the front of his truck (the other one having been shattered by friendly fire). Sunk in the haze of the tear gas, Alwyn drove away at no speed at all, blowing his horn incessantly to warn people of his clumsy passage. A minute later, he was stopped by Adolphus and Kareen Thomas, a young couple, members of his group of protesters, who were able to take care of him and the white Ford.

Once the water calmed the swelling in his eyes, Alwyn Cooke took control of the situation again, jumping back inside his truck and traveling up and down the only road that communicated the eastern end of the island with the "capital," The Valley, looking for fellow victims of the police force's heavy hand. After his first trip, where he found more refugees than he could carry and no police presence at all, he understood an unsigned truce had been granted by the authorities for the night. He continued his mission of search and rescue for two hours, until he was certain there were no more men and women trying to make their way back to the east. On his ninth and final trip down the road, he spotted Rude Thompson sitting under a tamarind tree. His face was swollen and his breathing heavy.

See wha' you crazy plan get us into?

Rude had been hit by a stone and was suffering somewhat under the effects of the tear gas, but he was absolutely elated about the events of the evening. *Al, dis only de start, you know.*

Alwyn Cooke didn't know, and, in fact, he didn't even want to know. But he still offered Rude a ride back home. *De police hidin' tonight, boy—but tomorrow dey goin' come lookin' for you. Is a good hidin' place I go find, if I was you.*

Little did Alwyn know that, in addition to Rude Thompson, Gaynor Henderson, and Whitford Howell, the police would come looking for him too. Because even though, in practical terms, Rude Thompson and Alwyn Cooke had ceased to work together, and their ideological tendencies had drifted apart, their fates would again be joined by the police force, who would throw every suspect of raucous behavior on the night of February 4, 1967 into the same lot. In the coming days they would visit East End and Island Harbour with arrest warrants for them all— but things would not go quite as they envisaged.

CHAPTER VII

THE RECONCILIATION

ALWYN COOKE WAS UP BEFORE THE SUN the following morning, and his wife Ylaria was up with him, sipping from a cup of bush tea, when they received the first call of the day. Alwyn was not certain what to expect, as, during the night, the fear had grown inside him that the police would disregard the precautions he had taken in his planning of the protest and would try to blame him for the violence that took place at the Comprehensive School and its surroundings.

Alwyn had not yet decided what he would do when the knocking on his door startled him and his wife out of their morning routine. He jumped from his seat, spilling his tea, and dashed toward the back door, which led into a backyard and farther still into the bush, where, he knew, he would be able to hide for days without being found.

As it turned out, Alwyn Cooke did not need to run because the knock on the door came not from the police, who wouldn't venture into the eastern end of the island before the break of day, but from Solomon Carter, whose countenance, severe and pained at the same time, was met by the similarly stern expression in Ylaria Cooke's face.

Good day. Solomon Carter did not wait for an invitation to come inside the house, nor did he expect his greeting to be reciprocated by Ylaria. *You husband home, or he gone hide in de bush already?* Alwyn

Cooke, midway between his backyard and the shrubs beyond, stopped in his tracks when he heard the familiar voice. As he returned to the house, Sol Carter nodded in his direction and scornfully, *You man enough to make dis mess, an' you ain' man enough to stan' by it?* The long, loud, pronounced sucking of his teeth left no room to doubt the extent of his disapproval of the prior evening's course of events.

Alwyn Cooke was aware that, though he had played no part in Rude Thompson's ill-conceived plan, he would have to be right at the center of the reconciliation process among all sides of Anguilla's dissenters. Relieved that it was not the police, he welcomed Solomon Carter warmly into his home. But Solomon Carter had not come to Alwyn Cooke's house at this early hour of the morning to be treated as a friend, to have his ego massaged. Solomon Carter had walked through the goat path that led from his home to Alwyn Cooke's a good hour before the break of dawn because he wanted to make it completely clear to the man before he went into hiding, or better still, to prison, that neither he nor those around him would condone the sort of behavior in which Alwyn and his people had engaged the night before.

Alwyn Cooke tried to explain he had had no connection to Rude Thompson's group of troublemakers, but Solomon Carter was in no mood to listen—he had come to speak, and above all, he had come to deliver one clear, if hostile message: *I see too many people dead real close in my life already, you know, an' I ain' goin' t'rough dat again jus' because you say so.*

Solomon Carter was not so much a pacifist as he was suspicious of violence. That is to say, he did not always advocate for peace, did not stand staunchly by peaceful methods as the best solution to any problem. Indeed, Solomon had lived too long, had grown too savvy, to believe that honest-to-God goodness would be sufficient to produce any kind of long-lasting or even democratic change in Anguilla. However, what he had seen the day before had been close to honest-to-God stupidity; what he had seen the day before had been a display of thoughtless, wanton lawlessness; what Solomon Carter had deplored the night before had been the sort of pointless, infectious violence that he had first experienced thirty years before, as a child, working in the cane fields on the southeastern plains of the Dominican Republic.

I ain' never had de chance to go to school yet, Alwyn, and Alwyn Cooke didn't dare voice the "me neither" that formed in his throat. *But de Lord bless me wit' enough years to turn dem hairs behind my ears white, you know. An' it don' always have to be so, I tell you. Listen to wha' I say, so you understan' why I han' you over to de police when I do,* and suddenly Ylaria Cooke, eavesdropping behind the curtain, felt an urge to grab hold of the visitor by the neck and throw him headfirst out of her home. But Ylaria contained her anger out of respect for her husband, and Solomon Carter continued telling Alwyn Cooke how he had been to the Dominican Republic to cut sugarcane from the time he was twelve years old.

My mother, God rest her soul, she make me 1923, so when I was twelve, times were hard, you know. Alwyn Cooke knew all too well, because Solomon Carter spoke about a time of hardship and poverty in Anguilla which had affected them both—a time when only those who left the island faced any chance whatsoever of earning a decent living for themselves and for those they left behind on the Rock.

Back in those days, Alwyn had been blessed by God, Lady Luck, or the devil, who knows, but he had found a place in the workforce of D.C. van Ruijtenbeek's estate, the Lover's Leap, in St. Martin. The rest, as they say, is part of his unlikely twist of fate. Meanwhile, Solomon had had no choice but to embark with his two cousins aboard a local schooner, *The Warspite*, on a five-day journey westward to join his father and uncle at the alien cane fields of the Dominican Republic, where they had earned all the money in the family for the past ten years.

T'ree years straight I go cut cane for eight dollars a ton, an' den de t'ird year somet'in' deadly happen. When we go Santo Domingo, people in de island already crazy. Everyone lookin' at everyone else like dey is de devil self, like dey should not be dere, like dey de enemy.

One day we hear of fightin' in a plantation close by; some oder day we hear hell break loose in town. Den one day come de Spanish people self. Dem come wit' sticks, dem come wit' stones, wit' machetes, anyt'in' dem could find on de way, an' dey call us dogs, woose dan dogs: dem call us pigs, an' woose dan pigs: rats—de same people we cuttin' cane wit' for years, de same people bleedin' dem hands every day wit' you for t'ree years, de same people drinkin' you rum at night, night after night, now come treat we like we rats, hittin', kickin', t'rowing stones at we heads.

This was in the early despotic days of Rafael Leónidas Trujillo, and things were no longer what they used to be. Ever since his ascent to power in 1930, measures had been taken against the assimilation of black immigrants, even if they were only temporary workers, in favor of European blood, who would contribute to the general plan of "improvement" of the nation's natural stock, which was one of Trujillo's most altruistic ambitions. Nevertheless, Solomon Carter's family had been employed steadily by the same plantation for a full decade, and the passing fancies of yet another autocratic ruler in the country was not about to govern the way in which the bigger—more potent—plantation owners ran their businesses. Consequently, the Carters, along with a number of proven West Indian workers, were asked year in, year out to spend January through July working the cane fields.

One choild, younger dan me, get hit in de head, fall stone cold. We start fightin' back, you know. We fight as we can, we get de machetes from dem, we cut dem wit' dem own weapons, we hit dem wit' dem own stones. When police come, four people dead on de groun'. We t'ought police come help we, but dey only aks questions an' leave dem Spanish alone. Den dey come aks we more questions—some senseless questions dat have not'in' to do wit' not'in', like how we go say parsley in Spanish: perejil. *Who kyan't say it go inside de truck. I don' speak Spanish. I go inside de truck wit' plenty fellows from Haiti.*

Alwyn listened carefully. Solomon's words were matched by an intense silence that emanated both from Alwyn's eyes and from Ylaria's presence, concealed behind the curtain. And yet, the atmosphere in the room had changed: there was no longer any of the aggression Ylaria had felt against Solomon Carter, nor any of the fear Alwyn had felt when he first heard the knock on the door. Instead, there was a heavy charge of energy, of undiluted passion, being invested in the same cause.

Dey 'bout to take we to de river, when one Spanish fellow look me in de eye, call the police, an' say I okay, I English. So dey take me out, while every person in de truck screamin' an' shoutin' an' tryin' to come out wit' me.

Dem take more dan twenty people from de plantation dat day. Dem take me friend Winston too. He seventeen—older dan me. We cut de cane side by side every day for t'ree years. Dem take he an' de rest to de river an' make dem drown, for no good reason. Or dey kill 'em before an' make it look like dey all drown. De same people we work wit' every day for t'ree years. Some more dan t'ree years. Dem say dey kill ten t'ousan' people in de river. Ten t'ousan' people. You kyan picture ten t'ousan' faces in you head? You know how much blood dat make? A whole new river.

Dawn was about to break; the roosters in Alwyn Cooke's yard and all around his home had begun their daily round of crowing, making it past yards and fences and up the hill toward Harbour Ridge to the east and in the opposite direction, along the shoreline toward Welches Hill; and Alwyn knew the time to hide was right now, in the twilight, while there was enough light to find his way through the tangled shrubbery and yet not enough to be seen by the police.

We come back before time dat year. We leave when we kyan catch de first good wind and we make it home in twelve hours. Normally, plenty schooners would make de way back at de same time, racin' eastward wit' de wind to see who make it home first. Normally, it have a big party in Anguilla when we men come home, de women dress like dey goin' to church, and de children dress de same way, waitin' by de beach wit' music an' food an' all kind of jollification for de men to reach. Dis year dere ain' no race, an' dere ain' hardly no talk at all on de way back. Dis year de beach empty wit' not'in, as de men come back before time, we hands empty like never before, wit' no money, but happy to be alive. I remember de mornin' sun come out, shine on de white sand of Sandy Groun', an' I t'ink I never seen somet'in' so beautiful yet in my long life.

I know dat day in de truck someone up dere pardon my life, an' I know it for a reason. I ain' know for wha' reason yet, but dat mornin' when I lay foot on Anguilla soil I promise to God, I promise to myself, I ain' never—never— goin' let somet'in' awful like dat happen in Anguilla. Not even somet'in' simi- lar. Not even ten persons dyin' jus' like dat. Not'in'. An if God let me live to stop you from performin' you stupidity, Alwyn Cooke, den so be it.

Before making his way out into the open field, Alwyn turned in the direction of Solomon Carter and, rather solemnly, *I give you my word, Sol, you ain' never gonna have to stop me doin' not'in' at all, because wha' you want an' wha' I want is one an' de same t'ing.* His words lingered in the room a lot longer than his presence, as he simply turned his back on his unexpected guest and on his concealed wife, and walked out of the door, through the backyard, and into the bush.

That was at the break of dawn of Saturday, February 5, 1967. The police task force sent two units and four officers, more than one-third of its full contingent, less than one hour later with express orders to arrest Alwyn Cooke. But Alwyn Cooke had already gone into hiding, and he entered the thick hinterland of Anguilla dressed in his usual pressed gray trousers and crisp white shirt, and by the time Sergeant Raymond Edwards became the recipient of all of Ylaria Cooke's spite, Alwyn Cooke was lost without a trace between the shrub and the thicket.

Sergeant Edwards, a heavyset man in his early forties, found in the orders he gave his subordinates the only route to escape Ylaria's scathing attitude. Thus, the four policemen entered the land of the goats and brushed the bush that led from the back roads of Island Harbour, a few hundred yards south of the bay, up White Hill, directly behind the town, westward, toward Welches Hill. Four hours later, now caught right in the middle of the high-noon heat, the three constables reemerged from the shrub, uniforms torn at the edges, boots muddy to the heels, dusty at the laces, sweat running down their faces, forming pockets of wetness underneath their armpits, along their spines, between their nipples. Sergeant Edwards, some thirty or forty yards behind the rest of the men, was the last to rejoin the road. His light-brown complexion was tainted with an intensely red hue that might equally have been caused by the physical exertion or by his bout of anger. Either way, his clever plan had provided him with no more findings than an old, rusty machete which had been cached behind a cactus in bloom.

By this time all the fishermen in town had returned to shore, and a lively crowd had gathered around the two police cars parked before Alwyn Cooke's house. A spontaneous collective guffaw ensued when a beaten and empty-handed Sergeant Edwards became discernible down the road. Children of all ages ran toward the four desolate policemen, bustling around them as they slowly made their tired way back to their cars, pulling at the torn pieces of cloth on their trousers and shirts, exposing their wounded flesh, their injured spirits. The women started

howling like cats, hissing like serpents, roaring like tigers, as a generalized sense of mocking gained momentum with a round of applause that
kept the beat set by the loud laughter. Finally, as the policemen reached
the haven of their official vehicles, Sergeant Edwards warned, as a final
(and futile) effort to recover an ounce of dignity: *Laugh all di laugh yer
coin take nuh, man, cause by di time I havin' my final say yer be cryin' like
babies, aksin' for forgiveness.*

The long cheer that ensued followed the two-car convoy on its
way out of Island Harbour, past Welches Hill, and back down the road
toward Deep Waters, into Little Dix Village, past North Side, and up
until the mahogany tree at the junction in The Valley. It followed the
men out of the cars, past the arid yard, into the plain, concrete, single-
story police station. It was still there as Sergeant Edwards recounted to
his superior, Inspector Edmonton, every detail of the most unsuccessful
search for a suspect to be recorded in the annals of Anguillian polic-
ing. Inspector Edmonton, feet firmly planted on the table before him,
hat slightly tilted, listened in disgust, as a drop of sweat traveled slowly
down his left cheek, irritating his nerves as severely as that goddamned
cheer burned the insides of Sergeant Edwards. Inspector Edmonton
fixed his large black eyes on Sergeant Edwards for a brief instant, and
the irritation, the cheer, and everything else paused for a moment—
until a brazen fly landed on the inspector's prominent nose. Then, one
dry, deep roar liberated all the tension of the moment and chased the
fly away with the full contempt of a choleric *Idiot!*

Meanwhile, at Island Harbour the party spirit had not really taken
hold of the village because, despite the moral victory provided by the
police that morning, Sergeant Edwards's threat had to be taken seriously,
*for dem wit' power will want to abuse it, an' even more so after dem make de
ass.* Indeed, while Alwyn Cooke wandered through the bushes in search

of the perfect cave in which to lay low until nightfall, some five hundred people braced themselves for the torrid backlash they expected to suffer from the hand of the law. So it was that Rude Thompson, still feeling triumphant from the havoc he had caused the night before, was shaken out of his revelry by a buzzing suspicion that reached way past White Hill, behind Island Harbour, that traveled through the open fields of low brushwood and cuji, that hovered over the pond at East End and told him that, having failed to capture the man they had searched for, Alwyn Cooke, whom they thought was the main man behind the rioting, the police would come back for anyone on whom they could lay their hands.

Gaynor Henderson was warned by the same open secret, traveling from door to door, from voice to voice, along the dust roads of East End, through the goat paths of Island Harbour, but while Rude Thompson jumped out of his hammock and over the heads of his two dogs—two scruffy little street animals with lean limbs, long snouts, and sad expressions in their eyes—heading into his kitchen, where he picked up an old piece of cloth to prepare a bindle with the provisions necessary to spend the night out in the bushes—some kerosene, a lamp, matches, a change of clothes, a quart of water, a roll of toilet paper, some johnnycakes, and a Guinness—then tied it to the barrel of his Smith & Wesson rifle and, gun and bindle on his left shoulder and machete in his right hand, stepped out into the wild, Gaynor simply stood by his own doorway with a stubborn, angry pose, shouting out to the four winds, the seven seas, and beyond, *Gaynor Henderson ain' goin' nowhere tonight! No sir! Anyone wan' speak t' Gaynor Henderson, he know right well where he be. Anyone wan' take Gaynor Henderson somewhere will have to deal wit' me here, nuh.*

Several hours later, as the convoy of three police vehicles—two cars and a van to transport the detainees—made its way back out of the eastern portion of the island, well before six in the afternoon to beat the sunset, Gaynor Henderson was one of the only three suspects whom the police intended to take back to the station for interrogation. That was before, of course, the armed convoy, already on its way back to The Valley, was intercepted by a group of twelve or thirteen Anguillian matrons, equipped with pans and stones, blocking the road. The face-off was something out of a comic book.

Sergeant Edwards, again in command of the operation, looked in wonder at the group of colorful bandits ahead, wearing headscarves and long dresses. Time stood still, tumbleweed tumbled to the hesitant tune of a distant harmonica, even the goats fell silent, and for an instant the whole world shrunk down to the short corridor of hot air rising visibly between Sergeant Edwards's fearful eyes and the outlaws, when suddenly, out of the crowd, Bathsheba Henderson stepped forward and, *Where you takin' me man, nuh? Leave me husband alone!*

It was the loud, reverberating thump of her stone against the metal door of the car that shook the rest of the women out of their stupor. They did not all venture as far as Bathsheba, whose gigantic black arms and ferocious expression fed her courage beyond reason, but they did start to tap the bottoms of their pans with the stones in their hands, making a raucous clatter that gained in tempo progressively, as they encroached upon the policemen. *Leave de men alone!* cried a shrieking voice from one of the women, clad in a blue dress that hung to her voluptuous hips, to her protruding stomach, to her powerful thighs. *Ain' no one goin' take me husband from me* issued forth from another throat, and for a moment everyone was slightly puzzled, because the young girl in shorts and a T-shirt, with rolls in her head covered by a ragged scarf, was neither married nor engaged. "Girl, watch who you mout' call husband—you better start makin' sense or go home, nuh!" was a thought that (simultaneously) crossed more than one of the women's minds, but the time was not right to show any rifts in the group, and questions of semantics and fidelity would have to be addressed—if not solved—later, when the well-being of the men had been safeguarded.

So, while a catalog of candidates was mentally reviewed in order to make sense of the war cry let out by the young girl with the rolls in her head and the rugged scarf, Melinda Isaacson, a tall, lanky woman with matte dark skin as hard as a shark's and see-through eyes, announced with a deep, otherworldly voice, *You ain' gettin' outta here wit' de men tonight, you know.* Whether this was a threat or a divination is anyone's guess, but as soon as she finished her sentence a blue pot tumbled through the skies, making three full circles before colliding against the windshield of the police car, shattering the screen right in the space between Sergeant Edward's eyes.

The women gained courage as the police lost control. They reached the cars and brazenly banged their pans, their stones, their fists against the frames, the windows, the roofs of the vehicles. The policemen were too afraid, too intimidated, to react. Eventually, it occurred to someone to open the door of the van. The three suspects stepped out victoriously, greeted by hugs and kisses as if they had been locked away for decades. Only Bathsheba Henderson grabbed Gaynor by his hair and, with one quick movement, pulled him to the ground as she reprimanded him for allowing the police to lock him in the van. Away from the attention of the women, the three police units raced in the direction of The Valley, once again empty-handed.

Later that night, shielded by the cloak of darkness, Alwyn Cooke emerged from the shrub and paid Ylaria a visit. His trousers were all torn at the sides, his pressed white shirt muddied, wrinkled, his face ragged, mottled with whiskers, his hair gone wild. Ylaria greeted her husband lovingly as he approached the house from the backyard: *Alwyn Cooke, you look like truck run over you head.* Alwyn knew she meant it in the best of ways, and he simply acknowledged her gesture with a *Boy, I all mash up, man,* as he walked into the living room and crashed on his wicker sofa. Ylaria undressed her husband carefully, examining his body for wounds as she stripped him naked, then sent him straight to the shower while she cooked him a meal.

The shower was a balm for his broken spirit and the fish and johnny-cakes were exactly what he needed before a few hours' sleep. But there would be no time for that, because as soon as he finished devouring everything from the plate, a knock on the front door startled the two of them out of their skins. Apprehensively, Ylaria walked toward the door as Alwyn moved in the opposite direction, ready to dive straight back into the bush. But he did not have to run away again, since the stranger at the front door was a messenger sent by Rude Thompson to inform Ylaria Cooke that he wanted to speak to her husband in all haste, and that as soon as she saw him, she should tell him to meet Rude by the flamboyant tree between the school and the East End pond.

Ylaria Cooke quickly dismissed the messenger, saying she had not seen Alwyn since the night before and promptly shut the door behind the loose, thin curtain that hung from the threshold. But she didn't need to tell Alwyn Cooke where the meeting should take place, because he had heard everything the boy had said to Ylaria, and he had chosen a new pair of trousers—not his usual gray ones, but much thicker blue denim ones that would better cope with the bush—and a jacket to keep himself warm, and he was now tying the laces of his boots before heading toward East End.

You comin' back tonight? and Ylaria's worried countenance went unnoticed by Alwyn, face turned downward toward his shoes.

Dunno. But he might as well have said no, because both of them knew this emergency meeting was likely to be too long for him to be able to return home for any meaningful amount of time before having to head back into the wild again for cover, prior to the break of dawn.

Ylaria put the rest of the fish and some johnnycakes in a bag with water and ginger beer. *Jus' in case*. Alwyn kissed his wife on the lips and went out the front door, as if he were not hiding from anyone in the world, before turning around and, with a calm, self-assured voice, *No worry, nuh. We all goin' be okay*. Whether Alwyn meant the men at the flamboyant tree by the school in East End, he and his wife, or the island at large with that "all" was unclear, but reassurance was precisely what Ylaria Cooke's heart wanted that very moment, and as soon as she heard the words, they soothed her beyond reason.

Alwyn Cooke traveled in his green Ford Anglia eastbound on the single road of the island, climbing the sharp hill over Harbour Ridge, through the scrubby hinterland that lay behind Island Harbour, past the stony path that peeled off to the left, leading to the easternmost spot of Anguilla, Windward Point, next to Junks Hole Bay, with its dense forest of coconut trees, and Savannah Bay, the last beach on the Atlantic shoreline, before he reached the left-hand bend down Mount Fortune, which ended across the East End pond from the school.

As soon as he saw the flamboyant tree, Alwyn Cooke could make out the silhouette of Rude Thompson gesticulating wildly at Gaynor Henderson. The men were discussing the events that had taken place that same afternoon at Gaynor's home and then on the road. Gaynor's version of the incident somehow made him look a lot braver, a lot more self-sufficient, than he had seemed a few hours earlier, but Rude was not so much concerned with the image that Gaynor was trying to convey, nor with the heckling of the men around him, as he was with the precautions that should be made the following day to prevent the police from taking any more prisoners.

Is some sentinels we needin'.

Nobody quite understood what Rude Thompson meant, but there was no doubt he would presently elaborate on his idea, so nobody dared speak a word.

I tell you wha' we goin' do, and Rude Thompson explained that he wanted men placed atop Welches Hill, on both sides of the road, and on the smaller hill that drifted eastward from it (*How you call dat hill, nuh?* and an anonymous voice from the back gave it such a sharp and unforgettable name—*Liberation Hill!*—that, although nobody had ever called it this before, Rude Thompson gallantly acknowledged the inventiveness with a *Par'ner, Liberation Hill is de name from now an' forever!*), and he wanted the men to be in full view of each other, such that they could exchange signals from a distance (and here again a spontaneous outburst proposed the use of conch shells to communicate—*Two blows, an' we know police on de way*), and Rude's arms flailed in the dark as he spoke, when Alwyn Cooke interrupted with, *Is youself you should take care of, you know. Not everyone dis side of Anguilla agree wit' wha' you done.*

The arrival of Alwyn Cooke brought back a sense of reality to the dialogue.

Wha' you t'ink you kyan achieve by attackin' de police? Sooner or later dey come attack us bad-bad. If dey intention be to crush us tomorrow, dey could come an' do it, you know, to which a roar erupted from behind, from the men gathered around the flamboyant tree, who all bounced brave interjections against each other.

No sir.

Not me.

Dey ain' crushin' me.

No one go crush East End while I here.

But an impending sense of danger weaved its way around the silent consciousness of the men present, until Rude finally gave the order for everyone to look for stones for the watchmen to carry and throw at the police when they came through the narrow path between Welches Hill and . . . Liberation Hill.

You still insist wit' you nonsense? You ain' see violence goin' take we nowhere at all? But Rude Thompson had not seen that violence would not take the Anguillian cause anywhere at all. In fact, Rude Thompson thought the violence that erupted on the night of February 4, 1967 was the first palpable step forward they had taken in months and months of struggle. What is more, Rude Thompson felt that in the wee hours of the night of February 5, leading to the morning of February 6, Anguilla was closer, much closer, perhaps not to escaping the tyrannical hold that St. Kitts, and Robert Bradshaw in particular, held over the affairs of the island, but certainly to what Alwyn Cooke and he had identified as the first step necessary for the island's cause to be taken seriously: to let the world, i.e., the British, know about the situation in Anguilla. Hence, there was a sense of accomplishment in Rude Thompson as he sat surrounded by his followers—his supporters—by the flamboyant tree, halfway between the school and the pond at East End; a sense of accomplishment that was in accordance with his practicality, with his need to get things done, regardless of the consequences, and this, undoubtedly, blended with the not-so-muted admiration of the men around him to make him feel the complacent pleasure of a garlanded hero.

So you t'ink you Anguilla Fidel? You t'ink you kyan hide in de bush an' fight for mont's out here?

Rude Thompson did not hear the *Fool!* that Alwyn Cooke muttered to himself, or if he heard it he chose to ignore it, because Rude had called for Alwyn to work out a common strategy between the villages of East End and Island Harbour, to work together from this point forward, because Alwyn and Rude had had their differences, and *I know you never approve wha' we done las' night*, and not only had Alwyn not approved, he had openly, outspokenly disapproved, he had tried everything in his power to dissuade Rude from carrying out such foolishness, until Rude had gone beyond the point of dissuasion, *But now de t'ing done, an' dere ain' no goin' back, an' like it or not de police t'ink you one of us, an' if we don' go work together we go make de police stronger*, so Rude wanted Alwyn to come back into the fold and help him and his men devise the best strategy of resistance against St. Kitts.

All dis time, Rude, an' you still understan' not'in' at all, at all, and Alwyn Cooke paced back and forth before the static figure of Rude Thompson. *You sit here for everyone to know, surrounded by you hoodlums, like Anguilla jus' a game. But plenty people don' like wha' dey see las' night, you know. Plenty God-fearing people, who wan' de same you say you wan'. Plenty right-t'inkin' people who would call de police right now to put us all to jail, if de police had de guts to show dem faces in de east dis late at night.*

Rude Thompson took the comment more as a threat than as a warning, and his men behind him encroached upon Alwyn Cooke, asking him, *Who you mean?* pressuring him into naming the traitor.

Easy, fellas. Easy.

Alwyn Cooke might not have been an educated man, in the formal sense, but he had been through enough in his life to develop a strong judgment, and he had been rewarded by Lady Luck with a hefty fortune, and he had nerves of steel, which made it unlikely that anyone that night was going to get anything out of him in the first place, so

Alwyn just looked straight into the night and *I ain' namin' no names, fellas, so cut it out. But I ain' sayin' no lies, neither. Is be careful, all I sayin', be careful wit' de games you play—you may burn youself hard*, and he turned his back on the crowd, walked away from the flamboyant tree, jumped into his green Ford Anglia, and made his way back to Island Harbour, into the bush, to find a suitable place to follow the example set by Jesus and meditate for a while, to spend the following day, to digest the whole situation.

Rude Thompson had not envisioned this end to his meeting with Alwyn Cooke, much like he had not foreseen the events that would unfold over the next few days: on the morning of Monday, February 6, the police force landed its first victory against the group of insurgents from the eastern portion of the island as Inspector Edmonton himself took control of the situation and, notwithstanding the shell-blowing, the stone-throwing, the fist-waving, the manic screaming, the threats, the anger, the complete indignation of the people, a new convoy entered East End and departed the area with not three but six detainees, filling, for the first time ever, the island's jailhouse.

But Inspector Edmonton was not really interested in hauling in three, six, ten, or twenty prisoners from his excursion into the eastern end of Anguilla. What Inspector Edmonton wanted more than anything else was to get hold of that loudmouth Alwyn Cooke, who had tormented him and his force incessantly on Saturday night, when the Statehood Queen Show had had to be brought to a premature end with the use of tear gas. And now that the man had gone into hiding, Inspector Edmonton was also keen on getting hold of Rude Thompson, because running away was akin to confessing that he was one of the leaders, one of the two leaders, of the group of troublemakers who insisted on making Anguilla the home of unruliness. So Inspector Edmonton

detained six nobodies, Gaynor Henderson and Whitford Howell among
them, more because he could than because he wanted to; and he questioned them, more to have them go through the trouble than to gather
any information, because Inspector Edmonton already knew everything
he needed to know, and he certainly did not need these six good-for-
nothings in his jail, but he charged them anyway before releasing them.
He charged them with disturbing the public order, he charged them
with rioting, he charged them with assault, he charged them with oc-
casioning bodily harm, and he even charged them with impropriety for
swearing in public. However, regardless of all these charges, Inspector
Edmonton headed to Island Harbour the following day with the intention of brushing every single inch of the bush, of turning every goddamned stone, until he found Rude Thompson and, more importantly,
Alwyn Cooke. That was the decision that spiraled into havoc.

The men of East End, the men of Island Harbour, infuriated with
the police force, took to the positions indicated by Rude Thompson the
previous Sunday night and, without further instructions or consultation, they awaited the return of the convoy. Except this time they were
armed not with conch shells and stones but with rifles and handguns,
such that when the three police cars that brought Inspector Edmonton
and his lot into an area where they were unequivocally not welcome
took the sharp bend to the left that took them from the village of Deep
Waters up Welches Hill, two shots from opposite directions warned
them that they were ambushed, and when they sought to push through
the hill onto the other side, a flurry of gunshots made Inspector Edmonton change his mind, give the order to turn round, and head back
toward the station with a whole lot of trouble on his hands.

From that point onward, Island Harbour was an open city. Or an
open village—call it what you will, but the police were most definitely

not going to be allowed into town, and whenever a new convoy arrived from The Valley on the days that followed, the reception became increasingly hostile, not least because the police force countered fire with fire, despite the fact that the strategic positioning of the rebels in the hills made it almost impossible for the officers to know at what or whom they were shooting. Speeding past the ambush point was precluded by the poor condition of the dust road, so on Tuesday and Wednesday the task force organized excursions into Island Harbour, with the convoy advancing slowly, in formation, covering all corners. But on both occasions it all came down to a standoff before Welches Hill, and the unexpected firepower of the rebels prompted a retreat. Meanwhile, the six prisoners had bought their provisional liberty through hefty bails, and they had rejoined their friends and families on the eastern end of the island, when, on Thursday evening, it occurred to Gaynor Henderson that the best way to get revenge on Inspector Edmonton and the rest of those pigs was to organize a nighttime raid of the police station.

Again there was no consultation, again there was no order from above, not a word from Rude Thompson, nothing from Alwyn Cooke— the operation was as spontaneous as Gaynor's initial idea. So, on the night of Thursday, February 9, a squad of "sharpshooters" from East End ventured out into The Valley, positioned themselves upon the low hills that rolled toward the southeast of Wallblake Airport and that offered a privileged vantage point, just a few hundred yards away from the government building, the jailhouse, and the police station, from where they could attack the latter. The whole affair lasted about two minutes, and only eight or ten shots were fired, but in spite of the fact that each of them missed the concrete building far wide or high, it seemed like a whole battery of infantrymen had just besieged the neural center of the island, because gunshots were not usually heard in the still Anguillian

188

nights, and gunshots had never before been directed consciously, pre-meditatedly, at the authorities in Anguilla. The message delivered was loud and clear, and all that was left for the rebels to do was head back east and wait for the response from the police.

East End was a bag of nerves on Friday morning. Several men took their shotguns and, of their own accord, made their way by foot down the two-mile dust road to Welches Hill and Liberation Hill, where, it had now become part of the local lore, just two armed men were enough to keep any force, no matter how strong, from passing through. And if two men were enough, well, imagine what could be accomplished with four, with eight, with fifteen, with twenty bold and eager armed men. Except nothing at all had to be achieved during that Friday, because Inspector Edmonton, in light of the previous night's attack, decided against entering the eastern side of the island, instead asking for rein-forcements from St. Kitts for his thirteen-man strong (or weak, rather) force, and putting in place a daytime roadblock that would essentially isolate the rebels and safeguard peace in the rest of the island. Inspector Edmonton figured the supplies of the dissidents were relatively limited, particularly when it came to ammunition. He also assumed that, hav-ing attacked the station at night, nothing would stop the rebels from striking again on subsequent nights. *Le' dey be anxious. Le' dey build dey confidence. Le' dey shoot all night, if dey wan'. Den we come inside, when dey have no bullets no more.*

All through the day the tension grew among the hotheads gathered at Welches Hill, at Liberation Hill, awaiting the convoy of policemen that never arrived. From time to time a shot could be heard, fired at the sky for no other purpose than to vent some anger, to let out some of the frustration, to rile the troops, or simply to dare the authorities to do something about it. But the authorities were in no rush to make any movement at all, and when the sun set, Inspector Edmonton told his men, all twelve of them, to go home and avoid being seen until the following day. So, when the same men who the night before had taken aim and shot at the police station with impunity reached Rey Hill to inflict much heavier damage on the task force, there was no one to shoot at inside the police station. Except the rebels did not know this. Far more collected than the night before, encouraged by the passive attitude of the police, the four men became more daring, more precise in their shooting on Friday evening: more than thirty shots were heard howling through the thick of the night in Anguilla, and twice as many, it seemed, shattered windows, splintered doors, echoed in the empty rooms of the building. The inspector's foresight had saved the lives of his men, and spared the revolution its first episode of bloodshed.

Rude Thompson's "Letter from Anguilla," written in pencil out in the bush, made no mention of the explosive meetings between the police and the people of the eastern portion of the island that week. Rude Thompson's "Letter from Anguilla" was mute about the raid Gaynor Henderson had organized against the police station on Thursday evening, simply because Rude Thompson knew nothing about it. Rude Thompson's "Letter from Anguilla" was oblivious to the standoff between official forces and dissidents on Welches Hill on both Tuesday and Wednesday, because he did not want to give the government in St. Kitts more information than it already had about the situation on the island. Therefore, Rude Thompson's "Letter from Anguilla" did not mention his or Alwyn Cooke's condition as fugitives, and it remained ambiguous as to whether either of them were still in Anguilla. Instead, his article focused that week on the events of Saturday, February 4, 1967; on the ill-advised use of tear gas by the task force; on the excessive use of force by the police, both that night and on the following days, when they imprisoned without reason just about anyone they could lay their hands on.

Rude Thompson's "Letter from Anguilla" made no mention, either, of the hideous attacks that took place on the night of Saturday, February 11, exactly one week after the Statehood Queen Show, primarily because the article had already been published when a group of young men hijacked Rude's green Sweptside pickup truck and made rounds of the island targeting individuals who were either outspoken supporters of the union with St. Kitts—Bradshers—or were merely suspected of siding with Bradshaw, the tyrant. That night, the rascals drove past the house of Constable LaRue and fired a blaze of shots at his property, before driving down the road toward Crocus Hill, the highest point of the island, on the north coast, where one of Anguilla's very few guesthouses was operated by a conservative politician, a member of Bradshaw's Labour Party and former representative of the island. The Sea View guesthouse was vandalized before the rebels decided to waste the rest of their ammo against the concrete building, the zinc roof, the shutterless windows. It was a miracle that no one, not the couple who owned it, not their seven-year-old son, not the one and only guest at the time, was hurt inside Sea View. On their way back to the east, the hoodlums stopped by the largest grocery store on the island and looted it, taking food, kerosene, anything at all, really, in the name of liberty. The ideal had been ravished in full.

If they had had any time, any choice, the people of Anguilla—of all of Anguilla, east and west, north and south, The Valley and beyond—would have voiced their indignation, their consternation, at the events of the night of Saturday, February 11. Because, while they were overwhelmingly against their association with St. Kitts, Anguillians—God-fearing, right-thinking, righteous—were not prepared for their island to sink to the depths of banditry to achieve recognition. Alas, fate was equally outraged as Anguillians would have been, and before anyone had the chance to know for certain what had happened the night before, dawn broke from the east of Island Harbour and greeted the village with the threatening presence of a two thousand–ton F32 frigate from the British navy, the HMS *Salisbury*, whose two hundred–plus crew included scores of trained marines who, soon enough, came ashore onto the beach at Island Harbour. One gunshot would have been enough to trigger a bloodbath. But it was too early for that, and the irresponsible thugs who had gone wild the night before still slept lazily in their beds, and the people of Island Harbour, caught halfway between awe and disbelief, greeted the soldiers with a genuine, spontaneous sing-along of a well-known ditty: "God Save the Queen."

While British marines, armed to their teeth, responded to Inspector Edmonton's cry for assistance and patrolled the goat paths of Island Harbour, of East End, where they found little other than harmless locals voicing their common national anthem, Alwyn Cooke checked the few hiding spots where, he knew, Rude Thompson would be laying low. The meeting of the two haphazard leaders of a revolution gone astray took place before, even, the marines had reached the government's headquarters in The Valley.

De whole t'ing gone out of hand, Rude, and Rude looked in wonder at Alwyn, as he asked him to hand himself to the police. *Dem boys gone out at night shootin' at random people, you know.* Rude didn't know. Alwyn didn't know, either. But everyone suspected, everyone had heard the buzz of gossip which distorted the facts, embellished here, elaborated there, but which always carried an element of truth. *I know dis ain' wha' you planned. I sure know dis ain' wha' we want for Anguilla. Is time we make it stop, an' start all over again.*

By the time the police task force regained control of the island, by the time Inspector Edmonton, supported by fifty British marines deployed along the eastern portion of the island, entered Island Harbour first, East End later, Ylaria Cooke had already received word from her husband. All in all, the police made fourteen arrests that morning, but the leaders of the insurrection, Rude Thompson and Alwyn Cooke, were nowhere to be found. Any other day, Ylaria Cooke would have greeted the knock on the door, which she knew came from Inspector Edmonton's hand, with a tirade so threatening he would have lacked the balls to ask for her husband. But this time, Alwyn Cooke had appointed her with the task of making the authorities understand that *You men kyan search an' search all day long if you wan', you know. But you ain' findin' me man unless he come to you.* Alwyn Cooke was not about to trust these newly arrived white men from Britain with his life, and he sure as hell was not going to allow Inspector Edmonton to come anywhere near him, unless he was certain he would be treated fairly. *Is only one man me husband trus': Solomon Carter. If Solomon Carter come wit' he, he come wit' Rude Thompson to de station to clear up dis whole mess.*

Before the end of the day, the HMS *Salisbury*, with its full contingent of royal marines, sailed from Island Harbour, bound for Antigua. Its call on Anguilla was not recorded in its logbook, and has been lost forever in the fissures of history. Meanwhile, Sol Carter, Alwyn Cooke, and Rude Thompson were put together in a room, where they awaited the interrogation of Inspector Edmonton. For over twenty hours, they waited. Twenty hours of arguing, of reasoning, of discord. Whether this was a strategy by the inspector to make them talk among themselves and thus extract information, or just a punishment for the pains they had caused him remains unknown. The fact is that those twenty hours provided the most productive dialogue the three men would ever enjoy.

Unbeknownst to Inspector Edmonton, he had paid the revolution a great service.

CHAPTER VIII

KICK 'EM OUT!

THE WEEKS AND MONTHS THAT FOLLOWED the ghost-visit paid by the HMS *Salisbury* to the tranquil shores of Anguilla took the island into uncharted territory. Inspector Edmonton and his police task force had regained nominal control of the island and, indeed, an agreement between Sol Carter, Alwyn Cooke, and Rude Thompson had put a momentary end to the spells of violence that characterized the days (and nights) that followed the abortive Statehood Queen Show. Nevertheless, there was a palpable tension in the air that impregnated everything in the daily routine of the islanders, from the slow glide of the elderly woman on the edge of town as she stepped outside in the early morning to tend to her goats, to the parsimonious stride of the youths trying to look cool on the way to school, to the methodical strike of the fellow down the road breaking the ground with a sledgehammer to set the foundations of an extension to his one-bedroom house—everything seemed to be done under the burdening shadow of a suspicion, in the troubling knowledge that *somet'in' jus' ain' right*. It was the end of February, and there was still a chill in the air, although the rainy season had come to an end; but in this lousy atmosphere everything seemed stale, and the days dragged with a surreal sense of being both long and short—short because nothing could get accomplished with this heavy load, this utter discomfort, on your back, and long because every minute that went by in this venomous environment carried the weight of an hour, of several hours, making every day an endless ordeal.

Alwyn Cooke was very much under the effect of this draining atmosphere when he sought advice from the only man he had come to trust in Anguilla in the midst of all this trouble: Solomon Carter. *I see everyone goin' crazy in Anguilla as de days go by an' in no time at all we all goin' dead under de rule of St. Kitts, you know. We mus' do somet'in' quick-quick.*

And double-quick it was that Solomon Carter came up with the idea that would keep the whole island busy for the days to come. *If Anguilla soon dead as you say, why we don' go make a big funeral?*

It was a stroke of genius. The idea spread around the island like a virus. Every sermon in every church in Anguilla, from O'Farrell's Anglican congregation in East End, to the Methodist church in South Hill, to the Seventh Day Adventist temple down by The Valley, to the Church of the God of Prophecy in West End, and among the few Catholics around Wallblake, all of them, without exception, touched upon the small matter of a general strike to paralyze the island and to express, graphically, the unequivocal rejection of the Anguillian people, their sense of bereavement at the thought of forming a single state with St. Kitts, through a public, all-embracing funeral procession.

Even Rude Thompson, ever the antagonist, had to give it to Alwyn the day they met to discuss, as always, the corrections Alwyn deemed necessary with Rude's use of colons and commas in his latest "Letter from Anguilla." Disgusted, Rude let out an impolite *I ain' know why you always wan' make changes like dat, like dis you piece or somepin'*, but soon enough he loosened the frown on his face and brightened up with an enthusiastic *Is good idea you have at last, Al.*

Alwyn thought of giving credit where credit was due by admitting,

"Is Sol idea, Rude—is Sol idea," but he suspected Rude would be less convinced about it if he knew from where the idea had come, and Alwyn feared Rude might even try to boycott the whole plan, or come up with some alternative one, a violent version of a funeral, a sort of bandit's farewell, or some other nonsense like that, and Rude hadn't even asked who had come up with the idea, he just assumed it was Alwyn's baby without Alwyn saying anything at all, so instead of turning Rude's attention in a dangerous direction, he just took the credit and, *You better not let you trigger-happy frien's ruin everyt'in' for us.*

And he didn't. Because Rude Thompson believed in this plan, in this new form of civil disobedience, in this challenge to the authorities, more than he had believed in anything he had done so far in the name of the revolution. Hence, on Monday, February 27, it was Rude Thompson who held the banner at the front of a procession in which thousands of Anguillians—Anguillian women, Anguillian children, Anguillians from West End, from South Hill, from Sandy Ground, from Blowing Point, old and young—came together at Burrowes Park, right at the heart of The Valley, and marched all around town. They walked past the small white building that was the government house, next to the simple wooden structure that read *Courthouse* on the outside, and up to the one-story police station, which was adjacent to the island's only prison, recently visited by the likes of Gaynor Henderson and Whitford Howell. And then they crossed over to the near side of Wallblake Airport and went right past the old Wallblake plantation house, through the dusty roads that lead to the factory, the largest store on the island with its long structure divided into several aisles, next to the remains of the old cotton gin, where once upon a time the (meager) island riches were obtained. And then they continued northward, through a narrow road that led to the Landsome House, home to the island's warden, who would be presiding over the raising of the new flag of the associated state of St. Kitts-Nevis-Anguilla—the very same green-yellow-and-blue flag which Alwyn Cooke had soaked in gasoline and set aflame while he hung precariously from the corner of his white Ford truck in the total darkness of the darkest night yet in Anguilla's history, Saturday February 4, 1967, just three weeks before, during the failure of epic proportion that had been the Statehood Queen Show.

A failure, too, was to be the symbolic act during which the Union Jack would be taken down and replaced by the tri-island-state flag, as a representation of the handing over of power from the old colonial master to the new indigenous autonomy. But the thousands—quite literally half the population of Anguilla—who gathered in their most formal outfits, fully adorned to attend the largest funeral they had ever seen, to put an end to their wishes—to bury their dreams—would not allow the staging of a political transition that was already taking place. So, Alwyn Cooke, not in his usual gray trousers but clad in equally well-pressed black ones, with his trademark white shirt—this time with long sleeves—and wearing a discrete, narrow black tie, was joined at the front by an old matron from South Hill, Cleothilda Hart, whose slow steps set the pace for the sea of people behind them, as the elaborate arrangement that hung from her black wide-brimmed hat bobbled at the rhythm of her burdened knees and orchestrated the motion of the widows and widowers who carried over their shoulders the black coffin in which lay—dead—Anguilla's future. Banners, old and new ones, crowded the street and voiced—in large black lettering—the same old concerns, the same old requests Anguillians had futilely expressed for months. But none was larger than Rude's banner at the front, which he carried almost like a staff, and which read in huge, dripping red letters: *ANGUILLA R.I.P.*

All of a sudden, in the middle of the procession, an unintelligible wail broke out from the back of the crowd, filling the hot afternoon air with a sense of both hope and despair, which spread quickly among the crowd, until the tune became familiar at the front too, and Alwyn Cooke and Cleothilda Hart, hand in hand, sang in unison for God to save the queen. Rude Thompson, puzzled at the choice of words and uncertain as to whether this was really the message he wanted delivered that very instant, hesitated for a moment, when, from behind, emerged the thin figure of Glenallen Rawlingson, only just fifteen years old but already tall, if lanky, and with that anthropoid gait of his, and, with both hands, he grabbed hold of the wooden pole wherefrom hung the banner announcing the death of Anguilla, and he relieved Rude from his duty, not giving him much of an option, before moving ahead, pole in hand, shouting from the top of his lungs, "God save the queen!"

So it was that all through the day on Monday, February 27, 1967, a peaceful, though visibly volatile crowd of Anguillians stood before the warden's house with the candid—almost childish—intention of pre- venting a (childish) representation of that which above all else they most wanted to avoid, simply because they were not entitled to do anything—not even give their opinion—about the real thing. And so it was, too, that three thousand Anguillians stood for hours on Monday, February 27, 1967 before the warden's house, to prevent him from rais- ing the flag of the new governing entity on the island, performing their defiance by chanting continuously a tune that prayed for the health, for the well-being, of the queen whose very government had been the main, the direct culprit of the neglect in which Anguilla had found itself for the previous three hundred years. Go figure.

The warden of Anguilla, intimidated by a crowd larger than anyone had ever seen on the island, thought better than lowering the Union

Jack from its flagpole and, instead, let things be for a while. In fact, for a long while, well into the night, when no official flag should fly loosely at all. But this was a special case, and the situation was, quite literally, extraordinary, and so, to commemorate the occasion expediently, the warden of Anguilla awoke in the middle of the night and peeked out of his window, and he made certain that the crowd had dispersed, and indeed every single one of the three thousand people who had congregated before his house earlier that day—or the day before, even, because it was four o'clock on Tuesday morning—had gone home, or they had gone to the Banana Rod, or they had gone somewhere else, but they were certainly not there, before his house, and if some of them were still around, they were not enough in numbers to intimidate him, to mitigate his initiative, to stall his sense of duty, so he called on the police officer who was his guard for the night, and Constable LaRue, our utility man, rubbed his eyes open and shook his head out of its slumber, and he stood firm, attentive, rolling the sleep he had cleared from his eyes into a small ball with the fingers of his left hand as the warden ordered him to go outside, to lower the flag of the United Kingdom, and to hoist the flag of the associated state of St. Kitts-Nevis-Anguilla, with its laughable three little palm trees in the middle, while he, the warden, officiated the act in his pajamas. (I kid you not. This one *is* recorded—go look it up, if you must, St. Thomas.)

Naturally, this did not go down well with Anguillians—so the warden made no friends among the people he was supposed to ward, and his days in Anguilla were numbered, and the dice had been cast, and the dice were tumbling. News spread around Anguilla with the speed of light, which is why in the total darkness of four o'clock in the morning on an island with little electric power, no one knew what had happened. However, as soon as the day broke on Tuesday, February 28, and the first rays of sunlight illuminated the horizon line far out in the east, the supple waving of the three silly little palm trees on a green-yellow-and-blue flag against the background of the warden's house left its imprint of anger and indignation on the Anguillian population, most of whom had gone to sleep triumphantly the night before, filled with a sense that, for once, their wishes had been voiced clearly enough for somebody to listen, for the British to understand. *But Lahrd, how so dey treat us so? How so de white man wait for Anguilla to be in she sleep to stab she in de back? I t'ought de man here to protect us! But he ain' protectin' nobody but heself. De man a Judas! De man a traitor!*

Before the sun had lifted over the clouds gathered in the distance, right where the sky meets the sea, still during twilight, between night and day, every person in Anguilla knew foul play had taken place in the wee hours of the night. Spontaneously, a continuation of the previous day's mourning was staged, and the banners were fished out from the yards, and the coffin was reassembled, and new garments were chosen by those who had so much, and the ones who didn't took every step to make their black dresses, their dark trousers, their white shirts or blouses look as if they had not been worn all day, such that well before seven in the morning the crowd gathered outside the Landsome House was so large, it seemed as if it had never dispersed at all.

Except something was missing from the previous day—there was none of the expectancy, none of the vibrant excitement there had been. Absent, too, was the soft tune of "God Save the Queen," replaced, instead, with a good degree of restlessness and a pervading sense that, coffin or no coffin, mock funeral, general strike, civil disobedience, and all the rest, it was already too late, as, indeed, it had been for the past two and a half months, since that fated meeting, belatedly called to-ward the end of December 1966, when Anguilla's destiny had been decided without so much as the presence, let alone the consent, of the island's representative, Aaron Lowell. Ever since that moment, Anguilla had been sentenced to rest in peace and desolation under the thumb of Robert Bradshaw and whatever shape or form his successor in the future might take, doomed to remain for the rest of its days an unrecognized colony of a "sister" island that could hardly be made out in the distance on the clearest of days, of a "neighboring" isle that was separated by five other islands, thus perpetuating an association rooted in the incongruous, incompetent, ignorant practicality of a colonial administration utterly disinterested in the state of affairs in Anguilla, now as then.

It might have been a lack of energy, or perhaps no one had the eloquence to express it in such words, or perhaps, even, no one was fully aware of the historical chain of events which, since 1825, had conspired to produce the situation in which Anguillians, clad in their darkest clothes, found themselves. So, perhaps the thought was not articulated in full, but the magnitude of the event, the scale of the treason, escaped nobody. Anguillians mourned their own death in stunned silence the rest of the day. But too much of their spirit—more than just energy—had been sapped by the latest blow for anybody to be ingenuous enough even to think about performing the same nonsense the following day. So it was that on Tuesday, March 1, peace returned to the streets of the island and a semblance of normality fell upon The Valley. Only just a semblance, though, because things were far from back to normal on that Tuesday morning and on any of the many mornings to come, because Anguillians felt betrayed, yes, but Anguillians also felt impotent and helpless and angry and played and at some point, everybody knew, something had to give.

Therefore, nobody was particularly surprised when, seven days later, the warden woke up to a sweltering heat inside the Landsome House, and to a distinct smell of charcoaled wood, and a dense cloud of black smoke that hardly allowed any oxygen to filter through his pituitary membranes and reach his lungs, such that the warden—choked, bright red eyes bulging out of their sockets, drenching his face in tears, throat tied in an impenetrable knot that presaged the very worst—abruptly stirred from his sleep and, invigorated with the resolve and the final thrust that spells alarm in an asphyxiating body, pulled himself out of bed, and, without bothering so much as to open his Demerara windows, threw himself, head and shoulders first, out of the top—second—floor of his lodgings, pulling off a perfect forward flip as he traveled down the fifteen feet that separated him from the ground. The pathetic whimpering that could still be heard close to an hour later, as the futile efforts by a fire brigade that consisted of simple civilians rushing to and from the Old Valley well with buckets that were roughly half-empty of water by the time they reached the Landsome House, was attributed to the left ankle the warden had sprained while saving his life, which he would be unable to treat in Anguilla, simply because there was no hospital.

No one was surprised when they saw the warden, clad in the same pajamas he had worn to raise the flag of St. Kitts-Nevis-Anguilla for the first time, just eight days earlier, desperately running—or leaping, rather—for his life, and no one was surprised, either, when they heard the epicene sobbing that followed, out of terror more than pain, some suggested. But what really no one was surprised at all about was the fact that some angry young or old Anguillian had decided to take matters in his own hands and pay the British back with a pyrotechnical display that set the oldest building in Anguilla aflame.

No one was surprised, and yet, at the same time, no one was particularly pleased or proud of the deed, either. As soon as the news of what was happening in the northern end of The Valley reached Island Harbour, Alwyn Cooke looked for his gray trousers and pressed white shirt to pay a visit, not to the injured warden, but to Rude Thompson, whom he suspected would be behind the act of arson. To Alwyn's surprise, however, it was he who broke the news to Rude about the warden's near-death experience, which was greeted with a cackle and an exuberant *Yeeeee-ha!*

Alwyn Cooke was not amused by Rude's approval of the methods and, indeed, questioned whether, truly, he knew nothing of the incident, yet Rude's matter-of-factness returned to him as soon as his integrity was questioned: *Is 'bout time someone teach dem English idiots a lesson, you know. I wish it was me come up wit' de idea. But is not me goin' say he ain' done somepin' he do, an' it ain' me goin' take credit for somepin' somebody else done.*

Alwyn was uneasy with Rude's position, but he knew confronting him was not going to help, so *Wha's done is done, Rude—bu' we cannot have people t'inkin' in Anguilla is no law an' dey kyan do whatever dem please. Is you started all dis violence nonsense,* and before he could finish his sentence Rude Thompson reassured him, *An' if someone from East End have somepin' to do wit' dis, I will know, you know.*

But days came and went, and Rude Thompson did not know a thing, because whoever caused the wooden structure of the Landsome House to go up in smoke was either too frightened of the consequences or not terribly proud of his actions, because he or (rather unlikely) she was not letting anybody know that he had done it, and in an eminently boastful society such as Anguilla's (then and now) that usually means something isn't quite right. Hence, after being left out in the dark for four days, Rude went to Gaynor Henderson's doorstep to ask him straight out, *Who de hell done dis foolishness?* This was the first time

Rude heard the prevailing rumor that the Landsome House fire had been caused not by arson but by the carelessness of that darned warden, whose habits had remained unchanged since he had first been sent in exile by the Crown's foreign office, still wearing the same satin pajamas to sleep, to which all of Anguilla had been privy following his more clumsy than great escape from the fire four nights earlier, and still, too, dining on his own at a fully set table with the steel cutlery carefully placed on red acrylic tablecloths, as if it were a set of Christofle knives and forks, and the full regalia of cheap china spread out on the dining table with the same elegance as if we were speaking of Spode plates, and a pair of copper candlesticks that sometimes had nothing finer than tea lights, though on the night in question, it was rumored, the warden had received a package straight from England with a box of long, thin candles, twelve of them, which had so excited him that he immediately lit two of them in the dining room and, straight after dinner, carried two more into his room.

De man fall asleep wit' a book in he hand an' next t'ing he know de curtains catch fire, de whole house covered in smoke, an' he havin' to jump out de window to save he life.

The warden had not helped his cause with the Anguillian people, and whether or not there was any degree of truth in this tale is completely inconsequential to our story, but no one ever stepped forward to claim any knowledge or involvement in the burning down of the Landsome House on March 8, 1967, and the only thing ever to come out of it was the warden himself, who hobbled onto a plane and flew to Antigua for treatment, never to return. Anguilla, meanwhile, lost yet another guise—another symbol—of authority, and was left to drift more or less boundlessly.

The situation, now beyond desperate, remained idle—stagnant—

for several months. Aaron Lowell, a figure as helpless as he was powerless, seemed even more hopeless than usual in his efforts to communicate with a British senior official, who, constitutionally, no longer had any jurisdiction, any power, nor any interest at all, for that matter, in any affair whatsoever involving Anguilla. Sol Carter, Rude Thompson, and Alwyn Cooke met often during this time to discuss the possibilities, to work out a plan of action, to give the impression, at least to themselves, that they were working toward a solution. Then, finally, Rude Thompson could take it no longer. He descended upon his people, he questioned every soul he found in the streets of Anguilla, he demanded everyone get together to speak, to protest, to act, and all of a sudden a meeting was officially called to take place at the park in The Valley on May 29, 1967.

For wha' dis meeting? Sol asked, full of suspicion.

We go figure it out right dere—de whole bunch of we. That was the best Rude could fashion for an answer, but it was enough to calm Sol's greatest fears, and the word was spread at the pace with which it was always spread in Anguilla: the speed of light; and soon enough everybody knew about the meeting, and everyone was getting excited, and everyone wanted to take part.

A massive crowd of people gathered in and around Burrowes Park, not really certain of why they were there or what they were going to do, other than to express their discontent, other than to protest against the present arrangement, other than to take comfort in the fact that each of them was not alone, in the fact that the vast majority of people on the island suffered in similar degree. Early on the afternoon of May 29, 1967, hundreds of Anguillians arrived at Burrowes Park to listen to their leaders' appeals, alternatives, solutions, ideas, and a dialogue began with each of the speakers, with Rude Thompson and Alwyn Cooke,

The Night of the Rambler

but also with less actively militant members of the community, who took the chance to jump under the limelight, to take center stage and voice their opinions. There was John O'Farrell, the Anglican canon from East End, whose pipe danced frantically between his lips as he entreated the people to look deep within their souls to find the courage to face the challenges posed to them by the Lord, for regardless of their will, their fate had already been written since eternity and for eternity in the Book of the Lord, and therefore they should not be stifled by fear of earthly punishments, for nothing, not fear, nor pain, nor hunger, nor the total neglect in which Anguilla had been left since ever and ever, would be able to prevent the divine edicts from being carried out and each of their destinies from being fulfilled. And as the generalized *Amen* was echoed in Catholics and Methodists and Anglicans and Evangelists among the crowd, the imposing figure of Gwendolyn Stewart, firstborn child of Connor Stewart from Island Harbour, emerged with her commandeering voice: *I does wan' to fulfill my destiny, Father, but how I kyan do dat an' not eat I ain' understandin' yet.* And suddenly it did not matter anymore who was on the wooden speaker's box and who was on the floor, because the discussion had grown alive, it had gained a soul of its own, and it made the rounds all through the cricket ground that was the original design of Burrowes Park.

But on this day, on May 29, 1967, Burrowes Park was anything but a sports ground, because the issues that were discussed within the stadium had nothing to do with wickets and runs but rather were fully concerned with the wishes and anxieties of the people of Anguilla, with their expectations and the way available to them to achieve them, with the future of the island and the well-being of its inhabitants. As a matter of fact, on that remarkable day, Burrowes Park was the closest thing the modern world might ever get to an ancient *agora*, where citizens would openly discuss the matters of their state and decide upon them through direct elections, and nobody in Anguilla might have known it at the time, and if they did, they might not have realized the magnitude of their achievement, but on May 29, 1967, as the afternoon dragged on and more and more people made their way to the park, and the discussions grew more heated and the opinions more agitated, more committed, more extreme, Anguilla put to practice a concept that for centuries had been studied and analyzed, that had been proposed, adopted, amended, discussed, theorized, developed, and redeveloped: the concept of Democracy.

Burrowes Park became the center of the most democratic process witnessed in any contemporary society, as the swelling crowd contemplated the events that had led directly to the state of desperation in which they had lived for the past four months, with each person exercising a right that was there in practice, if not in law, giving his or her views and affecting directly, without the need for representation, the course of the day and of history. This was the situation when Alwyn Cooke, suddenly aware of the potential of this forum, took to the platform and spoke through a megaphone: *Fellow Anguillians, is today we mus' show St. Kitts how bad we wan' break up wit' 'em. Is today we mus' determine how we go split wit' St. Kitts for good.*

And before any possibilities could be explored, before the consequences of their actions could be measured, before, even, the meaning of the words sunk into the consciousness of the people, a slogan spontaneously devised by Rude Thompson, heckling Alwyn's speech, grabbed hold of the collective imagination and spread like a wildfire from person to person, from one character dried out of any hope to the next, and the rumor grew into a chorus that demanded to *Kick 'em out! Kick 'em out! Kick 'em out!* and before anyone realized who *'em* might be, Rude

jumped right next to Alwyn and shouted into the megaphone, *We ain'*
wan' no orders from St. Kitts! We ain' wan' no not'in' from St. Kitts! and
as the women looked at each other, and the men, and as the big dark
eyes of one mirrored the enthusiasm of the other, the thought suddenly
made itself clearer in the minds of some of the audience, and their eyes
glowed with a dose of courage, and their fists got clenched in a sign of
defiance, and the chorus now turned into a roar that was intoxicating,
and the *Kick 'em out!* could now be heard as far away as the police station, and those who were not totally convinced by the resolution were
persuaded by the general hysteria, and the few dissenting voices were
drowned in the deafening unison of the chant, and those who were
overcome by doubt or fear at the thought of outright rejection of the
legal authority as stipulated by the new constitution were comforted by
the thought, *Wha' dey goin' do? Look how much people we be*—or was that
not a thought? Had Rude Thompson just uttered the words so many others were thinking that very moment? And, *For real, wha' dey goin' do? Dey*
t'irteen, we some t'ousands, and no sooner had Rude Thompson announced
that they should march toward the police station than the crowd was cut
through the middle to allow him and Alwyn Cooke to make their way to
the front, to lead the way toward the only bastion of Kittitian authority
left on the island, to *Kick 'em out! Kick 'em out! Kick 'em out!*

Inspector Edmonton was as baffled when he heard the news that
the mob that had congregated at Burrowes Park had determined that
enough is enough, that the police task force should leave the island,
never to come back, that the time had come for Anguillians to take
care of their matters by themselves, as, indeed, was Aaron Lowell, the
man whom Alwyn Cooke had chosen to deliver the nonnegotiable message. As the river of people flowed out of Burrowes Park in the general
direction of the police station, Alwyn Cooke called on Aaron Lowell

to take charge of things, because *You de man de people choose to represen'
dem. Now, you go ahead an' tell Inspector Edmonton wha' it is you people
who elect you wan' you to do.* And Aaron Lowell could not muster the
strength to come up with a response, and all he could do was hide his
small black eyes behind a fit of blinking that had his eyelashes fluttering
away, and Alwyn, *No worry, nuh, man—we have de Lord an' de people of
Anguilla on we side: wha' could hurt us now?*

And verily, Inspector Edmonton had precious little at hand to deal
with a crowd of this nature in Anguilla that day, and the only thing left
for him to do was buy some time and try to stall the situation in the
hope that the wildfire of popular courage would choke itself, or grow
weary with the passage of the hours, and if the authorities in St. Kitts
resolved to act with the urgency merited by the situation the following
morning, then maybe, just maybe, something could be salvaged out of all
this mess, so *How yer expect me to get me men out of here dis time of day?*

And, indeed, it was almost five in the afternoon by then, and there
were not enough planes to get all thirteen men out of the island simultaneously, and there would not be light for long enough to make two
journeys to St. Kitts, and the last thing the people of Anguilla wanted
was to send out just a portion of the contingent of policemen, for Bradshaw and his people to have all the details at hand to devise an attack
on Anguilla overnight, so *All right: you kyan stay tonight, but you leave
tomorrow mornin', before it turn to afternoon.*

Thus, an initiative that had begun as a collective exercise to figure
out what to do next turned into a rigorous night-long vigil outside the
police station. The vast crowd thinned out progressively as the night
settled over the Anguillian sky, yet Alwyn Cooke, Rude Thompson,
and, now, also Aaron Lowell presided over a group of people that was
never smaller than one hundred, camped along the main road in The

Valley. Contrary to what might have been expected, it was not a joy-
ous, festive, or even exciting night, but rather a bunch of tense, anxious
hours during which sleep was not even a possibility. Anguilla had taken
its leap of faith, but the fall would last all through that night and most
of the following day, and it was anyone's guess whether they would be
able to land on their feet, or land at all.

Hour after hour the crow of the roosters reminded the men, sitting
by a makeshift bonfire, around a game of dominoes or a bottle of rum,
that time had not stood totally still, that the next day was approaching,
until the first people from Sandy Ground, from South Hill, from Stoney
Ground, started to congregate outside the police station again, even before the break of dawn. They brought with them some fish, some bread,
maybe a banana cake or some fresh fruit—sugar apple, soursop, paw-
paw, pomme-surette, mango—to share with the men everyone knew
had stood guard all through the night.

Long before eight in the morning, Aaron Lowell went to speak again
with Inspector Edmonton. By then, Diomede Alderton had readied *The
Pipe*, his Piper Aztec, to take the first batch of policemen back to St.
Kitts. The inspector showed himself less collected, less self-assured than
the day before, and he had no other option but to order his men to
leave him and his fellow officers behind, and *I sen' di men out shortly*. It
was not even an hour later when the Piper Aztec, full to the rim with
members of the police task force, glided just above the heads of the
crowd gathered on the main road at The Valley before turning sharply
south to make the sixty-five-mile journey that put in motion an evacu-
ating operation which didn't even have a name.

All of a sudden, the unthinkable was happening in Anguilla, and as
the ball kept rolling there was nothing, anymore, that could stop it. Not
even the belated reaction of the central government in St. Kitts, whose

decision to act came roughly at the same time as Diomede loaded his "Pipe" full of unwanted guardians of the public order, such that somewhere along the skyline between the two islands he must have crossed paths with a de Havilland Twin Otter operated by the Leeward Islands Air Transport and packed to the last seat with twice as many guardians of the public order as were being removed in the Aztec.

Luckily for the sake of the unthinkable and for the fate of Anguillians in general, there was absolutely no way the plane carrying the members of the police task force had arrived in St. Kitts, delivered its package, and headed back home in such a short period of time. Therefore, the most alert among a crowd that included many haggard and hungover members understood immediately, as soon as they heard the drumming of the Pratt & Whitney piston engines in the distance, that unwelcome visitors were on their way. Wallace Rey then provided the inspiration that would save the day when he jumped in his red pickup truck and drove it to the middle of the dust strip. From behind a cloud of smoke emerged the aging frame of Wallace, the old fox, wildly beckoning the rest of the cars parked near Wallblake Airport to join him in blockading the runway and preventing anyone from accessing the rebel island. A few minutes later, the Twin Otter approached the airport full of intent, seemingly unaware of the spontaneous barrier, or perhaps assuming that the drivers were still inside their cars and would be pushed into moving out of the way by the sight of this modern-day kamikaze. Except, nobody was anywhere near the cars, and no one had any intention whatsoever of breaking the blockade, such that the de Havilland Twin Otter arriving from St. Kitts with highly armed and badly psyched-out reinforcements for Inspector Edmonton was forced to fly in circles over the airport and its adjacent areas, searching in vain for a suitable landing spot.

The roar of the Pratt & Whitney piston engines got lost in the distance as abruptly as it emerged. Oil drums were sought to liberate some of the cars; for the rest of the day, and for many months to come, these drums would protect the island by making it inaccessible. Inspector Edmonton was left to face the fact that he would be forced out of the island that was meant to be his jurisdiction, and the group of improvised rebels made the arrangements to dispatch the rest of the task force. Three of them would board the weekly freighter that, like every Tuesday for the past twenty-odd years, would head to St. Kitts with the post. The other five would have to wait until the return of the Piper Aztec that would take them on its second run for their final banishment. Among those five was Inspector Edmonton, who was carrying a bag of guns and ammunition when he was intercepted by Gaynor Henderson and Rude Thompson, who told him to *Drop de bag an' go on*. Then came the inspector's reticence to obey, Gaynor Henderson's need to restore his injured pride, and the .32 pistol he shoved right inside the man's mouth, until it polished his uvula. *You better drop de bag unless dis is da last t'ing you ever wan' taste.*

Escalation had, indeed, reached its peak. A few moments later Diomede Alderton would be on his way again, his dark gray flier sunglasses and wooden pipe clearly visible in the cockpit as he tipped the wings of his Aztec from side to side, flying low over The Valley in a saluting gesture to the men and women who had dared to rid the island of its oppressors. Just like that, an insignificant speck of coral in the northeastern corner of the Caribbean had revolted, and Anguilla found itself, very much by accident, "independent."

PART III

PART III

CHAPTER I

ATTACK!

HARRY GONZÁLEZ WAS STILL FIDDLING with the wires connecting the five sticks of dynamite to the detonator when a distant drumming of shots forced an angry *Shi-it!* out of him. Titus Brown, one-armed, lay low on the ground, having diligently mounted the Browning M1919 machine gun on its tripod, pointing its long barrel in the direction of the Defence Force camp ahead.

The ride from Half Way Tree, anxious and reckless, had taken the men through the vast cane fields to the left, and the black emptiness of the sea to the right, as they moved past Old Road Town, the first British settlement on the island, now bereft of glory and simply dotted with a row of run-down wooden houses crowned with ripped or rusted galvanized roofs. They had cut through the poor quarters of Challengers, along the edge of Palmetto Bay, until they reached the western outskirts of Basseterre and joined the main road, Cayon Street, which led them into Springfield Cemetery, where the endless rows of limestone tombs and crosses glowed despite the moonless sky.

This was as far as the Kittitian at the wheel of the car that had taken Rude Thompson, Glenallen Rawlingson, and two bags of guns, dynamite, and detonators would venture.

How you mean?

And the young Kittitian, *I waitin' all night out in di boat for yer—I tired of dis business now. I done too much a'ready an' bring yer dis far*, and with a gesture that hovered halfway between fear and violence he turned around on the front seat of the car, reached with his left hand, and, opening wide the back door of his Rover 60, *Is up di hill to yer left, di defence camp. Now, out! All of yer.* Rude Thompson thought about letting the automatic .25 handgun he carried in his pocket do the talking, but by then Glenallen Rawlingson was already out on the street, carrying the bag he had not set down from the moment Alwyn had instructed him to pick it up and stand by the port side of *The Rambler*, ready to throw it overboard. Glenallen was joined by Harry González, who, upset and confused, wondered *What the hell is going on?*

Rude Thompson let out a long sucking of his teeth before pulling himself out of the Rover. He barely had a chance to snatch the bag out of the trunk before the man gunned it, steering wheel pulled all the way to the left, tires screeching as the car made a U-turn, both suicide doors at the back still open, and returned to the depths of the Kittitian countryside.

Corporal Gómez and Titus Brown emerged almost simultaneously from the vehicle behind and Rude began to explain the situation when Harry González cut him short: *How 'bout we get out of the main fucking road? Jesus—don't get what all the fuss is about: we could blow up the whole damn island and we'd still be doing them a favor.* By then, all that was left of the dark-blue Land Rover that had taken the three Americans into Basseterre was a faint echo of its two-liter diesel engine racing down Cayon Street, but the five men hardly noticed, as their hunched shadows disappeared into the night en route to the headquarters of the Defence Force at Camp Springfield.

Meanwhile, Alwyn Cooke and his party in Ronnie's Austin truck continued along Cayon Street until they met the imposing stone structure of the Anglican church, where Ronnie turned to the left, to reach the police station from the quieter north side, heading out of town before turning right at Taylors Road and then right again, rolling slowly past the wooden structure of Warner Park, the island's cricket grounds, until they got to Lozac Road. Ronnie decided to park his truck in a dark patch beside the road, and to make the short distance from there to the station by foot.

At this point Alwyn split the group in two. *Sol, Dwight, Desmond: go by Cayon Street to de front of the buildin' an' take de position dere.* Whitford Howell, Ronnie and his child, and Alwyn Cooke stayed on Burt Street, looking to break into the station through one of its side doors.

Empowered by the weight of the M1 rifle strapped to his shoulder, Ronnie found the courage that had seemingly abandoned him at Half Way Tree, and he straightened his back and puffed his chest out, adopting a rebellious swagger. *We goin' get 'em good!*

Alwyn, terrified, hunched his back, lifted his shoulders, and stooped instinctively at the roar of Ronnie's voice. A finger to his thick lips and a fiery glance that sparkled into the night was enough to make the Kittitian understand he should not speak another word.

The police station in Basseterre was a relatively small redbrick building, practically attached to the island's prison. It was two stories tall and it made the corner that joined Burt Street with Cayon Street, where a small watchtower rose into the night. Ever since the expulsion of Inspector Edmonton and the rest of his crew from Anguilla ten days earlier, a guard had been deployed in that post to look out into nothingness, in case it was replaced by something suspicious. Every night a different corporal was placed in the tower, following the orders of Inspector Edmonton, who chose to ignore the ignominy of his submission to the Anguillian mob with the constant reminder of a very clear, very present danger: *If dey be crazy 'nuff to kick we outta de island, dey crazy 'nuff to come here.*

Whether it was a faint echo of Ronnie's reckless boasting, the fear that could be sensed—smelled, almost—in Alwyn Cooke's reaction, or simply an unusually diligent dose of care prompted by Inspector Edmonton's constant warnings over the past week and a half, the case remained that Constable LaRue, performing his rounds along the narrow corridor on the rooftop, on his way to the sentinel post, paused and took a deep breath. He took a long, careful look into the darkness of the night, trying to make out something—anything at all—that could tell him if things were happening out there that didn't qualify as nothing.

Alwyn was frozen still by the glare in the eyes he thought—he was certain—were looking straight into his. His knees bent slowly, progressively, and to make sure he would stay on his feet, he grabbed hold of the two men at his sides—Ronnie to his left, Whitty to his right—with a motion that they took to mean they should very slowly lower themselves to the ground, as Alwyn was doing.

Meanwhile, Sol Carter and the O'Farrells wondered what was happening, not so much with Alwyn and the rest of the gang as with Rude Thompson and the unit deployed to the Defence Force at Camp Springfield, who were supposed to trigger the whole operation with one big blast. But the dynamite in Harry González's rough hands was wet, and *Maybe we can save some of these sticks*, and *Maybe we can use some of that*, and everyone sat around watching in silence and disbelief as Corporal Gómez opened the damp bag and went through its contents, handing Harry what he thought could be used, while he, Harry, mixed the powder from different sticks, made a new bundle, taped the cylinders together, fiddled with the wires that connected the dynamite to the detonator.

The watch on the wrist of Sol Carter, the only Anguillian wearing one that evening, read twelve minutes past three when the first shots were heard from Burt Street. Alwyn had come back from his stupor and taken the reins of the situation, whispering to Whitty and Ronnie, *Time to get in de station, nuh. Ronnie, you take de tear gas. Whitty, take a real gun, man, in case t'ings get nasty*, and the M16 changed hands while Alwyn insisted that the element of surprise was their most important weapon. *T'row two canisters of da' stuff, upstairs firs', den downstairs, an' when I see smoke coming out de buildin', I cut out de power. Whitty, cover Ronnie. I cover you*, and the men were on their way.

As soon as Ronnie and Whitty moved in the direction of the station, Alwyn summoned the child by his side. *You can shoot?* The boy's nod of the head could have been taken for anything at all, but there was no time to waste on details, so Alwyn just pulled a .32 pistol from behind his neatly pressed gray trousers and *Hammer, trigger, bang—jus' like de movies, okay? When I tell you, shoot six holes into dat switchboard right by de building, okay?* Again there wasn't much in the way of response from the terrified kid, whose eyes danced bewildered in the night as he listened to the rest of the instructions: *Take t'ree steps behind, point at de t'ing like dis, empty de gun, and den run, run, run, an' you no stop runnin' till you reach home by you ma, you hear me? You hear me?*

But the boy had no chance to answer this time, because smoke already seeped from the lower floors of the police station, because Ronnie, precocious through his excessive eagerness, had thrown the tear gas canister upstairs without activating it, such that all it did was alert the guards with its loud thump that something was wrong; but for the job downstairs, Ronnie prepared himself better and he walked into the telecommunications room alongside Whitty, whose *Nobody move!* was indeed like in the movies, except he didn't know what else to say, because this wasn't a holdup, and he wasn't sure what it was instead, and "Dis a rebellious attack" just didn't have the same cling, the same swagger to it, and it wasn't really even necessary to say anything else, because the four men inside the telecommunications room had simply turned toward the outlaws, noticed Whitty's M16, and thrown their arms up in the air, but while Whitty wondered how to follow his *Nobody move!* Ronnie wasted a canister of tear gas, throwing it (activated) into a room that had already been taken without a fight.

And Alwyn, under the threshold of the side door to the police station, instinctively ordered Ronnie's child to *Go!* He could see Whitty, who, alerted by the heavy sound of boots running down the stairs, turned toward Constable LaRue arriving from above, took his aim, and, without saying a word, *click.* Except Anguilla's was a bloodless revolution from start to finish, despite the visit of the HMS *Salisbury* and the subsequent invasion by the British troops, which would follow roughly two years after one of the most naive failures in the history of military aggressions; through the frustrating demonstrations, the meetings at Burrowes Park, the visits paid to the island by Bradshaw the tyrant, by Johnstone the nobody; despite the havoc that marred the Statehood Queen Show, and the open challenges directed at the police task force; despite Rude Thompson and Gaynor Henderson, the nighttime raids, the looting of the supermarkets, the burning of the Landsome House; despite, even, the unthinkable taking place and the unlikeliest of crews embarking on one of the most ridiculous episodes anyone will ever find in the annals of revolutions, Anguilla's was still, and would remain throughout, a struggle that was waged at the expense of not one single human life.

Which is not to say, as it has often been claimed, that Anguilla's was a *peaceful* revolution, nor one that succeeded without firing a single shot. Plenty of bullets sailed through Anguilla's tropical latitudes, and the atmosphere on the island was anything but peaceful in the days and months both immediately before and after the clumsy—laughable, almost—execution of a sinister plan to carry out a coup d'état in St. Kitts in the early hours of June 10, 1967.

And yet, no lives had been claimed by the Anguillian cause to that point, and Divine Providence, human incompetence, or Whitty's cracked nerves made certain it would stay that way because, though the Anguillian had calmly taken aim and could see the pathetic expression on Constable LaRue's face through the gun sight as he pulled the trigger, he had not released the safety of the M16 after Alwyn Cooke had handed it over to him, such that Constable LaRue's pathetic expression got suspended in a timeless dimension for the briefest of moments as he distinctly heard the dry click of the hammer landing on the safety. Whitty pulled the trigger again, to no avail. He shook the M16 frantically, as if a good lick might make it work, and then the tear gas began to affect his eyes. Constable LaRue finally unbuttoned the holster of his gun, as more men approached from above in numbers. That was when the first shots could be heard in the Kittitian night. They came from Ronnie's child, barely fifteen, who had been pointing at the switchboard for a minute or two, trying to find enough courage to pull his index finger—curled around the trigger—toward his palm. He emptied the .32 revolver as Alwyn had instructed him, although his quivering pulse only allowed him to hit the target once, before dropping the gun on the spot and setting off on his long run.

The one accurate shot from Ronnie's child on the switchboard momentarily sunk the police station into the darkness of the night, before the lightbulbs were hesitantly reignited by the damaged circuit. The smoke-filled telecommunications room came in and out of the dark as the lights flickered dimly and filled the air with the haunting rattle of a circuit about to explode. Like the slowed-down reel of a movie, Whitford Howell saw the pallor in Constable LaRue's countenance be replaced by an ounce of composure, as he unbuttoned the holster hanging on his right hip and pointed his gun. The next frame was black, but the thunderous roar of a shot and an instant flash that shook the scene out of the night and right back into it told Whitty that time had not expired along with the generator. Whitty patted himself with disbelief, trying to find where he had been hit, though the shot had been fired not at him, but rather at Constable LaRue, by Alwyn Cooke, still standing near the threshold.

Except Alwyn Cooke was a hopeless shot, and the bullet flew right past Constable LaRue, hitting the metal stairs that led to the second floor before bouncing with a high-pitched whine against the far wall of the building.

The drumming of shots fired at the generator had put Ronnie on full alert, and now the loud blast of Alwyn's gun, together with the blindness that grabbed hold of his eyes, the burning feeling that grasped his throat, and the rotten smell inside the station—a smell of powder, a smell like de buildin' up in flames, a smell like de devil self 'bout to show up to fork every one of 'em straight into hell—simply made him forget everything about the mission, his duty, his comrades, or even his son, and, making use of the darkness into which they had finally been plunged, darted out the door, feeling his way up Burt Street, stumbling from side to side as he searched for his Austin truck.

Whitty, meanwhile, in the darkness of the station, came to realize he was not fatally wounded. He was, however, blinded by the tear gas, and though he had drawn the pistol he kept behind his back, he was as good as useless. Alwyn's cover had served to take the attention away from him, and two policemen arriving from the second floor fired in the general direction of the doorway. Alwyn had anticipated this reaction and had taken shelter behind the wall. Whitty, desperate, fired two blind shots that landed in the radio system. The darkness and the tear gas had dispensed with the last trace of orientation in him and he now spun around in circles, right arm outstretched, gun firmly pointed at nothing, left arm curled upward, as if he were a cowboy in a rodeo trying to hold firm to a raging bull beneath him.

The four men inside the telecommunications room were suffering from the same delirious agony as Ronnie and Whitty, and their cries got confused in the general hysteria. Then came Whitty's turn to let out a choking sound that turned into a loud grunt which woke Alwyn Cooke from his static shock. Alwyn reloaded his carbine, double-checked the cylinder in his .32 pistol to make certain he had six bullets to spare, and, in one movement, rolled out of his hiding place, arms opened at roughly forty-five degrees from his head in either direction, fired two shots from the pistol in his left hand and four in quick succession from the carbine. *Whitty, I comin' for you, nuh!* He glided around as he crossed his arms, guns pointing in opposite directions, let out another shot from the pistol, three more from the M1, which now jammed, so he threw it in anger as far as he could and with the same impulse grabbed hold of Whitty by the collar of his shirt and pulled him out of the room, emptying the rest of his pistol in three different directions as he backed up into the road.

Not a single bullet fired by Alwyn Cooke came anywhere near the policemen in the station. Indeed, most of them had flown into the roof of the building. But everything had happened so quickly, it had all been

so implausibly violent, that nobody inside the station had had the presence of mind to fire back. Constable LaRue, for one, had been busying
himself with a canister of tear gas, against which he stumbled as he
sought shelter from Alwyn's storm of bullets. As soon as he could lift
his head, Constable LaRue grabbed the burning can and threw it hard
toward the doorway, such that, as Whitty crossed the threshold, a wake
of gas whipped through the space between his downcast head and Alwyn's crazed expression. The Anguillians were out of the station, the
tear gas now clouding Burt Street with a distinct yellow hue. The gut
reaction of the policemen inside was not to follow the gangsters, but to
slam shut the side door and lock themselves in the relative safety of a
tear gas–infested room.

Meanwhile, the men from Cayon Street were caught off guard by
the round of six shots that had announced to the night the beginning
of a nameless operation. Although the watch on Sol Carter's wrist read
three twelve a.m. and the whole affair ran with a delay of a good two
hours, Sol's first reaction was, *Wha'?! Dem go in ahead of time.* He meant,
of course, that the men from Burt Street had not awaited the blast from
the Defence Force camp. More likely than not, Sol Carter was aware
of the disastrous implications this would have for the successful siege
of the military camp and, ultimately, for the whole operation, but right
now there was no time to think about that, because right now there was
no time to think at all, just to act conclusively and boldly, and so, Sol
Carter instructed the O'Farrell cousins, *You, come wit' me—you, cover
we,* and he and Desmond made their way to the front door of the police
station, while Dwight looked out for any danger.

Quite understandably, however, the police station in Basseterre was
closed at quarter past three in the morning, and while this was by no
means a fortified complex of the kind of, say, Brimstone Hill, neither

Sol Carter nor Desmond O'Farrell had any specific ideas as to how to gain access to the brick building. Desmond's reaction was to empty the magazine of the .25 handgun he carried in his back pocket, which totally obliterated the lock but did little else to solve their problem, because the front door of the station was bolted, and no matter what the Hollywood-fed imagination of the two freedom fighters dictated, the door would simply not give to the pathetic attempts by Desmond to kick it down.

Suddenly, all the parsimony of the two front men was drained by a shot from Dwight O'Farrell, sheltered a few yards back, behind a car. But this time the policemen did return fire, sending Sol and Desmond running in opposite directions. From that point onward, the men from Cayon Street would assault the police station from three different angles at varying intervals, making the men inside the station believe that there were many more rebels outside than there really were. The battle turned intense for some time, until the policemen figured they could not be hurt from the outside. Then, no further shots were heard from the station, except for when the Anguillians made any attempt to reach the front door. For the rest of the night Sol Carter and Desmond and Dwight O'Farrell would fire volley after volley of unanswered shots, but the contest was at a deadlock, and the Anguillians found themselves on the losing end of the draw.

Shi-it! was all that Harry González could muster as his head swiveled in the direction of Basseterre, where the distant drumming of shots fired ahead of time left the men inside the Defence Force camp wondering what the hell was going on. Harry's hands continued fiddling away as he taped the wires that went from the recycled sticks of dynamite to the detonator. The six shots coming from the hand of Ronnie's child had sunk into the empty darkness and the loud roar of Alwyn Cooke's

M1 had already reverberated in the distance, before Harry was ready to hand the dynamite to Glenallen Rawlingson to place in a small hole by the side of the building.

By far the youngest of the men who had landed on St. Kitts, Glenallen Rawlingson could not find the courage to refuse to play his part in the operation, to sprint the final hundred yards or so to the Defence Force camp, to dig a hole right next to the building, to place the dynamite inside it, in contact with the pink concrete structure, and to race back unseen to the position where his comrades awaited him. In fact, Glenallen Rawlingson would have been perfectly happy to perform his duty, had the site chosen not lay directly opposite the largest graveyard he had even seen in his life. *Is more dead people living in dere dan ever was in Anguilla, man,* and the limestone tombs seemed to gain an eerie glow in the moonless night. "No good t'ing kyan come from vexin' de deadman so" was the thought that most troubled the boy's mind, as Harry González explained to him what he should do once he reached the wall surrounding Camp Springfield. But Glenallen did not find it in him to express his utter terror to Rude Thompson, or to the three American mercenaries standing next to him, because once he had weighed his options for a moment he realized that there was no way out of this one, and that he was forced now to either face the wrath of the living, armed to their teeth and ready to murder; or to vex the dead, whom he could not see but he sure as hell could sense.

Thus, Glenallen Rawlingson, far removed from his skin with fear by now, made it to the Defence Force camp unobserved and reasonably quick; once there, however, he stumbled, and he thought he heard the twigs on the ground at the cemetery stir, and he felt a hidden presence pushing him against the ground, and a shadow raced past the corner of his left eye, though he could see no creature to correspond to it, and he was certain he felt the weight of boots pounding against the floor, running in his direction from the monumental Springfield Cemetery just a few hundred yards to his left, and he thought he noticed eyes watching him—through the sights of shotguns, perhaps—and he had no shovel, no pick, no axe, no tools to dig the hole, and the soil was dry and hard, and his hands could barely get any depth at all, and "I be damned if I comin' back here t'night," so he just placed the sticks of dynamite on the ground, and he surrounded them with a handful of stones that lay scattered near him, and he balanced the bundle between them, and then he got on his way back with his peculiar gait, carefully unrolling the wire as he retraced his steps, until he gave Harry González its bare ends.

Good job, kiddo! and Harry González did not notice the drops of sweat flowing from the temples of Glenallen Rawlingson's head, his crazed eyes, his dried-up mouth, and the overall agony that gripped his spirit, as the American rolled the peeled cables around the two poles of the detonator, before *Boom!*

A small puff of dust and smoke tainted the night with a blotch of gray as it rose from the ground along the concrete structure of the building, but soon enough it was evident that the wall of the camp had suffered no damage at all and that the siege of the garrison would prove a lot harder than initially imagined. There was no time to bicker, and it would forever remain unclear whether the blame really lay on the young Anguillian, or whether the dynamite had been too damp in the first place, the new sticks not sealed properly, or whether the recycled material had been contaminated with dust and sand and a touch of spite from the ghosts residing in Springfield Cemetery.

Whatever the case, Glenallen Rawlingson escaped a vicious scolding from Harry González, whose *Fucking moron!* simply served as prelude to his final instructions. It was well past three thirty in the morning by then, and the only hope for the Anguillian cause was to take advantage of the confusion inside the Defence Force camp to take the whole place by storm. In the distance more blasts resounded, providing the men inside the camp with vague details of a battle that was not meant to take place.

Harry González led his group from the front, firing left and right at the sentinels deployed around the military complex. He assumed the attention of the commander inside the garrison would be turned toward the area where the dynamite exploded, toward an assessment of the damage it had inflicted. That was all the time they had to skirt around the building and try their luck by the front entrance. Which was no time at all, because the main entrance was heavily guarded on the quietest of days, which is why the Anguillians had planned to break into the building through one of its side walls; and even if the rebels made it past the main entrance, once inside, they would be outnumbered by at least twenty to one. Harry's plan, however, was not to break into the Defence Force camp but, rather, to trap the army men inside. This would give the rebels by the police station enough time to move according to the plan and, ultimately, to gain control of the central government.

To this effect, the five men fired incessantly upon the military base for some twenty minutes. But much like what had happened to Sol Carter and the O'Farrell cousins on Cayon Street, the reply this crew got was, actually, no reply at all. Following a short exchange with the four guards by the main entrance, the army inside Camp Springfield opted to stay sheltered behind the thick concrete walls and wait it out until the light of day brought some clarity to the proceedings. Harry González was happy to play the waiting game: thinking the men by the

police station would be able to carry out their part of the plan, he kept
the thick of St. Kitts's military force in check for well over an hour. It
would not be until half past four in the morning that he would take his
men down from the hill at Springfield and onto Cayon Street, either
to join the triumphant rebels or to make a desperate dash toward Half
Way Tree. Little did he know that, by then, *The Rambler* would no longer be there to take them home.

CHAPTER II

RETREAT!

THE FIRST ONES TO CALL OFF THE OPERATION and cut the rest of their men loose were Alwyn Cooke and the blinded Whitford Howell. Deafened by his own exertions as the modern-day Wyatt Earp, Alwyn never heard the thumping blast of the dynamite explode one or two miles away from the police station. Whitty had dropped his M16 in the telecommunications room, and Alwyn had dismissed his M1 carbine as soon as it jammed during the rescue mission of his friend and comrade. Consequently, both were left with only .32 pistols and a handful of bullets. The noise from Cayon Street, just around the corner, intimidated Alwyn, who was as good as alone with Whitty suffering the consequences of his extreme fear of death and Ronnie's decision to activate a canister of tear gas to evacuate a room that had already been taken without a fight. Standing underneath a lamppost on Burt Street, Alwyn fired three shots before he managed to hit the bulb that shone on him, and he briefly considered his options.

Get up, nuh, man—we gotta go!

Whitty had no strength left to ask where, he just followed, a blur filling his eyes, a burning sensation tormenting his respiratory tract, his right arm on Alwyn's shoulders, feet dragging underneath him, trying hard as he could not to fall while his comrade carried him, almost, back up Burt Street and along Lozac Road, half-hoping they would find Ronnie's truck where they had left it.

But Ronnie was long gone, of course, and so was his truck, so Alwyn kept walking in and out of the shadows of the night with Whitty hanging from his shoulders until they reached the end of Lozac Road, and then they turned north at Park Range and intended to head out of town by whatever means possible, even if it meant walking it, and *Gimme dat*, and Alwyn tossed the two pistols as hard as he could into a bush on the side of the road, even though he could still hear the rounds fired at the police station by the men on Cayon Street, and now he heard, too, in the distance, the echo of shots fired at the Defence Force camp, and *Lord, forgive us!* though even he did not know whether he asked the Lord to forgive the men aboard *The Rambler* for coming to St. Kitts to raise this unstoppable hell, or whether he meant only himself and Whitford Howell, by now almost a part of his own back and shoulders, for deserting their comrades.

But no sooner had Alwyn uttered his little prayer than he saw a car parked by the petrol station about half a mile ahead, and *Jus' preten' you real drunk, okay?* and Whitty's nod got lost in the darkness of the night, because Alwyn wasn't even looking in his direction. Not that it mattered at all, because Whitty did not have to pretend to anyone that he was drunk, simply because there was no one to be seen for miles in the quiet of the Kittitian night, and when they reached the petrol station they found the car unlocked, as was to be expected, and the keys by some small miracle in the ignition, so in no time at all the two men were racing up Park Range and turning left toward the western end of town, and turning left again to reach Old Road, which would take them through Challengers and Old Road Town, and finally all the way back to Half Way Tree.

Alwyn's pulse quickened behind the wheel as he thought, with every pothole he hit, with every bend he took along the road, that a tire might just blow, that something might go amiss, that their great escape might still go wrong. But Alwyn's worries proved ill-founded as he and Whitty reached the dark, ugly bay of Half Way Tree sometime before five in the morning. Out at sea, the men on *The Rambler* were getting ready to head back southward, but Alwyn remembered the sequence of lights they were supposed to exchange with the Kittitian boat off Sandy Hill Point, and Gaynor Henderson spotted the signals sent out by the car on the bay, and Alwyn and Whitty were so desperate to get out of there that they jumped straight into the water and swam all the way to *The Rambler*, where they were fished out by the remaining crew.

Meanwhile, the siege of the Defence Force camp had come to an end. At four thirty a.m. sharp, after a long hour of periodic attacks against the concrete wall of the building, Harry González ordered one last heavy offensive led by the Browning M1919 machine gun handled by Titus Brown, before signaling the final retreat. *They're too afraid to face us in the night. We have an hour to get out of here, if we're lucky. After that, we're dead meat.*

The five men stooped on their way down Springfield Hill, but once on Cayon Street the outlaws brazenly took to the main road, walking in a formation that oozed an air of invincibility, that identified them as the Caribbean version of *The Untouchables*.

Except, once on Cayon Street, Harry González turned right and headed out of town, instead of leading his men in the direction of the shots that could still be heard coming from the area next to the police station. And Rude Thompson's *How you mean?* did nothing to convince Harry González that *we kyan't leave dem men fight we fight alone.*

Each to their own, Rude. Harry walked on, M16 in his right hand, .25 in his left. *You can join them if you want—but you won't get out of there alive, if you do.*

Rude said no other word and simply moved along, puzzled about the man's exit strategy.

Harry González would have explained that if their comrades were still, over an hour later, fighting at the police station, it was unlikely they would be able to take it with or without the extra men; and even if they managed to capture the police station, Harry González would have argued, had he wanted to do so, in all likelihood the government had been informed of the attack already; and even if, Harry González might have continued, they managed to abduct Robert Bradshaw, even if they were to get hold of Paul Southwell, who or what was there to stop the hundred-plus-strong Defence Force from coming to their rescue the following morning?

Harry González was acutely aware that the operation had gone sour, that they would be unable to accomplish their targets, and that the best they could hope for now was to come out of this godforsaken jungle in one piece. Harry González would have explained the situation to Rude Thompson, had not his ticket out of that godforsaken jungle shown its headlights less than a quarter of a mile up the road. The run-down Morris van making its way into town drove straight into the barrels of Harry González's M16 machine gun and .25 handgun, each pointing at a different eye of the driver's head from the end of his outstretched arms. He didn't even have to say a word: as soon as the Kittitian made out this strange jumbie jumping him on the road in the middle of the night, he stopped the van in its tracks and ran for cover into the mottled darkness of Springfield Cemetery.

Hop in, gentlemen—and off they went, back toward Half Way Tree.

Although the Morris van with the three American mercenaries and Rude Thompson and Glenallen Rawlingson was just some ten, fifteen minutes behind Alwyn Cooke and Whitford Howell, when they reached Half Way Tree *The Rambler* was already on its way back to the safe shores of Anguilla.

As soon as Alwyn was lifted onboard, he asked around if any of the others had made it back.

You de first ones. You lucky we still here, you know: we saw dem clouds liftin' yonder an' we gettin' ready to go.

Alwyn immediately asked for the time.

I ain' know, but it soon be daylight. There were eight men aboard *The Rambler*, not one of them had a watch.

True—but we go reach Statia in de night an' we safe after da'. This was as good as an order from Alwyn Cooke to Gaynor Henderson to lift the anchor and leave his best friend from childhood behind, stranded in a hostile land with no way out.

It wasn't even five minutes later when the headlights of the van carrying Harry González and the rest of the men from the Defence Force camp flooded the dark sand of the bay at Half Way Tree. Only Walter Stewart noticed the lights, but when he informed Alwyn Cooke, all he got back was, *Boy, how we know dey de oder men an' not de police come look for we? We mus' take we chance right now an' hope de revenue cutter no come for we, nuh. We mus' hope for de best.*

Harry González could see the white foam of the wake left behind by *The Rambler* as he stepped out of the van at Half Way Tree. He looked at his watch. 5:02 a.m. *Bastards! They must have taken off ahead of time . . . How well you know this place, Rude?*

Harry González wanted Rude Thompson to take them to the closest point to St. Eustatius, where they could steal a boat and sail across
the channel.

*Le' we go Newton Town an' farther out so—between de village and St.
Paul's is plenty fishing bays.*

Back inside the van the five men watched the twilight illuminate
the horizon, while the sky above their heads remained pitch black.
Harry González drove past the imposing shadow of Mount Misery to
his right, with Brimstone Hill hanging high above the other hills, and
he continued along the coastal road past the ruins of Charles Fort and
the slight rolling of waves along the bay at Sandy Point, before the road
veered inland and took the five men through a shantytown on the edge
of a long stretch of cane fields.

Dat Newton Town a'ready, take de nex' turn nort' an' we reach de beach.

But the sun was about to rise, and slowly the sky was turning dark
blue. *We don't have much time. We're gonna have to ditch the van and find
a place to hide for the day.* No sooner had Harry spoken the words than
he steered into the thick of a cane field and penetrated the tall rows of
grass at full speed, driving the van as far as it would take them before
the narrow wheels got so heavy with mud they could no longer find
traction. *This'll have to do. Rude, lead the way; take us to a place where we
can check out these fishing boats you're talking about.*

Making way through the sugarcane with no tools other than a cutlass found underneath the front seat of the van was a minor torture.
The sticky leaves clung to the bodies of the men, who, in the shadows
of the twilight, sought a safe haven before the break of day proper. Rude
Thompson opened a narrow path with blows flying from side to side,
but still the grass cut through the flesh of the men behind him, stems
caught between their feet, the thick sweet secretion of the plant rub-

bing against their legs every step of the way. The sun hung high in the sky by the time Rude found a way out of the field, his right hand bleeding profusely from his exertions with the cutlass, blisters cutting deep into his palm and dampening it with a mixture of water and blood as he climbed a steep hill that overlooked a small cove.

Where's the boats? And Harry González looked in utter dismay when Rude pointed at a small skiff with no engine beached on the sheltered end of the bay. *You're joking!*

But Rude Thompson was dead serious, and no matter what Harry González, Titus Brown, or Mario Gómez thought about it, he would jump on that boat as soon as it got dark again, and he was plenty sure Glenallen Rawlingson would be ready to join him.

And what do we do until then?

They sat in the relentless sun, with no food and little water, taking turns keeping guard, two at a time, should anyone take note of the five armed men hiding in the bushes on the northern coast of St. Kitts.

By this time, Sol Carter and the O'Farrell cousins had already abandoned their efforts to take the police station. Sol had been misguided by the final offensive against the Defence Force camp ordered by Harry González before he signaled for his men to retreat. Sol had already decided it was time for him and the O'Farrell cousins to head back, to try to somehow make it to *The Rambler* on time, when the sudden flurry of shots he heard coming from the Defence Force camp made him reconsider, because *Dem havin' havoc up dere, man.* Thus, emboldened by a sense of solidarity, Sol tried to deliver a message to the policemen inside the station—*We in control of de military buildin'! Surrender! You defeated, nuh!*

Much like the previous hour, however, nothing came out of the station at all: not an answer, not a shot, no sign of life. Sol signaled to Dwight and Desmond to redouble their shooting, to intensify the siege, to *scare de Bradshers till dey shit dem pants*. In his excitement, Sol failed to notice the total silence that emanated both from the Defence Force camp and from Burt Street. Until, finally, he told the O'Farrells to stop shooting. Suddenly, the Kittitian night went totally quiet. Sol pointed his left ear to the wind and there he stood, motionless, for over a minute. Nothing. He turned in the opposite direction, curled his fingers around his right ear in the shape of a shell, and, again, nothing. He called the O'Farrells over with a wave of his right hand. *Dem get de Defence camp already, or we on we own.*

Sol Carter decided they should wait a little while longer, in case the men from the Defence Force camp, presumably victorious, came to lend a helping hand with the police station. For five minutes Desmond O'Farrell looked through the sight of the M1 carbine he pointed in the direction of the station, while he waited for something, anything, to happen. Ten minutes. Fifteen.

We by weself, boys—le's get outta here.

Desmond O'Farrell left his M1 carbine lying there on the ground when he got to his feet to follow Sol Carter, who chucked his into an open plot of bushland as he moved away from the station. Dwight O'Farrell discarded his a few steps farther down the road, when Sol explained he had some relatives in Tabernacle, a small town on the Atlantic coast of the island, so *Drop you guns—we goin' catch de bus an' visit my cousin.*

It had just gone five in the morning and life began to spark up in Basseterre. Sol Carter, Dwight O'Farrell, and Desmond O'Farrell hurriedly walked up Cayon Street until they reached a large fork past Independence Street. At the crossroads, Sol Carter took the diagonal Wellington Road, which led out through the northeast corner of town, before suddenly slowing his pace. *Easy, fellows, easy.* He calmed his own nerves by telling his companions to keep cool, to act as if nothing had happened.

How far we goin' go, Sol?

And Sol wanted to reach the sugar factory, at least, to get to the outskirts of town, where they could catch a bus that would take them through the cane fields of Cayon and Ottley's and, finally, into Tabernacle.

It took the three Anguillians the best part of a tense hour to walk along Wellington Road, past Manchester Avenue and outward, past Taylors Road with the large, run-down sugar factory cutting an ugly figure to the left—its galvanized roof looking strangely matte in the early-morning light, its wide, low chimney still impregnating the air with the sweet smell of molasses derived from the processed cane. Sol breathed somewhat less heavily once they left the factory behind. *Le' we wait for de bus here, man.* Sure enough, the bus to Saddlers, a rural area toward the northeast end of the island, came around less than ten minutes later.

It was now well past six in the morning. Sol, Desmond, and Dwight hopped onto the bus and stood in the back of it without saying a word, lest their Anguillian accents give them away. All the talk, even that early in the morning, was about what had happened the night before.

The atmosphere was laden with an uncomfortable sense of suspicion, or at least that was what Sol Carter was thinking when he was suddenly kicked to the ground by a group of four Kittitians who were sitting behind the Anguillian men on the bus. The driver pulled over to the side of the road and a great turmoil ensued as the angry Kittitians threatened to lynch the three Anguillians. Dwight O'Farrell, fully at one with his role as rebel, had disposed of his M1 rifle when they'd left the police station; but he had not been so quick in getting rid of the automatic .25 he kept tucked in the back of his trousers, because he had grown fond of the gun, and because you could not know what lay ahead that day. So Dwight O'Farrell had lied to Sol Carter and told him he had thrown away all his guns and ammunition, when, in fact, he strolled along Wellington Road in Basseterre with an automatic .25 handgun behind his back. Until, standing on the bus, holding onto an iron bar that hung from the ceiling, Dwight's T-shirt had crawled up slightly and there, between the black fabric of his shirt and his green trousers, the men sitting right behind him could discern the glowing black metal of the gun.

It was only through the levelheadedness of the bus driver that the three Anguillians were spared their lives, although they weren't spared a good beating. Before things got out of hand, the driver had risen from his seat and shouted, *Out! Out! Out! Out, yer hear me. Out, I say*, and he off-loaded his passengers, and the gun had been taken from Dwight O'Farrell, and one Kittitian pounded Desmond's face hard, and *Gimme dat*, and taking the gun in his hands, *A'right, fellows, a'right. Da's enough, stop it now*, and in the fear that the bus driver might shoot Anguillians and Kittitians alike, everything did, miraculously, stop. The bus driver paid his passengers their fares back, and he took Sol Carter, Desmond O'Farrell, and Dwight O'Farrell, escorted by the men who had jumped on them and who now salivated at the thought of a reward being paid by the government for their service to the country, toward the police station in Basseterre.

For the second time in just a few hours, the three Anguillians were denied access to the police station through the main entrance at Cayon Street because the damaged door could still not be opened. Instead, Sol, Dwight, and Desmond were thrown straight into the jailhouse, where they would remain for months to come.

The rest of that day was chaos in St. Kitts. The wheels of power had been set in motion to act decisively and inclemently in the face of these wanton attacks. This much was made clear by Premier Robert Bradshaw in a press conference even before Sol Carter and the O'Farrell cousins were acquainted with the penitentiary facilities of the island. Decisively and inclemently. *Appropriately* was never a concern. It was at this stage that the question of *who* had opened wide, in the wee hours of the morning of June 10, 1967, the gates of hell was cast aside and left to go down in history begging. The situation was used by the government, instead, to tighten its already watertight grip on the country's power structure. Before the end of the day, Robert Bradshaw had declared a state of emergency across the islands of St. Kitts, Nevis, and Anguilla, even though, in the absence of a party representative, a single member of the police task force, or even a warden, the personnel available in Anguilla to enforce the measures were exactly none.

The personnel available to enforce the measures in St. Kitts and Nevis, however, were both substantial and, in the case of St. Kitts at least, desperate to redeem themselves from the affront they had collectively been dealt the night before. The situation demanded, by all reckonings, swift and exemplary administration of the law by its letter. In this respect, both the police and the government were at one in thinking that the time and energy spent searching for the actual culprits should be minimal, because everyone knew—it was plainly evident—who had been the intellectual, if perhaps not the actual, perpetrators of the crime. At least a dozen arrest warrants were issued during the course of June 10 in St. Kitts, and another two were produced in Nevis, every single one of them to individuals who had been identified during the previous year or so as citizens who posed a threat to the stability of the country, i.e., people who challenged or questioned the views put forward by the ruling party, and who were potentially powerful enough to stir some sort of popular response.

Within this framework of police activity, the fact that several of the Anguillians who had been directly behind the invasion of the island had been caught and delivered to the country jailhouse was not only completely accidental, it constituted almost a minor setback because it focused unwanted attention on the actual details of the night. There would be enough time, in due course, to deal with the issue of Anguilla at large, but right now priority had to be given to one thing, and one thing alone: securing the control of the island—and to that effect, the most imminent threat faced by Bradshaw came from within.

Consequently, the five armed men hiding in the bushland toward the northern shores of St. Kitts remained unseen and unperturbed all day. By human agency, that is. Because June 10, 1967 was a damn hot day, and the five men had nothing to eat, and between them they only had the little water left in the flasks brought by the American mercenaries, dressed to penetrate this miniature version of the Vietnamese jungle with total impunity. It was not quite noon when Glenallen Rawlingson began to hear the rumblings of his own gut after Rude Thompson was slapped with a *No more, fellow,* when he asked for *some ah da' water, dere.*

We have about five lidfuls each, and God only knows when we'll be able to get some more, so we're gonna have to ration from now on.

Rude Thompson and Glenallen Rawlingson went on a little excursion to see if they could find a well or a fruit-bearing tree to stock up for the journey back. But Glenallen was too scared to go far, and Rude would never own to it, but he, too, was as frightened as he had ever been in his life, so their pacing was hesitant and unadventurous, and their quest stopped short of being a rotund failure merely by the sighting of a small passion fruit tree. Except all the fruit was green and hard, and when Rude Thompson and Harry González, driven by hunger and boldness, opened a few of them, all that could be heard was regurgitation as Harry González spat out the bitter blend of seeds, fibrous meat, and acid nectar with a subdued *Jesus!*

Far from relieving the men's hunger, the passion fruit exacerbated their thirst and made the rest of their day even more miserable. The hours refused to pass, and the five rebels, hiding in the bush, sleeping below a tree, hopelessly waiting for the end of the day, grew in restlessness by the hour. Rude Thompson in particular found it unreasonably taxing to sit passively until the time came to move toward the bay. But whenever he or anyone else proposed an alternative plan, it was discarded for being too dangerous. In short, anything at all, other than stealing the small skiff, entailed moving in the light of day among a people who would now, no doubt, be paranoid about an invasion and obsessed with finding the invaders. If the five of them traveled together they would be picked out immediately, and neither the Anguillians nor the Americans wanted to split the group—the former because they felt comforted by the presence of *someone* with an idea of what they were doing, and the latter because they trusted the islanders' instincts at sea a lot more than they did their own.

Perhaps the most challenging moment of the long wait, however, came when the sun had finally set, and night had taken hold of the Kittitian sky. Rude Thompson jumped on his feet, tired and hungry as he was, and prompted the others, *C'mon, den!*

But Harry González would not risk it yet. *There might be people near the bay, still—let's wait for another hour,* and that was, quite simply, the longest hour in the life of Rude Thompson and Glenallen Rawlingson. But it passed, as most things do, and at last the five men were on their way to the skiff, and when his boots sank in the dark sand of Helden's Bay, Titus Brown jumped into the water and opened his mouth wide and gulped a mouthful of saltwater, opening his wild black eyes and shaking his head violently. *Ahhhh . . .*

Corporal Gómez and Glenallen Rawlingson pulled the wooden boat from the beach into the water and the men began to jump into it one by one. The skiff sank deeper and deeper into the sea, completely overloaded as it was, but eventually the five men found the right distribution to keep it both afloat and balanced, and Rude, sitting at the aft, instructed the men what to do as they faced the small waves rolling in from the channel that separated them from freedom. Titus Brown sat facing backward—facing St. Kitts—to the left of Rude Thompson, such that in due course he could use his one arm to row; next to him sat Harry González, M16 in hand, looking paler, altogether rougher, than he had all day. At the front sat Glenallen Rawlingson and Corporal Gómez, rowing at the pace set by Rude, who steered the skiff flat against the waves to avoid toppling over, and told the men to *Row, row, row, row, row,* every fifteen seconds or so, with each new wave that approached.

Just how the men escaped Helden's Bay under these circumstances and with that boat is hard to imagine. But the fact remains that they did, that after rowing against the waves for nearly an hour, they made it past the breaking point and then it was only a matter of time until they reached St. Eustatius. And luck, of course. But the famous Lady had already made it sufficiently clear that she was on the side of the rebels that night, so St. Kitts's revenue cutter was absolutely nowhere to be seen until the following morning, when a certain fisherman from the town of St. Paul's headed toward Helden's Bay at half past five in the morning, just like every other morning for the past twenty-five years, only to find that, for the first time ever, his boat was no longer there. He made his way back to St. Paul's (by foot) and reported the incident to the police, who put two and two together and instructed the revenue cutter to search the area for the boat. Which it did, successfully.

But by then, nearly seven a.m. the following morning, the coast guards of St. Eustatius had already detected the drifting skiff, and they had made contact with the men aboard, and Harry González, upon first sighting the police boat, had ordered, *All right, guys—time for us to drop these babies*, and all the guns had gone overboard, and the five men were sent to the detention room in the police station of Oranjestad, in St. Eustatius, for questioning, where they remained for three days—the maximum allowed by law. During all this time no charges were pressed against them by the government of St. Kitts, despite an effort to get the men deported back to Basseterre.

But Robert Bradshaw was seemingly unpopular in places other than Anguilla, because the authorities in St. Eustatius showed absolutely no desire to aid their counterparts in St. Kitts with any part of the investigation, and they openly refused to allow policemen from the neighboring island to question, or even see, the detained men, and every single request from the government of St. Kitts to extradite the suspects was met with a condition by the government of St. Eustatius that official criminal charges be made, which never were, so three days later the five men were released by the police, escorted to the airport, put on a plane, and shipped back to the safety of Anguilla.

EPILOGUE

THE DENOUEMENT

I F THE ATTEMPTED COUP IN ST. KITTS BY SIXTEEN MEN from Anguilla
on June 10, 1967 were a commercial enterprise, then the balance
sheet at the end of it would have read something along these lines: out
of sixteen men traveling aboard *The Rambler* that night, as many as six
of them never ventured out of the boat; only two made it back to *The
Rambler*; five men drifted to the relative safety of a jailhouse in St. Eustatius the following day; and three were caught and kept in prison for
over three months without charge, under the provisions of the state of
emergency declared in the tri-island state of St. Kitts-Nevis-Anguilla.
A homemade recipe for bankruptcy. Luckily for Anguilla and for the
men in question, the accountancy of life tends to draw figures in more
shades than just black and red.

Hence, although it might not have been immediately obvious to
Alwyn Cooke and the rest of the Anguillians who, sitting by the generator, listened to the news on ZIZ Radio St. Kitts at eight in the evening on June 10, 1967, the troubles through which the ten deluded,
ill-equipped, and thoroughly unprofessional freedom fighters had gone
the night before had placed Anguilla in a far better position to seek that
which it wanted most: secession. Naturally, this was not the general
consensus that night—not among the population at large, nor among

the fifteen men who, just twelve days earlier, following the departure of the Piper Aztec that carried the last remnants of the police task force, including Inspector Edmonton himself, had come together to form a temporary committee of sorts that would be in charge of ensuring that all Anguillians could still lead their lives in peace.

Among the members of this peacekeeping committee and, indeed, among the public at large, the fear that Robert Bradshaw would take the opportunity and use brute force to punish Anguilla for its indiscretion was only exacerbated when they heard the news on ZIZ Radio St. Kitts that the police station in Basseterre, as well as the Defence Force camp, had been attacked. *Dey makin' de whole t'ing up. Is jus' an excuse to come shoot us all.*

Alwyn Cooke was perfectly aware there was more to the story than simply scaremongering and manipulation, but he had resolved to play his cards close to his chest, and he was not about to declare himself the leader of a criminal operation which, had it been successful, would have claimed the lives of dozens, maybe hundreds, of his own people's cousins, so Alwyn went with the flow and shared everyone's concern, and reaffirmed the fear he had voiced ever since he'd returned from St. Thomas, roughly ten days earlier—that an invasion from St. Kitts was imminent.

If there had been any skeptics on the issue before June 10, 1967, every single doubter on the island had been convinced by the newsreel that night. No one in Anguilla would even dare to question the fact that their condition was, presently, critical. Precisely such certainty was the catalyst that led to Anguillians acting, for once, in unison and with urgency during what they assumed would be the final days of their standoff against St. Kitts. The peacekeeping committee continued to seek support from abroad, but in light of the total disregard the world insisted to pay to Anguilla and its affairs, the committee also turned inward and, with uncharacteristic haste, foresight, and prudence, sought to build the institutional edifice needed to rule a country.

It might have been that, every step of the way, Anguillians expected their efforts to crumble, their hopes to be shattered by the silhouette of one, or two, or three frigates anchored off their coasts, and that, therefore, they just carried on trying, without giving much thought to what might happen next. Or maybe it was sheer desperation that drove the Anguillian temperament to display an ounce of Teutonic efficiency amidst the Caribbean waters. Whatever the case, the peace-keeping committee contacted prominent émigrés, and it sought advice from private individuals, and it researched the requirements to play the part of an independent nation, and suddenly there was a red drape with a shell and two sirens, and *that* became the first unofficial flag of a republic that was yet to be declared; and then there was a noble, soft-spoken Anguillian-American, a war veteran, a successful entrepreneur who had moved to the States in search of that fabled dream, and this man visited the offices of the UN one day, but was asked to return the following day, so he did, but he was again asked to return the following day, so he did, but he was then asked to return the day after that, and every day he came back and knocked on the same door, and he raised the same issue, and he asked to speak to the chairman of the Decolonization Committee about the island of Anguilla. *Which island?* Anguilla, that little island that absolutely refused to be associated with the despots from St. Kitts. *From where?* And so it was that through patience and resilience and obstinacy and determination, the man was finally allowed to speak, not to the chairman of the Decolonization Committee, but rather to the undersecretary of a secretary—and yet, the process had been put in motion and the wheels of bureaucracy had begun to turn, and eventually the world would find out about Anguilla and its utterly reasonable claim.

The final piece of the puzzle was an internal referendum organized by the fifteen-member peacekeeping committee to decide upon the question of secession from the state of St. Kitts-Nevis-Anguilla. According to the census, there were 2,554 registered voters in Anguilla in 1967. Of those, 1,813 voted on July 11, 1967, in favor of secession, while five voted against it, during a process that was duly monitored by members of the Canadian and US media. By then, one month and one day after the shambolic attack on St. Kitts, Anguilla already had a small "army" of fifty servicemen who patrolled the twenty-odd bays where the landing of forces from St. Kitts might be possible; it had enlisted an important foreign advisor, who would draft the island's first constitution, a simple document with precious few provisos; it had an ambassador to the UN, a revolutionary leader, and an autonomous government in place; and, most importantly, it had caught the eye of the world through a transparent and peaceful referendum that had vindicated the island's cause with an absolute and undisputable majority.

And all this time, Robert Bradshaw was too busy settling the score at home, turning St. Kitts into a 100 percent safe, absolutely invasion-resistant bunker. Thus, the foundations were put in place for the people of Anguilla to enjoy that which they had been craving, officially, since 1825. The road ahead was still uncertain, and the battle that ensued—legal, diplomatic, at times even military—would not be resolved until well into the 1980s, but The Rambler had already played its part by then, and its claim to glory would forever remain the events that took place on June 9 and 10, 1967, between the islands of Anguilla and St. Kitts.

And what of Sol Carter, the most reasonable man in this whole tale?

It's well past my bedtime, but we cannot allow the words that were left untyped back on page 20 to hang in literary limbo, because this tale must end with a heroic feat, performed by a man who'd already had his share of adventures in life, and who'd sought to lead a more sedentary lifestyle by embarking on a real estate operation on the island of St. Barths. Jan van Hoeppel was a great friend of the five-island cluster in the northeast Caribbean, and when Anguilla found itself in need of a bold and capable pilot to carry out the most intrepid of rescue missions, Jan van Hoeppel felt the blood in his veins rise to his cheeks, and he sensed the simmering of his spirit cloud the power of his reasoning, and soon enough he was flying over St. Kitts's airspace, weighing his options, getting familiar with the layout of the airport to the north of Basseterre, sketching his plan in a tiny notebook he would then show to Alwyn Cooke.

Because after spending more than three months in prison without charge, Solomon Carter and the O'Farrell cousins were finally accused of conspiracy, of disturbing the public order, of profanity, and, in the case of Dwight O'Farrell, of illegal possession of a firearm. But with the charges also came the formalities of an official trial, which included the right to bail for the duration of the process. The court set the bail at an unreasonable sum, in the hundreds of US dollars, enough to buy a small parcel of land, but Alwyn Cooke had more than enough parcels to spare from Lover's Leap, and he was likely being eaten up inside for having forsaken his comrades in a hostile land with no obvious means of escape, so he approached Dr. Crispin Reynolds one day and handed the politician two envelopes, and he explained there was enough money in the first to pay the bail of the three men, and he didn't need to explain what was in the second, but he did pause for a moment to grab a pen from the man's desk, and he pulled a crumpled piece of white paper from the right pocket of his neatly pressed gray trousers, and he scribbled in red, *East End. Airport. One foot on tarmac, one foot on grass,* and he folded up the small piece of paper into a tiny cube which he placed in Dr. Reynolds's hand and explained, *Dey life in you hands, nuh: you give dis to Solomon Carter an' tell he T'ursday, five thirty p.m., okay?* and Crispin Reynolds was affected by the severity in Alwyn Cooke's tone, by the general sense of gloom in his demeanor, and, as he gently nodded yes, Alwyn reiterated, *Don' forget, nuh: T'ursday. Five thirty.*

Because on Thursday, September 28, 1967, Jan van Hoeppel chose to wear the hat of Otto Skorzeny, and sometime around five p.m. he departed Wallblake Airport in his red four-seat Stinson Reliant, dubbed *La Cucaracha,* the last surviving member of the fleet of aircrafts that once belonged to Air Atlantique, and, with a wave of his left hand as he sharply turned south over the houses of Rey Hill, he was on his way to St. Kitts, where, at the eastern end of the runway, the three Anguillian men who, less than a week earlier, had been released from the jailhouse in Basseterre upon payment of a bail of three hundred US dollars each, awaited his arrival.

It was a damp, clear September afternoon, laden with the high humidity characteristic of that time of year, and little more was expected to happen at Basseterre that day, so few noticed the rumbling of the single Lycoming engine at the front of the Reliant as it approached St. Kitts, but the Anguillians heard it straight away and with great anticipation they searched the horizon for signs of the plane.

At five thirty-four p.m. the control tower at Golden Rock Airport tried to make contact with an unidentified flying object heading in the direction of the island; three minutes later the ground crew had established the object was an airplane, and the control tower requested the aircraft to identify itself and provide its provenance and destination, over, but nothing came from the other side, so the question now was whether the aircraft was in distress, whether it had radio communication at all, and *This is Golden Rock control, do you read? Over*, and nothing but the seething noise of static on the radio, and *This is Golden Rock control, we do not read your signal, repeat, we do not read your signal; switch to frequency 121.5, repeat, one two one point five, over*, and again the busy nothingness of white noise taking over the scene at the control tower, such that the one fire truck at the airport was instructed to get onto the runway and stand by, and preparations were made for an emergency landing to take place in the next few minutes.

At first, it looked as if van Hoeppel had overshot the runway and a great tragedy was about to unfold, but the modern-day Red Baron knew perfectly well what he was doing, and he knew his *Cucaracha* like the palm of his hand, and he could judge to an inch how much tarmac he would need to bring the airplane to a halt, and so, to the horror of the three Anguillians at the end of the runway, he used every single yard of the strip and then a few more of the emergency runoff area, where he turned without letting the tail of the Reliant fall. Only then did the authorities at Golden Rock Airport realize there were three men lying on the ground at the end of the runway, who now got to their feet and ran in the direction of the airplane, and as the red Stinson turned to face the tarmac the fire engine raced from the other end toward the Anguillians.

Despite his age, Sol Carter was still an agile man, and the O'Farrells were swift in their movements, and it was Dwight O'Farrell who opened the small door underneath the left wing of the airplane, and no sooner had he done so than Desmond jumped into the back, and *La Cucaracha* was already in motion again when Sol Carter made it inside, and his eyes almost bulged out of their sockets when he saw the Rover police car turn into the runway and drive toward the plane. Jan van Hoeppel did not so much as ask the men behind to hold on, because he could tell the fire engine would not be able to intercept them before they took off, and the police car was far quicker than the truck, but even with four men inside he knew he would be able to force *La Cucaracha* up within five hundred feet, and as he did the fixed wheels of the Stinson flew just a foot or so above the top of the police car, and then mere inches from the windshield of the fire truck. Yet none of that mattered anymore, because *La Cucaracha* was as good as home and dry, and as the silhouette of the red aircraft turned north, it became progressively smaller to the stunned men looking out from the control tower.

Boy—you almost kill me of heart attack, but Jan van Hoeppel heard the distinct tone of gratefulness in Solomon Carter's words, and the adrenaline raced through his body and put him in a playful mood, and despite the fact that he was no younger than the Anguillian, *Don' die on me jus' yet, ol' man—they got a great little party goin' for you right now, you know,* and it was true, because hundreds of people had gathered at Wallblake Airport to greet the last contingent of the rebels who had risked their lives for the sake of their island, and as *La Cucaracha* emerged from the hazy distance, tainted with the intense pink and yellow hue of the sunset, van Hoeppel got on the radio and spoke the famous words that brought an end to the implausible plot of June 10, 1967 and its appendix: *This man thin-thin like a stick, you know. You better get some goat from the pen to bulk him up.*

Acknowledgments

This book would not have been possible without the support of the government of Anguilla, which kindly allowed me to stay on the island for close to two years between 2008–2010. The first seed of the novel was planted years before, when I first read a rare and carefully crafted piece on Anguilla's revolution, *Anguilla: Where There's a Will There's a Way* (1984), by the island's most rigorous chronicler, Colville Petty. Mr. Petty's assistance in collecting copies of the first newspaper in the island, the *Beacon*, as well as other material from the Anguilla Heritage Collection Museum, also proved priceless. Many details in the narrative have been recycled from dozens of interviews conducted with many of the protagonists of the events that inspired *The Night of the Rambler*. Equally valuable was Ronald Webster's *Scrapbook of Anguilla's Revolution*, published privately in 1987.

My thanks to Alan Gumbs for his continued support cannot be reduced just to the production of this book, and in fact must be dated back to a different millennium. I owe a special nod to the taxi driver who took me around Basseterre several days in a row: I'm sorry to keep a promise so poorly, but names elude me even in the best of days. Finally, traveling all the way back to the root, I hold fondly to the memories of Jeremiah Gumbs, the patriarch, conversing endlessly through my childhood and adolescence at Rendezvous Bay Hotel. This is is my tribute to him and all the wonderful people of Anguilla.